AN INFAMOUS
BETRAYAL

LYNN MESSINA

potatoworks press

greenwich village

CHAPTER ONE

As sympathetic as Vera Hyde-Clare was to the pain her niece suffered as the victim of a brutal assault that had left her badly bruised, she couldn't help but feel the situation had several advantages to recommend it. Naturally, she would never *wish* a pair of swollen, battered eyes on anyone, not in the least the poor parentless child who had been delivered to her care more than twenty years ago—even if that orphan, who owed her family nothing but docility and gratitude, had suddenly and inexplicably turned willful and disrespectful. But Vera hadn't countenanced Beatrice's sneaking out of the house in her male cousin's clothes to attend the funeral of her former beau, a law clerk struck down in the prime of his life. It went without saying that she would have expressly forbidden such an act if her permission had been sought, and given that her niece was fully aware of the wrongness of her conduct, Vera felt it was fair and just to hold the girl responsible for the unfortunate attack.

Having done nothing to create the situation, Vera felt no compunction in utilizing it to her purpose and claiming that Bea was still too injured to attend the Duke of Pemberton's ball. "Obviously, I wish you could come for your own sake, my dear, for being trapped inside this house for

1

three weeks cannot have been fun. But you must own that it would be beyond scandalous for you to appear in public with that discoloration on your cheek."

Beatrice Hyde-Clare examined her face in the mirror next to the grandfather clock and insisted that her complexion had returned entirely to normal. There was no trace—faint or otherwise—of the abuse she had suffered.

Her aunt tsk-tsked softly as she worried that the thrashing Bea had endured might have permanently damaged her sight. "For I assure you the signs of the injury are readily apparent to anyone who looks at you. No, you need at least another week to recover completely."

The thought of being confined in the house like a chicken in a coop for another full week horrified Bea. "I really don't think—"

But Aunt Vera was having none of it and swore it was her sacred duty to protect the reputation of her niece as well as the standing of her family. "Only when there is no hint of your terrible misfortune visible shall you be allowed to attend society events or receive visitors. For now, I suggest you retire to your room and think about how lucky you are to have your devoted family looking after you with such care. Other, more unfeeling relatives might let you step outside and risk censure and embarrassment. Now do be a dear and allow me to find Mrs. Emerson. I must discuss tomorrow night's menu."

Although Bea wanted to protest further, she knew better than to waste her breath, for her aunt was fully committed to the fiction that her skin still displayed evidence of her recent beating. Having found a way to control the movements of her unpredictable niece, she was determined not to give it up a single second sooner than was necessary. At most, Aunt Vera had another week left in the ruse, and as impatient as Bea was to leave the town house in Portman Square, she could submit gracefully to seven more days of confinement. Indeed, despite her discomfort, she couldn't really blame her aunt for manipulating the circumstance to her own benefit and actually found herself impressed with the woman's ability to successfully pull off the ploy. She hadn't credited the forty-six-year-old woman with either the cunning or ruthlessness.

Furthermore, Aunt Vera's interpretation of events was somewhat accurate: Bea was a little bit responsible for the attack, as she *had* snuck out of the house in her cousin Russell's clothes to insert herself in business that was no actual concern of hers. As to the particulars, of course, her aunt was wrong, for the story Bea had told her family was a complete fiction. No, she hadn't gone to the funeral of Theodore Davies, a law clerk with whom she had conducted a secret romance. And, no, she hadn't been attacked by his father, who thought she was flirting with his bereaved daughter-in-law—recall, please, that she was wearing her cousin's clothes—when in fact she was merely offering her condolences. Of course, Mr. Davies, in his grief, could not be relied upon to act sensibly or sanely when witnessing a strange young man, oddly handsome with his broad shoulders, paying attention to the sad, beautiful mother of his grandchildren.

What a ruckus it caused! And poor Beatrice—pummeled by a man overcome with anguish before his wife could pull him away.

It was all nonsense, of course, for she did not have a former beau who was a lowly law clerk at the Chancery. At six and twenty, Bea had never had any beaus at all. She was a plain-looking woman with brown eyes, slender lips, pale skin and a spray of freckles across her cheeks and nose. Her portion was small, her conversation limited and her social success nonexistent. What little confidence she'd had on her presentation—always modest and propagated on the belief that those freckles had an endearing charm—had been almost immediately undercut by the insidious Miss Brougham, who described her with gleeful malice as drab. Before Lord and Lady Skeffington's house party in the Lake District that her family had attended in the fall, she hadn't spoken three coherent sentences in public during the whole of her career.

And then she stumbled upon the bludgeoned corpse of Thomas Otley, a spice trader who'd made a fortune in India, and everything changed. Suddenly, she found herself embroiled in the great mystery of his death, for nobody else in the house seemed the least bit interested in discovering who had bashed in the spice trader's skull with a candlestick. It fell to Beatrice to investigate, which she did with surprising skill and success.

It was in pursuit of this larger truth that she had made up the minor fabrication of Mr. Theodore Davies, law clerk. Suspecting that one of the young guests at Lakeview Hall was engaged in an illicit relationship with an unsuitable man, Bea invented an illicit relationship with an unsuitable man for herself. It was meant to demonstrate empathy and elicit confidences.

Instead, it created a situation so complicated and absurd she was still trying to extricate herself from it five months later.

The problem was her aunt, who, taking it into her head that the secret to her niece's future lay in her past, had resolved to meet this remarkable young clerk and discern from him all the traits and characteristics her niece found appealing in a suitor in order to locate another man with similar qualities. It certainly seemed wiser than holding to the present course of trying to marry the chit off to a third son or a clergy with a small parish in the country, an exercise that had borne no fruit in six seasons. As an additional inducement, Vera felt Bea's behavior in the Lake District, so unaccountably bold, indicated that an arrangement just a little outside the bounds of polite society might be the best way to contain the girl's suddenly unconventional conduct.

If only Mr. Davies could be located!

Obviously, Bea could not let her family spend months looking for a phantom and she couldn't confess to inventing one, so she arranged for Mr. Davies to suffer a tragic, premature death. She wrote up the notice and brought it to the newspaper office to run in the next day's edition. That should have been the end of it and would have if not for the Earl of Fazeley, who chose her feet at which to drop in the entrance of the *London Daily Gazette*.

That charge was unfair, she knew, as a man who had been stabbed in the back by a fourteen-inch knife wasn't actually capable of deciding at whose feet to fall. Beatrice merely had the misfortune of being closest to him at the moment his legs could no longer support his body and his heart ceased to function.

Suddenly, she found herself embroiled in another great mystery.

It was in pursuit of his lordship's killer that she had obtained the twin black eyes, but she couldn't tell her family that. They would be horrified to learn she fancied herself an investigator and as such had inserted herself into matters that had nothing to do with her. How heedless! How ill-bred! How monstrously self-confident! They were already convinced that her faculties had been corrupted by the sight of Mr. Otley's bloody corpse. And, of course, they thought she was deep in mourning for Mr. Davies because they could not conceive of her being anything other than devastated by the loss of her only chance at happiness. Yes, despite the fact that her ersatz former beau had settled in Cheapside with a wife and two children, her family believed she'd still nurtured hopes of a future with him.

It was a humbling new low to discover just how hopelessly desperate they thought her.

And yet she made no move to correct them, for the less her relatives knew about her activities, the more likely they were to prosper. If her aunt had any idea she'd spent a week interviewing the various owners of the jade knife that cut down the Earl of Fazeley, she would consign her to the insanity ward at Bedlam. If she discovered that Bea had worked alongside the Duke of Kesgrave in the pursuit, her eyes would no doubt pop out of her body and roll down the front staircase in shock.

Bea could understand that reaction, for she herself had a difficult time digesting the fact that the esteemed peer who wanted for nothing—neither wealth nor looks nor status nor society—seemed to enjoy helping her identify murderers. He did not need to do it in tandem with her, as he had freedom and access and could easily follow every scrap of uncovered information on his own. And yet he sought her out and provided her with updates and asked her to dance even though leading her in the waltz at the Leland ball served no discernable purpose in the discovery of who killed Lord Fazeley.

It was almost enough to turn a foolish girl's head.

Fortunately, Bea wasn't foolish.

She was just imprudent enough to fall in love with him but too clever to believe for a moment that he could ever return her regard.

This clarity of understanding, she contended, was her saving grace, for it ensured she would not do anything so pitiful as pine for an unattainable duke. No, she would stiffen her resolve and throw herself into a new, consuming passion. All she required was an occupation to distract her thoroughly from thoughts of Kesgrave's crystalline blue eyes and his square jaw and blond curls and his impertinent sense of humor…

A murder!

Yes, a murder was exactly what she needed to keep her thoughts from lingering on the duke's many attractive attributes. As soon as she was released from her confinement, she would make a rigorous attempt to find one. During the three weeks she had been trapped in the house, she had given the matter serious consideration and realized it was the only solution to hopeless infatuation. Using her wits to identify a killer was truly exhilarating, and once she had a clue to decipher, she could think of nothing else.

It was the ideal solution.

The fact that she had promised Kesgrave that she would cease investigating the horrible deaths that kept crossing her path was immaterial to the situation, for she intended to seek one out. The difference between the two might strike some as a minor semantical distinction, but she thought it was enough to proceed with a clear conscience. She could find her distraction and keep her word at the same time.

All was well.

If only the duke would stop calling on her aunt to keep abreast of her progress.

It caused her heart to lurch every time her cousin Flora informed her the duke was downstairs inquiring about her health. She knew his concern was sincere, for he had been with her when the attack occurred and had witnessed the damage to her face firsthand. It had disturbed him greatly, she thought, to see a woman so egregiously battered. But that was all it was. His interest in her welfare was not personal. She firmly believed he would show just as much distress for any creature that was similarly abused—his groom, a footman, a horse—and it was only her aunt's determination to keep her home as long as possible that caused him to worry that the damage was more severe than her injuries had indicated. If he knew Aunt Vera was merely using the unexpected development to advance her own agenda, he would stop calling every third or fourth day to check on her condition.

Bea suspected Aunt Vera knew very well that Kesgrave's visits would stop as soon as her niece was deemed healthy enough to return to society and this provided her with another reason to delay her recovery. Having one of the most sought-after partis in London calling regularly to her house had raised her stock considerably. As far from dashing highfliers as mice were from tigers, the Hyde-Clares were situated comfortably on the margins of society, where they interacted with sedate precision with other fringe dwellers. The duke's notice, however, had thrust Vera to the center, and hostesses who had only tipped their heads in her general direction now engaged her in conversation. She insisted she put up with the treatment only to further the prospects of her twenty-year-old daughter, Flora, but it was apparent to everyone that she adored the attention. Indeed, it had put her in such a genial mood, she finally relented and allowed her son to take lessons at Gentleman Jackson's salon. It was a stunning reversal, as she had been irate with him when he'd revealed that he may have accidentally mentioned Bea's injuries to Kesgrave, whose attention and approval he assiduously sought. (The specifics of how the conversation somehow wound its way to his cousin remained a mystery to Russell, which Bea thought was rather to the duke's credit.)

Kesgrave was not the only member of the *ton* to take an interest in Bea's welfare, and her aunt was equally in alt over her other visitor: the exuberant Countess of Abercrombie. Unaccountably, the beautiful widow, who was famous for her wit, daring and numerous love affairs, had decided to make Bea her particular project for the season. She had resolved to do the impossible—to bring a plain-faced spinster into fashion—and she refused to be deterred from her mission, no matter how hard Vera tried to persuade her to mentor another young lady. Such an effort was necessary, of course, for her ladyship's objective of drawing attention to her strange, unpredictable niece was precisely the opposite of hers. Initially, she'd argued in favor of her own delightful progeny, but perceiving her ladyship's desire for a significant challenge, had switched her focus to Mrs. Marlton's daughter, a pretty girl whose pronounced limp had made popularity elusive.

No, Lady Abercrombie remained stubbornly focused on Beatrice and sent Vera Hyde-Clare regular notes asking when she could meet with her protégé to discuss her plans for the season. The missives, which were at once abrupt and effusive, drove Aunt Vera to distraction, as she'd been convinced the woman would lose interest in her niece after a few days. After all, she was famous for having the mind of a butterfly, always flitting from this thing to that. And now, suddenly, just when it pertained to Beatrice, her memory proved as long as an elephant's.

It was decidedly unfair.

Like her aunt, Bea had expected the countess's interest in her to wane quickly and she could not conceive why the other woman persisted in her scheme. Obviously, as a woman approaching the middle of her sixth decade, she had a penchant for novelty, for she kept an African lion cub as a pet and had decorated her drawing room in an Oriental style so extravagant it rivaled the Royal Pavilion at Brighton. But spinsters were not rare birds one sought to get a glimpse of in a tree. They were as common as dirt in the London ballroom, and if Lady Abercrombie was so committed to making such a creature the height of fashion, she could easily locate one who hadn't been secluded from society for almost a month.

Apparently, her ladyship had another reason for her interest in Bea. At first, Bea had assumed it was because she had discovered the truth about the widow's relationship with one of her son's friends. Having engaged in a light dalliance with Lord Duncan over the Christmas holiday, Lady Abercrombie hoped to keep the affair a secret by proposing a quid pro quo: the promise of popularity in exchange for a vow of silence. At the time, Bea had suspected her of murdering Lord Fazeley, for the widow had both a reason to want him dead (the earl had tried to blackmail her) and an opportunity to end his life (she was the original owner of the jade dagger that killed him).

But Bea had not been interested in any bargains and neatly rebuffed the countess's offer, an act that she'd expected would end their association. And yet the other woman persisted.

It was a mystery.

Was it enough of a mystery to keep her mind off the Duke of Kesgrave? She considered the question as she climbed the stairs to her bedchamber.

At once, the image of his blue eyes laughing at one of her remarks flitted through her mind.

Indeed, it was not.

She needed something gruesome and overwhelming and thoroughly incomprehensible.

Her thoughts turned now, as they had many times in the past few weeks, to the problem of finding just such a thing. She could think of no obvious path to locating a murder victim in need of justice. Naturally, the newspaper presented itself as the most logical place to begin, and she'd taken to reading the *London Daily Gazette* every morning as soon as her Uncle Horace relinquished the broadsheet. She'd adopted the habit with enthusiasm and vigor, but after three weeks of dedicated perusal, she was ready to abandon it. Day after day, it was the same tedious collection of political reports, theater reviews and shipping news. There wasn't a single violent, suspicious or inexplicable death to be found on its pages. In the entire time she had been reading the paper, only one body had been pulled from the river and it belonged to a whisky-soaked sailor who had stumbled drunkenly off the bow of his ship and knocked his head against a floating plank. Five of his shipmates had witnessed the event so there wasn't the slightest chance he was pushed.

There were advertisements for information about highwaymen and stolen property, but Bea wasn't interested in finding pilfered necklaces and missing snuffboxes. Her vision was grander than that, and her skills were more deserving of a larger challenge.

Patently, she required another approach, one that was more enterprising in its methodology, but she had yet to figure out what that should be. Even with her newfound fearlessness, which allowed her to openly mock intimidating, blue-eyed dukes to their faces, she could not bring herself to frequent the poorer districts of the city alone or pay an unaccompanied visit to the docks. Such behavior would be foolish and dangerous, and as much as she was in want of a consuming occupation, she was not so committed to its acquisition as to court personal harm. Already, she had been attacked twice while in pursuit of justice: the series of blows that resulted in the two black eyes, of course, and being knocked on the head and trapped in a shed. The latter occurred during her investigation into Mr. Otley's death in the Lake District and necessitated her breaking her way out of the ramshackle structure one wooden plank at a time. Fortunately, it was just dilapidated enough to make escape possible.

No, the better idea was to befriend a Bow Street Runner, who would already be tasked with investigating a crime, and ply him for information. That method came with its own challenges, for she wasn't exactly sure how to contrive such a meeting. Runners worked out of the magistrate's office on Bow Street, so perhaps it was merely as simple as patronizing a tavern nearby where the men went for a pint of beer after a tiring day of capturing criminals.

The scheme wasn't wholly implausible, for she made a fairly convincing young man when she donned her cousin Russell's clothes. As her aunt liked to point out, she had broad, masculine shoulders ("Ideal for fencing, my dear, which makes you only the more disappointing as a female"), a development that lent authenticity to the enterprise, and she was skilled at lowering her voice an octave so it sounded vaguely mannish. It was the timing, however, that presented a problem, for she could not sneak out of the house toward the end of the day. Nobody would notice if she was gone during the afternoon, but by early evening they would expect her to emerge from her room and join the family for dinner.

But if she could somehow manage to contrive it—

"Come now," Flora said, her tone urgent as she entered Bea's room without knocking. "Come right now before she realizes."

Bea spun around on her heels, confused as she looked at her cousin, whose hazel eyes were bright with excitement and mischief. "Come where?"

"To the drawing room," she explained, threading her

arms through Bea's as she pulled her from the room. "You have a visitor, but Mama doesn't know yet, and if you get down there before she does, there will be nothing she can do. Just think of it, Bea, company! After all these weeks. You must be going mad with nobody but your family to talk to. I know I would be."

Bea smiled at her cousin's hyperbole, for having the opportunity to read book after book without the onerous interruption of social obligations was hardly the sort of circumstance to undermine her sanity. Indeed, some version of her happiest life entailed her sitting alone in a cozy room filled with bookshelves and comfy chairs and plates of warm scones.

And yet as she thought about her cousin's words, she had to concede there was some truth in what she said. With each passing week, she had felt an increasing unease in her situation, an itchiness in her limbs that could only be described as restlessness. Something had been missing from her daily existence, and as she considered the problem now, she realized it was what one might call the society of others.

Astonished by the prospect, she moved instantly to deny it, for if there was one thing in the world that Beatrice Hyde-Clare absolutely did not crave, it was company. She was an awkward creature, self-conscious to a crippling degree and inclined to stammer and stutter answers to even simple questions such as inquiries into her health. Even when she knew exactly what she wanted to say, when the words were arranged in orderly coherence in her head, she could not get them out without stumbling clumsily over her own tongue.

She had been a disappointment to herself and her family from the very moment she had stepped onto the London social scene six seasons ago.

But as true as that was, it was no longer the whole truth. Since the events at Lakeview Hall, her temperament had undergone a radical evolution and she found herself less likely to be intimidated by the august bearing of her betters.

Standing across from Kesgrave in the Skeffingtons' deserted library at two in the morning with Mr. Otley's bludgeoned body between them had irretrievably altered something inside her. In that moment, when she believed him to be the murderer and bent on ending her life to remove a witness to his villainy, she'd discovered what true terror was, and the fear she experienced in various drawing rooms and ballrooms felt inconsequential in comparison. And surely she wasn't so timid as to be afraid of an inconsequentiality?

'Twas an alarming discovery to make at the age of six and twenty—that one desired the company of others. Her entire career had been devoted to the principle of isolation, to the ethos of getting through each social ordeal in order to retire to a quiet room to read. No effort had been made to further her connection with other people, no attempt to actually find a man with whom she could enjoy the pleasures of lively conversation.

Ah, she thought, cynically amused at herself, this was about the Duke of Kesgrave after all.

Everything was about the Duke of Kesgrave.

But no, a voice argued fervently, it was also about Viscount Nuneaton, another member of their little party in the Lake District and a charming dandy who made her laugh. It was even about Lady Abercrombie and her absurd scheme to render Bea fashionable.

"Come on, you silly," Flora insisted, tugging her across the landing to the staircase. "We have to get you into the drawing room before Mama finds out. Once you're engaged with a visitor, she can no longer claim that your face is too bruised for company and you will be able to come to the Pemberton ball tonight and flirt with the Duke of Kesgrave."

Bea halted on the first steps, incapable of going forward as she stared at her cousin. "What?"

Flora smiled. "You've been flirting with him for months. You skewer his self-worth, and he challenges your presumption. It's the way you communicate with each other, and he enjoys it as much as you do. I see that now. I didn't before because I was distracted by Mr. Davies, but once Kesgrave started calling every day to inquire after your health, I realized the truth."

What her cousin was proposing was so ridiculous, Bea could hardly breathe. She shook her head firmly and insisted he had not called every day. "It's only twice a week."

Her cousin laughed softly as she gently pulled her down the stairs. "I trust you hear yourself, my dear. A duke is concerned enough about your health to come *twice a week*. Obviously, he's smitten."

So many thoughts crowded Bea's head at this preposterous statement, she didn't know where to start.

No, that wasn't true. She knew exactly where to start— with the fact that the statement wasn't as preposterous as it should have been. Although her experience with men was limited, she had spent enough time with Kesgrave to realize he felt something for her. It wasn't love, of course, or even infatuation. But there was clearly some compulsion at work that kept bringing him back to her side. She knew he didn't understand it himself, and even if he did, it would not matter. He was one of the most privileged men in England, raised to expect perfection in all things. He could not accept a mousy spinster as his wife. He would choose among Incomparables and settle on an elegant hostess who would adorn his estate with grace and beauty. As he was approaching thirty-three years of age, she could only assume he would make his decision any day now.

"You don't understand," Bea said, her tone a little bit frantic as she thought about all the things her cousin couldn't know, such as the truth behind his twice-weekly appearances. Whatever Kesgrave did or did not feel, the only reason he kept returning to the house was a sense of obligation to make sure she recovered from the pummeling he had all but witnessed. That was all. It wasn't the result of an unbearable infatuation. "You can't understand."

Her vehemence, however, only further amused her

cousin. "All right, darling, we don't have to talk about it now. But please do let's hurry." Again, she tugged on Bea's arm to propel her forward. "I think I can hear Mama discussing tomorrow's dinner menu with Mrs. Emerson. She can't be very far."

Bea was so grateful for the change in conversation that she almost thanked Flora for her consideration. She held her tongue because such a comment would reveal a desperation she wanted to conceal as much from herself as from her cousin. And, indeed, the sound of Aunt Vera firmly assuring the housekeeper that nobody enjoyed watery blancmange grew closer every second they stood there at the bottom of the staircase.

Conceding the urgency, she dashed with Flora down the hallway until they reached the threshold of the drawing room. There, they both stopped abruptly to ensure a dignified entrance, and Bea, suddenly fearful that her aunt's contrivances had been sincere efforts and not self-serving machinations, worried that her face still showed evidence of her recent attack. She grabbed her cousin's hand before she could open the door and said earnestly, "My face is healed, right? There aren't faint traces that I couldn't see in the mirror?"

Flora laughed. "Your face healed ages ago. I know nothing of the standard progression of bruises from black to purple to yellowish brown, but you seemed to recover with preternatural speed. I assure you, my mother was desolate when she realized how swiftly you were improving. Now, come, no more dithering. We must go in at once or lose our chance to go in at all."

Bea nodded resolutely, and it was only as her cousin was opening the door that she realized the last few minutes had been too full of Kesgrave and mortification for her to wonder who her visitor was. And now, as she observed the handsome brown head of the Skeffington heir, she owned herself thoroughly confused.

CHAPTER TWO

Flora strolled smoothly into the room with an eager expression, as if greeting a long-lost friend.

"My dear Mr. Skeffington," she said, dipping into a curtsy as he turned from the fireplace mantel to observe her crossing the room. "This is indeed a lovely surprise. We are so glad you called. Please do take a seat. Dawson will be in at any moment with a fresh pot of tea. I do hope you have time to have a cup with us."

The young man, his eyes troubled as they darted a quick look at Beatrice, colored slightly and mumbled a reply that might have been yes or no or an observation about the weather. It was truly impossible to tell.

Flora made herself comfortable on the settee, and Bea, one eye trained on their visitor, lowered herself slowly into an adjacent armchair. Andrew Skeffington considered his options, settled on a rosewood bergère and sat down. Then he grasped his hands tightly together and studied them carefully for several long seconds. Whatever his errand was in the Hyde-Clare household, he was evidently uncomfortable with it.

Although Beatrice had excellent cause to take pleasure in his discomfort, she found herself oddly in sympathy with the young man who had hit her over the head with a wooden plank and locked her in a rundown shed to fear for her life. As she sat in that horrible shack, her head aching from the cut on her forehead, her mind racing with terror at the prospect of Mr. Otley's murderer returning to snuff out her life, she had no way of knowing that the villain who had trapped her inside was under the impression that she herself was the villain.

Having observed her in her secret investigation of the spice trader's murder, Mr. Skeffington became convinced that Bea was the killer. It was, she decided, looking at the matter from his point of view, a perfectly reasonable conclusion. For one thing, he had seen her sneaking into his room to search it for information. For another, he had found incriminating evidence—a blood-speckled silver candlestick—ensconced in his room soon after she'd left it. Naturally, the young heir assumed she had been trying to make it appear as if he were the killer in an attempt to hide her own guilt.

As she understood the motive for his behavior, she bore him little ill will for the attack. After all, his intention had not been to kill her but to merely restrain her in the shed while he fetched his parents from the house to witness his accusal. That the entire house party had accompanied him to the field, including her aunt and the duke, had not been part of his original plan, and she could not lay the whole of that mortification at his feet. If she had waited patiently for his return rather than scraping her way out, she would not have looked like a bedraggled wild creature when she finally emerged.

What she could find it in her heart to resent was his supercilious attitude and his stubborn refusal to listen to anything resembling reason when she tried to explain herself. Instead, he had insisted that she had an improper relationship with the dead Mr. Otley, citing the story he had heard about the fictional Mr. Davies as evidence of her questionable morality. He also claimed that she and Kesgrave were conspiring against him while professing himself amazed by the duke's interest and dismissing it as an act of country boredom. The precise term he used to describe her, if she remembered it correctly, was "freakish novelty."

It was every humiliation a young woman feared in a single, horrible speech, and that she found harder to forgive than the gash on her forehead.

But watching him now as he stared at his clasped fingers, which were slowly turning white from the pressure, she discovered she could absolve him for even that awful scene. She recalled how he looked when the truth had finally come out. At four and twenty, he was hardly a child and yet when he discovered the depth of his parents' cruelty and callousness, he seemed to wither into a baffled little boy. The last she'd seen of him, he had been led out of the drawing room by an unexpectedly gentle Viscount Nuneaton, who was a distant cousin.

Although he seemed inclined to examine his hands indefinitely, he suddenly looked up and said with forceful vehemence, "I must apologize, Miss Hyde-Clare, for my atrocious behavior at Lakeview Hall in the fall. You must think me the worst kind of blackguard, trying to sully your good name when my own...when my own..." He trailed off for a moment as his knuckles grew impossibly white, then he resumed speaking as if undisturbed. "When my own is synonymous with betrayal and duplicity. I'm sure I cannot fix the situation now by speaking honestly and plainly, but I'm determined to rectify the family legacy of disgrace by doing the right thing."

It was a dignified speech, full of ennobling sentiment, and even if Bea had not already forgiven him for his part in the affair, she would not have been able to withhold approval now. Before she could speak, however, Dawson entered the room with the tray, and Aunt Vera, immediately following on his heels, wondered what he could be thinking to deliver tea to an empty drawing room. Her brow furrowed when she spotted Mr. Skeffington in the rosewood bergère, then turned thunderous when she noticed her niece sitting across from him. Unaware of the under-current among the family, the young heir turned white as he anticipated a harsh scolding from the aunt of the wom-an he had previously abused. He jumped to his feet.

Bea rose too and sought to put him at ease by draw-ing her aunt's attention. "How wonderful that you were able to break away from planning tomorrow's dinner to join us for some tea. I know you can spare us only a few minutes, as you still have so much to do before we go to the Pemberton ball this evening. I will pour, Dawson, so you may put the tea on the table in front of me. Mr. Skeff-ington was about to tell us his plans for the season. Will you stay for the whole of it?"

Although Beatrice had never had an opportunity to play the gracious hostess before, she found the role easy to master and smiled soothingly in response to her aunt's angry scowl. Cautiously, as if she was still unsure what was actually happening, the older woman walked into the room and sat down next to her daughter. Mr. Skeffington bowed awkwardly in her general direction before regaining his seat.

"There," Bea said as she poured the first cup of tea and offered it to their guest, "isn't this cozy? I'm so glad you dropped by, Mr. Skeffington."

Bea knew it was wrong to gloat, but she just couldn't stop herself, for she had cowered for years. For decades she had been silent and docile and terrified her aunt and uncle would throw her out on her ear at the first display of temper. She knew now it would never happen. Her aunt would move heaven and earth to see her leg-shackled to a man, any man, yes, it didn't matter how low—the village blacksmith would do just fine, thank you very much—but she would never eject her husband's brother's daughter from the family. In the smallest corner of her miserly heart, Vera Hyde-Clare loved her niece.

Or so Bea liked to assure herself.

Mr. Skeffington thanked her for the tea and declined the addition of sugar.

"You are looking well," her aunt said, even though the color had yet to return to his face. "I'm relieved to see it after the…um…"

And there, in fewer than a dozen words, Aunt Vera had wandered into treacherous territory, only a syllable or two away from mentioning the unpleasantness at Lakeview Hall. Hyde-Clares in general did not like to talk about hideous events and her aunt had a particular aversion, as she seemed to find it rude or uncouth to discuss anything that wasn't benign or pleasant.

Now she fumbled for a way to quickly change direction and decided to substitute the word *visit* for "dreadful murder of Mr. Otley by your mother."

"I cannot remember when we last had such an…uh…interesting stay in the country," she added, striving to appear unconcerned by the awkwardness of her own slip. "I'm sure everyone else did as well. Although, of course…"

But she could not bring herself to make an exception for the victim or the villain and trailed off awkwardly with an angry look at Beatrice, as if this, too—the discomfort she felt in her own drawing room—was all her fault. She considered the unmasking of Lady Skeffington as the killer to be the sole responsibility of her niece and resented the fact that the meddlesome young lady had forced them all to confront the truth.

Vera Hyde-Clare firmly believed in the graceful evasion of distasteful information and preferred reality to be served with a satisfying sprinkling of sugar.

Mr. Skeffington, however, would have none of her discretion, stating the matter forthrightly and making her complicit by crediting her with raising the topic in the first place. "I'm glad you brought it up, Mrs. Hyde-Clare, for I don't want to tiptoe around the subject. The awful events of the fall happened, and there is no use in pretending they didn't," he said, his tone defiant even as he managed to avoid saying the words. "My parents are in Italy now and plan to move on to Greece when the weather warms up. I don't know if you heard how the matter proceeded with the magistrate."

They'd heard—of course they had. 'Twas not every day that a baroness was remanded to local authorities on the charge of murdering one of her guests. And yet the occupants of the room remained silent, for none of them wanted to discomfit their visitor or, in the case of Aunt Vera, herself.

"It did not go as smoothly as my father had hoped," Mr. Skeffington explained, "for, although Gosport was inclined to be reasonable about the whole thing, he could not dismiss the fact that my mother had confessed to the crime in front of a Runner. He was in quite an awkward spot—unable to dismiss the case and unwilling to refer it to the Crown—so he placed my mother under house arrest and quietly urged my father to remove her from his jurisdiction."

Although fleeing one's country seat to avoid criminal prosecution hardly constituted embarking on a grand tour, Aunt Vera chose to see their escape to the Continent as an opportunity to travel. "How delightful. Helen always did long to explore more of the world. When we were in school together, she would frequently talk about having wonderful adventures when she grew up. She had a particular interest in the Parthenon, so I'm not the least bit surprised to hear she will be traveling to Greece soon. I'm sure your father is quite pleased as well, for he is a great angler and the Mediterranean is known for its abundance of fish."

But Mr. Skeffington would not allow her the consolation of a silver lining. "Actually, they're both wretched, for my mother hates discomfort of any kind and my father is deeply suspicious of foreigners and they are surrounded by both at every moment. I suspect my father will see her settled in Athens and then return to England. He has said repeatedly in his letters to his steward that he has done nothing wrong and sees no reason why he should be punished too."

He put his teacup down with unexpected force, causing it to rattle loudly against the saucer, and turned to Bea with surprising intensity. "They're monsters, Miss Hyde-Clare," he said, plainly feeling some sort of connection to her after the ordeal they had both endured, albeit in significantly different ways. The violence he had suffered had been entirely emotional, but it left its scars just the same. "They're absolute monsters. I don't know how it's possible that they could have been like this my whole life and I not see it."

The pain in his voice was unmistakable, and Bea realized with dawning horror that he had come to Portman Square seeking its mitigation. He, like her aunt, considered her a central player in his parents' downfall and somehow believed that gave her a special power to make things better or different.

Overwhelmed by the impossibility of his expectation, Bea felt an almost irresistible desire to run out of the room. Alleviating his personal anguish was no more her responsibility than his parents' dreadfulness was his. Furthermore, she had her own difficult relations to contend with, including an aunt who would seek to lock her in a tower and throw away the key if only the house had been fortuitously blessed with that particular architectural feature.

But obligation did not follow the strict dictates of decorum and instead flouted them openly. It lay down on the settee and stretched it legs, so to speak.

With a deep sigh, Bea examined the young gentleman whose formidable black brows contrasted disconcertingly with his light-green eyes. He was only two years younger than she and yet seemed a generation apart. "You are being far too hard on yourself, for you are their child and cannot be expected to see them clearly. Your perspective has been molded by affection, both theirs for you and yours for them. But even those who had the benefit of a less sentimental connection did not see them clearly. Isn't that correct, Aunt Vera?" she asked, turning to consult the opinion of someone who had known Lady Skeffington when she was still Miss Poole. "You had been friends with Helen since you were classmates at Mrs. Crawford's School for Girls and you never suspected she was capable of repeatedly hitting a man over the head with a candlestick until he was dead, did you?"

The look her aunt sent her was murderous, but she managed to temper it to mild annoyance by the time she turned to her guest. "Although I disagree ardently with the brutality of my niece's description, for I cannot believe the event happened in quite such a heartless fashion, the substance of her observation is correct. I knew your mother for decades and never suspected she was capable of anything more violent than shooing away a fly," she said kindly. Then, as if unable to accept even the slightest hint of culpability, she was compelled to add that she had seen little of Lady Skeffington in recent years. "As you know, she held a privileged place in society and her presence was much in demand at routs and dinner parties. She did love hosting, as well, and there were several house parties at Lakeview Hall to which I was not invited. And of course her relationship with Mr. Otley must have demanded a fair amount of her attention, for one cannot conduct an extramarital affair without carving out some time for it."

As soon as the words were out of her mouth, Aunt Vera gasped at her thoughtless candor and slapped her hand over her lips. Although nobody else in the room reacted, including Mr. Skeffington, whose expression indicated that he'd had a similar thought himself, she could not withstand the egregiousness of the faux pas and fled from the room with the claim that she'd heard Mrs. Emerson calling for her. It was a blatant lie, for no housekeeper in a respectable establishment would ever think to yell her employer's name down the hallway, regardless of whether she was entertaining company or not.

Flora apologized at once for both her mother's abrupt departure and Mrs. Emerson's supposed rudeness. "It's the blancmange, you see. The peace of the household rests on its successful execution."

Unsurprisingly, Mr. Skeffington did not see at all, but rather than seek clarity, he returned his attention to Bea, whom he considered to be the more sensible woman. "I cannot thank you enough for your kindness. You must know that for months I've been haunted by my treatment of you. It seems impossible to me now that I actually hit you over the head with a wooden plank. It's far too similar to my mother's treatment of Mr. Otley for me to breathe easily."

Ah, Beatrice thought, realizing it was this possibility that bedeviled him the most. "I believe the simple fact that you are aware enough of your own actions to wonder such a thing means you are incapable of it."

"I agree," said Flora, leaning forward on the cushion. "You are already too thoughtful, Mr. Skeffington, and more thoughtful still, having seen the horror up close."

"Yes, that's precisely what Miss Otley said," he announced with a pleased smile.

"Miss Otley?" Aunt Vera said, sticking her head into the room with alarming swiftness. Either she had been listening at the door from the moment she'd left or her sense of a rival's presence was so finely honed she could appear within a fraction of a second of one's mention.

"Why, yes, we have been in almost constant communication since the events of the fall," he explained. "It turns out that having monstrous human beings for parents creates a rather impervious bond among their offspring. In the act of consoling each other we've discovered a fondness and lasting affection. We are to be wed next Christmas, for we need to wait an appropriate amount of time after the end of her mourning period."

"Wed?" Aunt Vera asked faintly as she sat down next to her daughter on the settee. "As in married to each other for all of eternity?"

Although Bea knew the blow her aunt had just suffered was genuine, she couldn't help but be amused by her dramatics. No doubt she was thinking how unfair it was that Mrs. Otley, despite losing her husband to a candlestick and herself being revealed as an adulteress, still somehow managed to pull off the match of the century for her Incomparable daughter. Naturally, Aunt Vera had hoped to nab the Skeffington heir for her own daughter, which was why she had attended the house party with such alacrity and purchased two lovely and entirely unnecessary new gowns for Flora. At the time, Mr. Skeffington had seemed interested in neither young lady, but the events of the fall, as he chose to describe his mother's murderous attack on Miss Otley's father, seemed to have matured him.

They must have matured Miss Otley as well, for when Bea had known the beautiful young lady she had been dismissive of her parents' plan to rivet her to a lowly baron. Her sights had been fixed on a marquess or a duke.

"That is wonderful news," Flora said with sincere enthusiasm as her mother whimpered beside her. "I offer my warmest congratulations. Is Miss Otley in town? Is she accepting visitors?"

Mr. Skeffington said that she was indeed and would be quite delighted to see the Misses Hyde-Clare at their earliest convenience. He also rushed to explain that the engagement was not a matter of public record yet, as the *ton* would consider it indecent so hard on the heels of her father's death.

With each word he spoke, Aunt Vera's anguish increased, which was patently absurd, Bea thought, for her discomfort with unpleasant truths was so acute she could never have withstood the awkwardness of joining her family with a murderer's. As Mr. Skeffington had yet to return to society, it was impossible to say what his welcome would be, and although it was decidedly unfair to deliver the sins of the mother unto the son, the beau monde was hardly known for its evenhanded dispensing of justice.

Nevertheless, her daughter sought to ease her grief by speaking softly to her and gathering her hands in her own.

Not sure if she was more amused or disgusted, Bea looked at Mr. Skeffington and offered her congratulations as well. "I'm sure you will both be very happy. I think your temperaments will match very well."

"Thank you," he said with a distracted look at the settee. She was about to apologize for her aunt's ridiculous display, of which he couldn't possibly know what to think, when he stood up, crossed the couple of feet that separated them and sat down in the chair next to her. Then, leaning his head close to hers, he spoke softly but in an urgent rush. "I'd hoped to have a few moments alone with you to discuss a very troubling matter. It's an entirely indelicate subject and wholly inappropriate and I won't be the least bit surprised if you gasp in horror and throw your tea at me, but I'm thoroughly at my wit's end and have no idea where else to turn. Indeed, my decision to speak to you might be the result of a wild panic I seem incapable of overcoming, but that's only because I am beside myself with fear and anxiety. Something must be done."

His frantic speech was by far the most remarkable one Beatrice had ever heard and she stared at him in alarm, for he appeared to be on the verge of apoplexy. "Please speak, Mr. Skeffington, I will do whatever I can to ease your fear and anxiety."

Slowly, he nodded and took a deep breath. "I would like you to investigate a murder."

CHAPTER THREE

Although Bea's first response was an eager and excited yes— *yes, yes, of course I will investigate your murder*—her thoughts instantly swerved to the source of the question and she stared at him aghast as she tried to figure out who the victim could be. Not Miss Otley, obviously, or her mother, for no man would have been able to sit in a drawing room making polite conversation with a tragedy of that magnitude drumming a beat in his head. By his own account, his parents were well and safe on the Continent. Could it be his friend Lord Amersham, who had accompanied him to Lakeview Hall in the fall…

Aware that her aunt would not be inconsolable forever, she chastised herself for wasting time with speculation and put the question to him directly. "Who?"

The young man sighed with relief at the calm practicality of her question, unmistakably grateful that she hadn't descended into hysterics. "Do you recall Mr. Wilson? He was Mr. Otley's business associate in India and Mrs. Otley's lover."

Beatrice required no reminder of who Mr. Wilson was, for she had convinced herself he was responsible for the murder of the spice trader. Despite having no reason to believe he was in England, let alone the Lake District, she had been certain he was secreted away somewhere on the estate, hiding in the guise of a new employee. It was while she was looking for him in one of the outbuildings behind the stables that Mr. Skeffington had knocked her on the head with a wooden plank and locked her in the shed.

"I do, yes," she said, barely able to comprehend the unlikely turn of events. That the man she had believed responsible for Mr. Otley's untimely death had suffered the same fate himself seemed extraordinary.

His composure somewhat restored by her cool acceptance, Mr. Skeffington explained, his voice too quiet for her aunt, who was moaning softly, to hear. "He was found dead this morning. It was horrible, Miss Hyde-Clare, simply horrible for he was discovered in"—here, he lowered his voice until it was a mere whisper—"Mrs. Otley's bed. She had sworn that the affair was over. Emily refused even to speak to her again until the connection had been severed, and her mother complied. Or, at least, she'd claimed to. But this morning Emily heard terrible, terrible sounds coming from her mother's room, and when she raced in to discover what the matter was, she found Mr. Wilson in her bed, his body wracked by convulsions he couldn't control. He was, she said, in tremendous pain and could not stop arching his back in the most alarming manner. Just when she feared he would split himself entirely in half, the convulsions stopped. She'd thought the fit of paroxysms had passed, but upon closer examination she realized that he had expired. Can you imagine what that was like for her?" he asked with growing despair. It was apparent that he could imagine, and had done, little else in the interval since discovery. "I am in agony on her behalf."

Although the story Mr. Skeffington told was shocking and repellant, a nightmare transposed to the drawing room, Bea wasn't shocked or repelled. She was genuinely horrified, of course, for Emily, who did not deserve to witness such a traumatic event so soon after her father had suffered his own violent end, and she spared a thought for Mrs. Otley, her lie exposed in a horrifyingly public manner. But she was also intrigued and curious, and her mind immediately went to the method the villain had used. What she knew of poisons was limited to the little she'd gleaned from her reading over the years, but she recognized the properties of a toxic substance in his description. The question, of course, was which one.

"No, Mr. Skeffington, I cannot imagine what that's like, and my heart aches for poor Emily. She has already been through so much, and now to have this devastating situation." She shook her head gently, uncertain if the Incomparable she'd met in the Lake District had the mettle to deal with Mr. Wilson's tragedy on top of her father's. She had seemed as hard as stone when discussing her marriage prospects during their walk to the folly but had crumbled like a castle of sand when confronted with the depths of her parents' depravity. "I agree there's no time to waste. We must start the investigation at once with an examination of the scene of death. There is always information to be gained from it."

Bea spoke firmly and with conviction, almost as if she were a Bow Street Runner herself, or, somehow more fancifully, an expert in detection who offered her services for a modest fee. But in truth she was simply making an educated guess as to the best way to proceed, for she had done this only twice before. At best, she would call herself an informed amateur.

The Duke of Kesgrave would call her a foolish one.

At once, she pictured Kesgrave's disapproving frown.

No, she thought, pushing the image away, for this circumstance could not qualify as crossing her path. The duke had been speaking to a very specific condition in which a dead body literally placed itself in her path, as it had in both the library at Lakeview Hall and offices of the *London Daily Gazette* on the Strand.

He could not quibble with her participation, she told herself.

And yet she knew he could quibble about anything, for he was a duke and a man and believed he knew best about everything.

Ah, but he could not know best about something he did not know about at all.

Mr. Skeffington let out another deep breath, and his whole body seemed to lighten. "You have no idea what a relief your attitude is, Miss Hyde-Clare. I trust it goes without saying that I hesitated greatly before coming here today. Even after I entered the house, I wasn't sure I would have the nerve to bring up the matter, for it's beyond inappropriate that I'm asking you. But when I recall all that I have already done to you—that is, whacking you with a plank, imprisoning you in a shed and accusing you of licentious behavior before a house full of people, including your family—asking you to investigate the suspicious death of my future mother-in-law's lover feels almost minor in comparison."

Bea laughed with unexpected force and darted a quick look at the settee, noting with relief that her aunt was still too engrossed in her own miseries to notice anything amiss. "As I said, I'm certainly happy to help in any way I can, but why seek me out? Would not the authorities be even more helpful in this situation?"

"Mrs. Otley refuses to allow us to alert them and wants to dispose of the body by contacting a physician who works at an asylum," he said with a growl of frustration. "She claims no woman's reputation could withstand two dead men. One, particularly a husband, was understandable, for whose life was without its difficulties. But a second suggests a recklessness. I tried to reason with her but she simply won't listen, and I can't allow Emily to live in a house that may or may not be occupied by a murderer. We must discover the truth, no matter how unpleasant, and I did such a shabby job of it last time. You, however, knew exactly how to put all the pieces together to make a complete picture. I cannot tell you how grateful I am that you're willing to assume this horrendous task."

She nodded gravely, as if the gratitude was solely on his side, but she could hardly believe he'd appeared on her doorstop with a mystery at the very moment she was on the lookout for one. Indeed, the absurdly providential timing of his request made it seem almost preordained, and silently she told the Duke of Kesgrave to take the matter up with his maker if he had a problem with that.

"And I, in turn, am deeply gratified by your trust in me. I promise I will do everything in my power not to let you and Miss Otley down," she said solemnly, sparing another glance at her aunt, who was now dabbing her eyes with a handkerchief. "Naturally, my family cannot know anything about this. They aren't as practical as I am about these matters. Aunt Vera, in particular, tends to get flustered. She also believes exposure to dead bodies corrupts one's faculties, a stance with which I heartily disagree. Speaking of exposure to dead bodies, how *did* Mrs. Otley respond to her lover's convulsive episode? I cannot imagine she remained composed."

"She tried to shush him."

Bea leaned forward, certain she could not have heard him correctly. "Shush him?"

He nodded. "Yes. You see, his suffering was quite acute and he was making a tremendous amount of noise and she wanted him to be quiet, so she tried to shush him. That did not work, as he was beyond sense at that point, according to Emily, so she tried covering his mouth with a pillow."

To her surprise, Bea discovered it was possible to be even more appalled by Mrs. Otley. "She *what*?"

"When she could not get him to regulate his volume on his own, she sought to do it for him by placing a pillow over his mouth. It was futile, of course, as the convulsions were so strong he flailed all over the mattress like a fish suffocating for air. He did not stay anywhere for long, but she kept flopping over the bed, trying to place the pillow over his mouth. When Emily first entered the room, she thought her mother and Mr. Wilson were engaged in some sort of bed sport," he explained tightly, his cheeks turning bright red at the hint of carnal activity.

Something in his bashful expression caught Aunt Vera's attention, pulling her out of the doldrums she had sunk into since hearing the news of Miss Otley's triumph. Promptly, she lifted her head from where it rested on Flora's shoulder. Knowing nothing of the situation, she assumed her niece was responsible for Mr. Skeffington's discomfort and apologized at once for Bea's behavior. "The fault is my own, for she has been under the weather most recently, and I should not have allowed her to have company."

"You mustn't be so hard on yourself," Flora said comfortingly. "I'm the one who decided Bea was ready for company, not you. The fault is entirely mine, although I must say I think this visit has been good for her. Her eyes are shining, and there's a healthy glow to her skin. It's quite an improvement."

Although Flora could hardly know it, she had all but said that murder was excellent for her cousin's complexion.

Bea had the grace to blush.

"I must thank you, Mr. Skeffington, for coming around," Flora added. "Your good news has brightened the day for all of us."

Naturally, Aunt Vera mewled again at this reminder of Mrs. Otley's unqualified success, and the image of the widow trying to smother her lover's cries of agony as he convulsed to death in her bed flitted through Bea's mind. As she watched her aunt's bottom lip tremble with disappointment, she wondered if her judgment would soften if she knew of the ghastly events of that morning or if her disappointment in losing a future baron to an old school rival was so entrenched nothing could mitigate it.

Despite this very great setback, Aunt Vera was still mindful of her duty and she managed to echo her daughter's thoughts with a modicum of grace and composure. She asked Mr. Skeffington a few brief questions about his plans, listened patiently to the answers, and then drew attention to the lateness of the hour. It was time they started getting ready for Pemberton's ball.

It was barely three o'clock.

Mr. Skeffington was too well-bred not to respond instantly to the hint and stood up to make his goodbyes. "Yes, of course. I had intended to go myself, but an unexpected issue has arisen that requires swift action." He darted a speaking glance to Bea that was as frantic as it was helpless. "But I'm very sorry to have to miss it."

At this indication of further bad news, Flora expressed sympathy, and while Mr. Skeffington tried at once to minimize its importance and hide his distress, Bea considered the best way to proceed with her investigation. As she had told Mr. Skeffington, the first step was to examine the scene where Mr. Wilson had met his excruciating end. To do that, however, she would have to leave the house without arousing Aunt Vera's suspicions. During her last investigation, she'd discovered how easy it was to slip out of the house unnoticed, but now that her family was aware of her tricks, she imagined executing a furtive exit might be slightly more challenging.

If she announced her intentions openly and honestly, her confidence might confuse her aunt into compliance.

"I will go with you," Bea announced.

Aunt Vera turned to look at her with bewildered eyes. "Go with whom? Go where?"

"To visit Miss Otley," she said simply, as if stating an obvious fact. "Mr. Skeffington is on his way to her right now, and he said she's despondent that I haven't visited since returning to town. After all, she is one of my dearest friends and I have yet to congratulate her on her coming nuptials. I'm sure you understand. I will just get my pelisse and my maid."

As far as baffling statements went, this announcement was probably the most confounding one she could have come up with and her aunt stared at her bewildered, as if she could not even understand the words. "One of your dearest friends?" she echoed. "But you don't have *any* friends."

Although Bea had not only invited this response but relied on it to attain her goal, she was still taken aback by the casual cruelty of her aunt's tone, whose matter-of-factness did not allow for the possibility that her status could change. "If Emily was not my dearest friend, then why would I have confessed my deepest secret to her? You knew nothing of Mr. Davies, for I had told nobody in the family about him."

To this point, her aunt had no answer because it was true: Bea had shared the details of her love affair with an unsuitable law clerk with only one person in the world and it had not been a Hyde-Clare.

By any account, this fact did seem to indicate an unprecedented intimacy.

"But she's engaged to Mr. Skeffington," Aunt Vera said—by which she meant: You cannot be friends with the Incomparable who stole a baronetcy from me.

Bea knew it was unkind to be amused by her aunt's distress, but she couldn't quite smother her mirth. "I know, dear. And that is why I must go. But do not worry. I will be back in plenty of time to get ready. I know how disappointed you would be if I missed the ball."

Unsure if she was being teased, Aunt Vera managed a half smile.

Flora, whose intense fascination with Miss Otley had faded as soon as her family's unsavory secrets were revealed in the drawing room at Lakeview Hall, gave her full support to the scheme. "You must go. I'm sure Emily has been made desolate by your neglect. Do pass along our kind regards and assure her we look forward to visiting with her soon."

It was a lovely speech and entirely self-serving, for Flora was convinced her cousin was up to something dashing and hoped to discover the specifics of it later. Bea knew what she was thinking because she'd spent weeks fending off Flora's curiosity. The story about the funeral had struck the other girl as implausible, for she felt certain nobody would be ill-bred enough to raise their fists in a cemetery, and every so often she would ask Bea to repeat a detail just to see if it varied from previous retellings.

Unlike the rest of her family, Flora did not think Bea's faculties had been undermined by grief and exposure to Mr. Otley's gruesome corpse. Rather, she believed the explanation for her recent behavior was far more straight-forward: They were simply seeing their relative clearly for the first time.

Bea had always been tricky and clever and full of mischief.

No other explanation accounted for how she had managed to conduct an entire courtship without anyone in the house raising an eyebrow, not even the servants. What was most astounding was how Bea *seemed* to have been present in the house the entire time she was off being wooed by Mr. Davies. No one could think of a single oc-casion when Bea wasn't on hand exactly when her pres-ence was required.

Flora's awe made Bea distinctly uncomfortable, for she did not relish the way her cousin treated her now, as if she were some magical creature who could achieve impos-sible things. The trick, of course, was that there wasn't a trick: She'd seemed always to be around because she al-ways *had been* around. Day after day, week after week, year after year, she'd been at her aunt's beck and call, ready to serve in whatever capacity was needed—and why wouldn't she have been? She had nothing to take her away from the drawing room: no clandestine assignations, no secret lover. As Aunt Vera had so helpfully pointed out only a few minutes before, she didn't even have friends with whom to pay calls or attend the theater.

Taking his cue from Bea and Flora, Mr. Skeffington thanked Bea for her willingness to visit his fiancée without hesitation. "Ordinarily, I would not admit this to company, but I was actually under orders from Miss Otley to engineer this exact situation. She will be so pleased—and perhaps a little amazed—that I was able to do her bidding exactly as she requested. I cannot thank you enough, Mrs. Hyde-Clare, for your allowing me to steal your niece away for a couple of hours. You are so wonderfully kind and generous. And you must not worry: I promise I will have her back in plenty of time to get ready for the ball."

Highly susceptible to flattery, Aunt Vera simpered at these compliments and almost forgave him for choosing a diamond of the first water over her very pretty but in no way ravishing daughter. "Yes, yes, of course, you must go. Poor Miss Otley has suffered so much shame and humiliation, and if she finds some measure of consolation from my niece's presence, we must not deny her it, no matter how little we comprehend it."

Bea shook her head in amusement and, swallowing a smile, told her aunt that her graciousness was humbling to behold.

"I try, dear," she said as if surprised by the amount of effort she was continually called on to make. "I try all the time."

"Of course you do," Flora murmured, wrapping an arm around her mother's shoulder as Mr. Skeffington escorted Bea and her maid, Annie, to the door.

CHAPTER FOUR

Mrs. Otley screamed when she saw Bea enter her front parlor. A high-piercing trill that continued for several unnerving seconds, it brought the housekeeper, two footmen and one of the girls from the kitchen to the room at top speed. They hovered in the doorway as if expecting to see something dreadful, perhaps another dead body, and it was only when Mrs. Otley spotted the scullery maid on the threshold that she modulated her tone. The volume of her shriek lessened and faded into silence. Then she laughed awkwardly.

"Oh, goodness, such a lot of bother," she said, coloring slightly as her butler appeared to gently direct the group of gawking servants away from the room. Annie, who had entered the room a few steps behind her mistress, was swept along with the assortment. Before he closed the door behind him, she requested a pot of tea to soothe her nerves. "Do sit down, Miss Hyde-Clare. I'm sorry for the reception. I truly don't know what overcame me other than I'm apprehensive and not quite in control of myself. It has been such a trying day. To be honest, I feel like a clock that is continually striking midnight. Bong. Bong. Bong. It's awful. And to take it out on you! My dear, I'm mortified. It's just that the sight of you brought back all those awful memories from Lakeview House, and suddenly I was in that drawing room again being subjected to the public revelation of all my family's private business. To be perfectly candid, Miss Hyde-Clare, I'd hoped to never see you again, and to have you here on this miserable day of all days is a particular cross to bear. I'm not sure I can stomach it."

Her daughter, who had entered the room in time to hear the second half of this speech, had no patience for her mother's dramatics. "You will stomach it, Mama, and much more besides," she announced coldly before greeting Beatrice warmly. Emily Otley was a beauty in that classic English way, with pale skin, rosy cheeks, pouty lips and dark lashes defining light-blue eyes. She was taller than her petite mother, whose coloring she shared, and prided herself on an ample collection of elaborately plumed hats. Today, her dark head was unadorned.

"Mr. Skeffington sends his apologies for not joining us in tea. He has an appointment with the solicitor, for which he must be particularly grateful, as he cannot enjoy listening to me and my mother bicker. Now you may have the pleasure," she said with a wry smile as she sat down next to Bea on the dark-colored settee. "I'm so glad you were able to come so quickly. I did not know what to do with myself this morning when my mother insisted we not call the Runners to investigate the matter. Given the recent discovery of my mother's heartlessness, I naturally assumed she was responsible for Mr. Wilson's unfortunate condition and that was why she resisted contacting the authorities."

It was quite a harsh indictment of her mother's character, and Bea was genuinely taken aback. Aunt Vera was a rather callous human being—a fact that was in no way a recent discovery for her—but Bea would never suspect her of murder.

"But she did succeed in making a reasonably sound argument for why she couldn't be responsible," Emily admitted.

"It's true," Mrs. Otley said with a wary glance at her daughter. "If I was keeping my relationship with Mr. Wilson a secret from you, why would I murder him in the most ostentatious way possible? Would I not have simply thrust him in front of a carriage on Bond Street or pushed him out of a high window somewhere far from here? I'm sure every person who has ever plotted the demise of a troublesome interloper knows the first thing to consider is location. Never dirty one's own nest if one can avoid it."

Emily sighed loudly and looked at Bea with an expression of sad resignation as if to convey the hopelessness of her situation. "In this way, I've ruled my mother out as a possible perpetrator, but she still refuses to let the authorities handle it."

Mrs. Otley shook her head. "Why can't we just plant him in the garden, or if that offends your sensibilities, we can hire an undertaker to emboss him properly, although if you ask me that is a needless and foolish expense that we cannot easily afford at the—"

"Embalm him," Emily said, interrupting.

"Excuse me?" her mother asked, torn between impatience and confusion.

"You emboss stationery," Emily explained. "You *embalm* a dead person."

Now Mrs. Otley sighed heavily, as if exhausted from all the details she'd been forced to keep abreast of during an already arduous day. "It appears you have the matter well in hand. I'm not sure why I need to be here." She turned to look at Bea. "You don't need me here, do you? The viper whom I've nurtured at my breast says it's vital that I talk to you. But it's not really necessary, is it?"

Although she had coolly announced her mother capable of murder only a few minutes before, Emily took offense at this description. "Mother," she cried in an injured tone. "How can you speak of me like that?"

Mrs. Otley shook her head. "How can *you* speak of *me* like that?"

"Must I remind you of your relationship with Mr. Wilson?" she asked. "That is how I can."

"I gave him up for you!" her mother exclaimed, outraged by the charge.

"You made a lavish spectacle of severing the connection and then continued your dalliance as if nothing had happened," Emily replied with passionate disapproval.

"Yes, and I went through that pretense because you're my daughter. Your feelings are important to me," Mrs. Otley explained gently. "I assure you, my dear, there's no one else in the world for whom I would make such an effort."

Emily did not find this statement quite as affecting as her mother had hoped and looked at Bea as if challenging her to come up with a reasonable response.

When Bea met the family in the Lake District in the fall, the dynamic between mother and daughter had been quite different. On that occasion it had been apparent to anyone who observed them that Emily ruled the roost and her parents devoted themselves to fulfilling her desires. She demanded and they delivered—not, it turned out, out of a desire to see her every wish granted but from the hope that she would make a quick, advantageous marriage before the beau monde discovered the true state of their finances. Mr. Otley's business, which was, as far as the *ton* knew, a very successful spice-trading concern in India that he had overseen ever since he'd returned to England a rich man decades before, had suffered an irreversible setback. The East India Company, the joint-stock firm that all but owned the region, discovered that he was running a small but highly lucrative opium operation. Considering the cultivation and smuggling of illegal opium to China to be its exclusive province, John Company, as the massive organization was informally known, seized his fields and drove him out of business.

With his family's fortune in desperate need of repair, Otley had ostensibly set up a new enterprise growing hibiscus and found eager investors to sink funds into his next success. In actuality, however, he planted not a single plant, for the venture was a fraud from the very beginning. He waited a few months, then claimed a devastating fire wiped out the entire crop. Alas, his investors were not as easily gulled as he'd hoped and, suspecting a trick, sought out the truth. The only reason the Duke of Kesgrave had been in Cumbria was to investigate Otley and the hibiscus scheme on behalf of an old family friend whose financial situation had been devastated by the swindle.

Andrew Skeffington, as well as his friend Lord Amersham, was also among the swindled.

Since the startling revelations at Lakeview Hall, the relationship between the two women had undergone a radical revolution. Mrs. Otley was no longer in awe of her daughter's beauty, even though it had achieved the very thing she'd wanted it to achieve, and Emily could not muster any respect for the mother who had lied to her about almost everything.

Bea imagined the situation must make for some rather awkward family meals.

Grateful to no longer be at a house party with the pair, Bea looked at Mrs. Otley and said, "He was a troublesome interloper?"

The older woman's brow furrowed in confusion. "Excuse me?"

"A moment ago you said that anyone who has ever plotted the end of a troublesome interloper knows not to sully their own home," Bea reminded her. "And I was just wondering if Mr. Wilson was a troublesome interloper."

"Goodness me, no!" she cried, amused by the accusation. "That you can think such a thing demonstrates precisely why this exercise is an utterly ridiculous waste of time. Only an interfering busybody with no interests would imagine something nefarious in a routine digestive issue gone tragically awry. And now you are here accusing me of harming a man who had been nothing but kind to me during a very trying time in my life. How could I wish to harm a hair on his head? I'm far too grateful for the comfort and support he has provided, unlike some people...." A quick look in her daughter's direction confirmed whom she meant, but it was not necessary to Bea's understanding. "He *might* have been a little overly ambitious in his plans, for how could he seriously believe I would consider marrying someone of his standing, a former steward who had cultivated opium in a foreign backwater, especially now that my daughter's advantageous marriage will put me in the reach of a much better quality of suitor. But surely that gives him cause to wish me harm, not the other way around?"

Bea wasn't entirely sure she agreed with that reasoning, for if Mrs. Otley had decided to end the relationship and her lover resisted, then slipping him a little poison with the morning tea might be the ideal solution to a potentially awkward problem. "How did Mr. Wilson feel about your rejection of his suit?"

"Gutted, naturally, as he positively adored me, but he understood the opportunities available to me, an attractive woman with many good years left," she said as Emily snorted at the description. Mrs. Otley was firmly situated at the upper end of forty, and although she most likely had quite a few years left, it was debatable how many of those could be categorized as good. Determined to ignore her daughter, she added, "Charles wanted me to have the best. Since he'd returned—"

"When was that?" Bea interrupted to ask.

"When was what?" Mrs. Otley said blankly.

"When did he return from India?"

"Several months ago," she said, furrowing her brow. "Poor dear. He had an arduous journey home, and he does abhor the sea. It's so violent sometimes. I don't quite remember when it was. Perhaps the end of October? I don't see that it matters. He had decided to set himself up as a farmer with the money he made and was looking for a property to buy. He knew such a humble existence would not appeal to me. Above all else, Mr. Wilson was a sensible man. When Otley insisted on sending him to India he didn't want to go, of course, but he recognized the assignment for the opportunity it was and agreed to go without ever letting on that he knew the real reason he was being shipped off to a foreign land."

Recalling his letter to Mrs. Otley grumbling about the inhospitable environment of India, which Bea had discovered and read during her investigation in the Lake District, she wasn't surprised to hear of his reluctance. "And what was that?"

"To separate us," she explained. At her daughter's shocked gasp, she snapped impatiently. "Of course your father knew we were lovers. He wasn't a ninny, and half the reason to have an affair is so your spouse may seethe over it. Really, my dear, it's as if you were raised in a convent, your notions are so puritanical."

Emily's lips turned white at this taunt, but she remained silent, and Bea, whose notions could also be described as puritanical, strove to keep her thoughts hidden. There was nothing to be gained in appearing to sit in moral judgment of one's suspect. Rather, she asked how long she and Mr. Wilson had associated before he was sent to India.

"A year," she answered promptly. "He had been in my husband's employ for a year before we could no longer fight the overwhelming attraction we felt for each other and was sent to India a year later. Otley was so churlish about the whole thing. If his own romantic liaison had not ended in acrimony, he would not have minded my happiness quite so much." Here, she sighed long and deep. "He had always been a stingy man."

Her daughter whimpered at this further glimpse into the cold indifference that characterized her parents' relationship. Most marriages among the *ton* were transactional, shoring up status and property, and the Otleys' lack of sentiment was hardly unique. Nevertheless, Bea felt the same revulsion as Emily. Even if her aunt and uncle had little affection for her, they respected and esteemed each other.

"In what way was going abroad an opportunity?" Bea asked.

"In every way," the widow replied. "Otley made his fortune there, and it seems as though every other month another second or third son returns from there a nabob. It could not be that difficult to accrue money in such an environment, and Mr. Wilson was clever. He knew how to make the most of a situation. I knew he would flourish there, and he did. He returned with several thousand pounds to his name, which is considerably more than he went with."

Although the widow made the accumulation of wealth sound as effortless as stepping off the boat in Bombay and catching banknotes as they flew by in the wind, Bea could not believe it had been that easy. Even in India, money was a limited resource and its acquisition frequently called for an aggressive stance. It would not be unusual if, in the pursuit of his fortune, Mr. Wilson had made an enemy or two. After all, the man had run a successful opium-smuggling operation for more than a year, which had to require a certain ruthlessness.

"Do you know how Mr. Wilson made his fortune while he was there?" Bea asked.

"Gracious me, no!" Mrs. Otley said with a dismissive chortle. "Talk about money matters? What do you take me for, Miss Hyde-Clare, a cit? No, I did not ask him about the source of his wealth any more than I'd asked Otley about his. As long as the bills are paid, it is none of my concern."

Emily snorted in disgust. "Yes, as long as the dressmaker is appeased, she doesn't care how filthy the lucre is."

With surprising patience, Mrs. Otley turned to her daughter and said, "If I've told you once, I've told you a hundred times that I had no idea your father was swindling nice young men like Mr. Skeffington."

"You thought he was just swindling senile old men," Emily said with spiteful cynicism. "Do stop trying to appear high-minded in front of our guest. She knows what you are."

Mrs. Otley shrugged her shoulders, as if unable to muster the interest in composing a response to the charge, and looked at Beatrice. "As I said, I know very little about Mr. Wilson's time in India and nothing about his associates there."

Bea nodded and imagined this was true, as Mrs. Otley seemed particularly devoted to remaining as ignorant as possible about many things. The better to enjoy the fruits of her husband's immoral labor. "I believe Mr. Wilson wrote you letters from India. Perhaps you or I could peruse them for information about his business dealings. They may contain a name or two that would help us find out who wished him ill."

"I'm afraid that's impossible," she said with a firm shake of her head. "I burned all his letters last year after I discovered Emily had rifled through my private things and found a missive from Charles. They were too dangerous to keep."

"I would not have had to rifle through your private things if you and Papa had been honest with me about our financial situation," Emily said defensively. "You both insisted everything was all right when in fact things were quite desperate. Perhaps if you or Papa had sought my counsel, you would not have turned to thievery."

"*I* didn't turn to thievery," Mrs. Otley protested with a calm smile. "Your father is the one who lied and set up the swindle. Perhaps if he had not, he would still be alive right now and you could direct your ire at him, where it belongs."

Knowing her mother was not as innocent as she claimed, Emily harrumphed loudly.

Bea also found it difficult to believe Mrs. Otley knew nothing of what her husband was doing, especially as she had admitted at Lakeview Hall to having suspicions, but she did not press the issue, as she considered it to be a digression from the main topic.

"What about current matters?" Bea asked. "Where did he stay in London? Did he rent rooms?"

"What a question to ask!" Mrs. Otley said sharply. "Of course he rented rooms. He certainly wasn't living here."

"Do you know the name of the establishment?" Bea asked.

"I do, yes," she said firmly.

But she did not volunteer its name, which convinced Bea the woman was determined to be as unhelpful as possible. Did that mean she was trying to hide something or was she simply that miffed at having to answer impertinent questions in her own drawing room? Regardless of her motivation, she required Bea to ask three more questions before ultimately revealing Mr. Wilson had been staying at the Melbourne in Piccadilly.

"Do you also wish to know the number?" Mrs. Otley asked irritably. "I cannot supply that information as I had no need to seek it. What I do know is that Charles frequently complained about the positioning of his rooms, at the top of the steps on the first floor. Such a bother with people tromping up and down the stairs all day."

As Bea had not dared believe the widow could be so informative, she was genuinely grateful to be spared the awkwardness of discovering which rooms were Mr. Wilson's. Marking the location in her head, she asked if Mrs. Otley knew what dealings her lover had in London. "With whom was he associating?"

The widow shook her head, as if exasperated by Bea's obtuseness. "As I've already said, I make it a practice not to involve myself in business matters."

"What about social matters, then?" Bea asked. "Do you know who he associated with socially?"

Mrs. Otley tittered with amusement. "My dear, he was a former steward and aspiring farmer. Such a creature doesn't have social engagements. Next you will be asking me to which gentleman's club he belonged."

"For God's sake, Mama, she didn't mean he attended Almack's," her daughter growled impatiently. "She just wants to know what Wilson did all day when you weren't together."

"How would I know?" she asked owlishly. "We weren't together."

Emily grunted at this intentionally disingenuous response just as the butler returned with the tea tray. He laid it on the table in front of Mrs. Otley before leaving the room as quickly and silently as he'd entered.

"You weren't curious what he was doing?" Bea asked.

"No, should I have been?" Mrs. Otley said as she reached for the teapot. "Would you like some, my dear? I always find a cup of hot liquid to be soothing when I'm riled up by unnecessary drama, which this entire ordeal has been. I do not understand why my daughter and her fiancé can't simply agree with my intelligent assessment that Charles suffered from a disagreeable gallstone he was unable to dislodge. Then we might arrange a private disposal of his body to a well-respected medical institution that is always in need of specimens for anatomical study. Truly, I don't know what Emily has against science, but she clearly does not esteem the advancement of knowledge. I suspect her illogical response to the situation is due to the fact that she's not used to adversity and hasn't yet learned how to handle it with equanimity. If the worst she has to deal with, however, is her mother telling her a little white lie to spare her feelings, then perhaps she will never have an opportunity to cultivate that skill. She has been coddled her whole life, which is my fault, as well as her father's, and we take full responsibility for that. I fear Mr. Skeffington will continue the practice. I've tried to explain to him the importance of holding her to account, but he resents me because of that minor to-do with the investments. I don't know why he thinks it's *my* fault, as I never told Mr. Otley to swindle the son of one of my oldest and dearest friends. Indeed, if he had consulted me, I would have counseled the opposite."

"What about his past?" Bea asked, realizing the widow would not be a useful source of information about the deceased's recent activities. "What position did he hold before entering your husband's employ?"

Mrs. Otley stared blankly at Bea, as if confused by the question, then insisted she had no idea. "Presumably, he was someone else's steward, for Otley would never engage a man without proper qualifications. It's *possible* he had inherited his previous position from his father, as he *might* have mentioned an estate in the wilds of Yorkshire. It's all so vague, you see, because I did not spend time with him for his conversation. He had other talents."

"*Mama!*" her daughter screeched.

"You see," Mrs. Otley said wearily, "a Puritan."

Bea was equally horrified to discover the widow's interest in Mr. Wilson seemed to be primarily carnal, but she was denied the luxury of avoiding the issue and asked her to narrate the events of that morning. "What was your first indication that all was not well with Mr. Wilson?"

"I heard him call out," she said, holding out a cup of tea to her daughter.

"Were you not in the same room?" Bea asked, confused.

"Good gracious, no. I rose before him, as was my custom," Mrs. Otley explained. "I awoke a little before eight and rang for tea, which I took in the sitting room so as not to disturb him. When he is not working Charles prefers to sleep late. It's the novelty, I think, of being on no man's schedule but his own. I don't know how long it was—perhaps an hour and a half, possibly a little longer—but suddenly I heard him call out. I thought he was calling for me, so I went into the room to remind him to keep his voice down, for we didn't want Emily to know he was here. I realized then that he was in tremendous pain, for he was doubled over on the bed, as if suffering from horrendous cramping. Almost immediately, however, he seemed to lose control of his body and began to convulse repeatedly, his back arching in a dreadfully awkward way."

Her voice was placid and smooth as she gave her account, which surprised Bea, for the events she narrated were quite disturbing.

"And the whole time, he was making such a tremendous amount of noise, all that screeching and wailing," Mrs. Otley continued, her voice growing agitated as she recalled the scene and her anxiety about being discovered. "'Twas as if he were at an ice fair or Vauxhall Gardens. No matter how I pleaded with him, he would not modulate his voice. Indeed, he seemed to hardly notice I was there. And then, as I knew it must, the ruckus drew Emily's attention. She came flying into the room to see what was the matter and instantly began castigating me about my relationship with Mr. Wilson. I thought it was heartless of her to worry about a minor thing like a harmless fabrication when a man was suffering so dreadfully. Only a minute or two later, however, he stopped convulsing and lay still on the bed—finally silent, thank goodness! I thought he was better, that the stone had passed and he would now be well, but Emily insisted he was dead."

Her daughter, who had remained silent during the entire recital, even at the charge of heartlessness, now spoke, confirming the events as her mother had described them. "I, too, assumed he would mend once the fit had passed and was very disturbed to discover that was not the case," she said mildly. "It did not help that my mother refused to accept my pronouncement and insisted I was lying because I did not like Mr. Wilson. We argued over what I consider to be perhaps the most absurd claim any human being has ever made, and it was left to Fillmore, our butler whom my mother deemed a trustworthy third party, to make the final determination. Naturally, he confirmed my report."

If Mrs. Otley felt any embarrassment at having the

butler examine her lover for signs of life, it was subordinate to her anger over her daughter's criticism, which she deemed unfair. "I was made overwrought by Mr. Wilson's suffering, yes, but you *didn't* like him."

Emily sighed deeply and said with enduring weariness. "I did not know Mr. Wilson well enough to like him or not like him. What I did not like was my mother conducting an adulterous affair with my father's steward. As the man was in my father's employ and owed him some loyalty, I did find his behavior to be treacherous as well. That is all. But even if I did loathe him with every fiber of my being, I still would find no value in pretending he was dead when he was very much alive. There isn't any claim I can think of that would be easier to verify than someone's continued well-being. All it requires to see that is a little bit of logic, which my mother appears to lack."

Mrs. Otley sniffed loudly at this jab at her intelligence and added that it required only a little bit of logic to see that her daughter was the obvious suspect.

Emily stood up, and although it appeared as if she was prepared to storm out, she calmly remained in place as she said, "Given your so-called little white lie about your relationship with Mr. Wilson, I had no idea you were still involved with him, which means I had no cause to harm him. Furthermore, I didn't even know he was in our house. So please do try to keep your ridiculous notions to yourself, Mama." She turned to their guest. "Bea, if you are ready, I will show you to the room now so you can examine the scene for yourself."

Bea reviewed the information she had been able to gather from Mrs. Otley, which was really very little, and decided that, yes, she was ready to move on to the next stage of her investigation. Hopefully, the scene itself would be more illuminating.

Calmly, she placed her teacup on the table, thanked Mrs. Otley for her time and followed Emily out of the room. As soon as they were clear of the threshold, the girl leaned against the wall, closed her eyes and sighed heavily.

"I'm sorry you had to witness that," she said after a moment, the exhaustion more pronounced now that she was out of her mother's presence. "It has been daggers drawn between us ever since our visit to Lakeview Hall. *My* anger and disappointment are completely justified, for I had the misfortune of discovering that neither of my parents is whom I thought them to be. But I can't understand why *she* is so angry at *me*. It's true what she said—I have been coddled for much of my life—but I didn't force her to cosset me. I did not come out of her womb with a gun pointed at her head insisting on indulgence. She did it because I am so beautiful and she knew my beauty reflected well on her and that she could use it to achieve certain material success she had been unable to accomplish for herself. It was never about me as a person, so why is she so resentful now? I confess I am baffled by the situation."

"Could it be grief over your father's death? Perhaps a little guilt?" Bea asked, knowing both could be destructive emotions.

Emily shrugged. "It's possible. Andrew says she is jealous of me."

Another destructive emotion, Bea thought, sparing a moment of gratitude that her own mean-spirited relation was merely thoughtlessly cruel rather than intentionally malevolent. Even after twenty years, Aunt Vera still seemed surprised that providence had handed her a little girl to raise and that she could not contrive some way to escape the responsibility. Mrs. Otley, on the other hand, appeared to nurture a genuine resentment of her daughter, which was surprising, given Emily had accomplished precisely what her parents had asked of her. She was to be married to a future baronet and restore the family fortune.

"Not my beauty," Emily rushed to add, "which is what I originally thought he meant because I am breathtaking to behold and that must be difficult for plainer women, but my youth. I am starting my life while she is ending hers. I don't know if that's accurate or not, but I do know it doesn't really matter. I will marry Andrew and be free of her forever."

So much about the Incomparable had changed since the last time Bea had seen her that she was perversely relieved to observe that her towering self-regard had been preserved. Five months ago her vanity had struck Bea as the would-be cause of her inevitable downfall, and yet now it appeared to be her saving grace. Bea didn't know why the other woman had viciously turned on her daughter, but she imagined Mr. Skeffington's estimation was not far off the mark. She openly resented many of the decisions she'd made in life and now held the one person who had nothing to do with the making of them responsible.

Thinking of the young man now, she said, "I was surprised to hear of your engagement to Mr. Skeffington. I must congratulate you."

Emily twisted her lips into a wry smile as she led Bea down the hallway to the staircase, which would take them to the next floor. "No doubt you are recalling my horrifying speech during our walk to the folly where I disparaged his lowly status and declared myself unwilling to settle for anything less than a dukedom," she said with a disquieting amount of contempt.

"You're being unduly harsh on yourself," Bea said, striving for the right mix of kindness and veracity, "for you were open-minded enough to consider a marquessate."

"And that is exactly what I mean," Emily said with a laugh. "I was insufferable—and probably would be insufferable still if you hadn't orchestrated that awful scene in the drawing room wherein all my family's secrets were revealed. It's very humbling to discover the comforts you take for granted were bought with funds swindled from unsuspecting, decent people. If you are surprised I'm engaged to Andrew, it's nothing compared with my astonishment. He's so good and kind and understanding. I saw no hint of it during our stay, for he and Amersham had struck me as particularly immature, but I also wasn't look-ing for it."

"I don't think it was there," Bea said frankly. "The scene in the drawing room appears to have matured him muchly, just as it appears to have matured you. Truly, I'm happy for the both of you."

Emily threaded her arm through Bea's as they climbed the stairs and squeezed affectionately. "You are so kind, and I know you know I don't deserve it. You haven't said anything, but you must resent me horribly for break-ing your confidence in the Lake District. You poured your heart out about your disappointment with Mr. Davies, and I told everyone about it. And the only reason I did was I thought it was vastly diverting that a woman of your ad-vanced years and uninteresting demeanor had found love with a dreary little law clerk." She shuddered at the memory. "Andrew says our parents are monsters, but I worry that *I'm* the true monster."

Bea, who considered herself too hardened a cynic to be shocked by anyone's opinion of her, found herself so taken aback by this admission, she missed a step and had to be righted by Emily. She'd known, of course, that the girl's indiscretion had not been motivated by kindness, but she had attributed the transgression to the general lack of thoughtfulness of nineteen-year-old Incomparables. It had never occurred to her that she had acted intentionally or out of cruelty. And yet it made perfect sense, for the idea of a plain spinster so desperate for love she would look among the clerks at the Chancery was quite diverting indeed.

Inevitably, she thought of the Duke of Kesgrave, for he had been one of the people Miss Otley had entertained with her tale at Lakeview Hall. Like she, he'd recognized the inherent ridiculousness of the story, but he'd had enough sense to realize it was all a hum. Bea had learned of his opinion weeks ago, and yet somehow the mortifica-tion felt fresh. It was, she supposed, the first time she'd looked at it fully aware of her feelings for him.

Fearing a self-pitying slide into sentiment, Bea reminded herself that she was investigating a murder, precisely the thing Kesgrave had ordered her not to do. He might be the most handsome and coveted lord in all of England, but he could not control her behavior or get everything he wanted simply because he wanted it. She'd succeeded in overcoming him in a battle of wits, she told herself with a wry smile.

And yet she knew it was a meaningless victory because Kesgrave wasn't engaged in the skirmish. It was an entirely one-sided struggle, which only made the whole situation worse.

Although Bea's stumbling on the stairs did not make Emily aware of her faux pas, her silence did. Undoubtedly, the Incomparable had expected Bea to assure her she wasn't a monster at all, and when the expected assertion did not come, she realized her honesty had created a problem. As they approached the top of the stairs, she apologized with surprising effusiveness and did not spare herself the recriminations she knew herself fully to have earned. "You see, I *am* a monster, and I deserve a mother as unpleasant as my own. But I really don't think I deserve this," she said, opening the door and there, amid the yellow damask curtains of her mother's mahogany poster bed, was the pallid corpse of Mr. Wilson.

CHAPTER FIVE

The second Bea fixed her gaze on Mr. Wilson's pale face—
the white chin, with its off-center dimple and the begin-
nings of a beard; the long bridge of a nose ending in a
point; the broad cheekbones; the high forehead—she realized her plan was as foolish as it was impractical. There she
was, in the Mayfair residence of a young woman whom she
barely knew preparing to examine the formerly pain-racked
body of her mother's dead lover.

How had this happened?

It was all the duke's fault, she thought, with his pro-
hibition against further investigations. How dare he forbid
her anything! He wasn't her family. He wasn't her husband. He wasn't even her friend. He was merely a peer
with a perverse interest in her activities that he himself
could not explain. Why should she conform to his expectations? Because she hoped to earn his approval?

For shame!

She could think of no surer way to undermine her
self-respect.

Angered by this presumption, she had fixated on his
directive and resolved to do the opposite.

And look where it had gotten her, she thought wildly,

staring at Mr. Wilson's feet where they hung lifelessly over the edge of the mattress.

Kesgrave had so much to answer for!

Yet even as she railed at the duke in silent dismay, she knew she was being neither fair nor truthful. His attempt to control her was maddening, oh, yes, but it certainly wasn't the source of the misguided self-confidence that had brought her to Mrs. Otley's bedchamber.

No, that sin could be laid only at her own door.

It had started with the successful identification of Mr. Otley's killer, which had convinced Bea she was clever. Then, when she figured out who murdered Lord Fazeley, she grew to believe she had a particular talent for comprehending the machinations behind mysterious deaths.

Spending three quiet weeks in virtual isolation while her family maintained a busy social schedule had provided her with too much time to appreciate her own ingenuity. With only books as a distraction, her mind wandered frequently to what she considered her two greatest accomplishments: the moment she realized how unsurprised Lady Skeffington was by her son's revelations and the instance she recalled the meaning of a sea turtle tattoo on Mr. Cornyn's forearm. Slowly, over the course of almost a month, she'd inflated her opinion of herself until it rivaled Miss Otley's own mortifying self-regard.

And now she had taken that hubris and brought it to Park Street to identify the person responsible for Mr. Wilson's pallid corpse.

Beatrice felt an unaccountable desire to laugh.

Oh, but it wasn't funny, for she had led Mr. Skeffington and Emily to believe she could somehow mitigate their desperate situation. Despite her inexperience, she'd committed her expertise to solving a problem so complex she could barely grasp it as she stood on the threshold of Mrs. Otley's bedchamber.

I must get out of here, she thought.

Emily would understand, wouldn't she? Surely, she'd

believed the scheme was farcical from the very beginning. She probably only agreed to appease her worried fiancé, who had felt compelled to do something to address the situation.

Straightening her shoulders, Bea turned to look at Emily and said, "I'm beyond embarrassed to admit this—"

But Emily wasn't listening. She was staring at Mr. Wilson's corpse with an expression of horror and murmuring, "Look at him. It's so much worse than I remember. How is that possible? It was thoroughly appalling before, and yet now it's somehow worse. Is that the passage of time, do you think? Is it because he's six hours more dead?" Shaking with distress, she grabbed Bea's hand and squeezed it hard. "I'm so grateful that you have come. Truly, you cannot imagine the relief I felt when Andrew suggested your name as someone who might be able to help us. My mother is a ludicrous creature in every way, but she is right. With the tale of my father's demise and the rumors of his swindle circulating about London, our family cannot withstand another scandal, especially one that involves a man in my mother's bed—a dead man, at that. I wouldn't mind on my own behalf, for I've never dreamed of social success, but Andrew deserves better. He has been through so much already, and I would not have him subjected to even more gossip."

Although Bea thought it was very unlikely that a girl who had hoped to nab a marquess or better had not expected to conquer the beau monde, she was not peevish enough to say it. Rather, she pondered the obligation Emily's gratitude imposed. Coming here had been a mistake, and allowing Emily and her fiancé to believe that she could somehow solve their problem was cruel. The kinder thing would be to quickly admit her error so they could come up with another scheme to dispatch the awkwardness and discomfort of Mr. Wilson's unfortunate death.

Even as she formed the words in her head, she could not bring herself to issue them. Part of her reluctance was a genuine aversion to letting anyone down, but her hesitance ran deeper than that. It was the way Emily was looking at her now, as if she were her only hope, and Bea, whose usefulness to her family had always been of the banal fetching-and-carrying kind, found something profoundly alluring in the appeal. She wanted to be the person Emily saw when she looked at her. It was the same person the Duke of Kesgrave had seen walking next to him on the return from Lady Abercrombie's house when he insisted that she not search for the memoir Lord Fazeley was purported to be writing. He'd believed her to be a woman of such courage and daring that she would steal into a dead man's town house and rifle through his belongings.

Oh, to be a woman who stole and rifled!

Confronted with the opportunity now, Bea decided there was nothing to be lost by making the attempt. Emily and Mr. Skeffington's options were limited, for there were not hordes of people in London who considered themselves capable of identifying a murderer with discretion, and if she failed to make any progress at all, they would be no worse off than they were now.

Indeed, they might even be in a better position, for in a few days, when she admitted she had discovered nothing, their anxiety would most likely have eased and they would be less resistant to contacting the Bow Street Runners.

Her failure would be a favor of sorts.

Bea smiled wryly at the thought, for she was not so prone to self-deception as to actually believe her ineffectualness had a positive aspect. Nevertheless, it amused her enough to propel her forward, and she entered the room with a confident gait she had not imagined possible only a few moments before. She stopped at the foot of the bed and considered Mr. Wilson in his nightclothes.

Emily, hovering in the doorway, coughed lightly and announced that if she was not needed, she would be in her room hiding from her mother until Mr. Skeffington returned from the solicitor's. Understanding her discomfort, Bea nodded and smiled deprecatingly as the Incomparable scurried down the hallway.

For a moment, standing at the foot of the bed, Bea felt an almost dizzying sense of freedom. In her two previous investigations, she had not been given the opportunity to examine the corpse with impunity. In the library at Lakeview Hall, Kesgrave had loomed protectively over the scene, insisting time and again that her sensibilities were too delicate for her to linger. In order to distract him long enough to get a satisfying look at Mr. Otley, she'd been forced to affect female helplessness and mild hysterics. With the Earl of Fazeley, who had seemed to deliver himself directly to her for her inspection by falling only inches from her toes, she had no chance at all beyond a passing glance. As they were in the offices of the *London Daily Gazette,* she had found herself immediately surrounded by reporters and decided it would be prudent to remove herself as quickly and as discreetly as possible.

But now there was nothing to stop her from gleaning all the information she could possibly imagine from the victim, and the prospect filled her at once with excitement and dread. Staring at something openly, wholly, with the full force of one's attention, was categorically different from glancing at it out of the corner of one's eye, and she feared suddenly the further revelation of her inadequacy. What if, after casting long, languishing looks at Mr. Otley's and Lord Fazeley's corpses, she proved unequal to the duty of studying Mr. Wilson's?

Knowing there was nothing to be gained from wringing her hands, she pushed her doubts aside and devoted herself to the task before her.

The body.

How still it was now. How oddly pristine as it lay on the bed slack and loose, its awkward arrangement bearing no relation to the repose of sleep.

She was surprised by how little evidence there was of his suffering. Although he was dead, she expected something of his pain to linger in the air, like an echo that repeated several seconds after the words had been spoken. Alas, there was nothing but Mr. Wilson in his nightclothes, his red brocade banyan having ridden up to reveal the top of his calves.

At once, she was struck by what was missing: bodily fluids. There was no vomit or excrement on him, his clothes or the sheets.

Immediately, she knew the poison used to end his life was not arsenic. A student of history, she had read Michael Holborn's four-volume account of the life of Pope Alexander VI, who, along with his son Cesare Borgia, made regular practice of killing cardinals with the deadly substance to increase their personal wealth. Arsenic mimicked food poisoning in its effects, and the fact that Mr. Wilson had not emptied the contents of his stomach while in the process of dying indicated another toxic element.

Bea tried to recall the other ones she knew.

Hemlock came readily to mind because every child learned of Socrates's fate while still in the schoolroom. But hemlock, she felt positively, did not cause terrible convulsions like the ones described by Mrs. Otley. Indeed, in the version she had read of the Greek philosopher's death, the poison had been almost gentle, with numbness slowly overtaking him until he could no longer stand. Then he calmly lay down.

Next she considered monkshood, which was the substance many suspected Emperor Claudius's wife sprinkled onto a plate of mushrooms to hasten his end. Did it cause painful convulsions? Bea did not know, but she did recall Seneca's description of the scene in *Apocolocyntosis (divi) Claudii,* which satirized the fallen Roman's death. "*Vae me, puto, concacavi me,*" he said, meaning he had soiled himself. As Mr. Wilson had not suffered that particular mortification in the act of expiring, she realized monkshood could not have been the culprit.

What about belladonna? she wondered. It had a long and illustrious history as a murder weapon, gaining a reputation in the Middle Ages as a reliable potion for disposing of one's inconvenient spouse. She closed her eyes and tried to recall details of how the poison progressed in the body.

All that came to mind was George Buchanan's *History of Scotland,* which claimed that King Duncan I mixed the juice of the berry with wine and fed it to the Danish army under the guise of a truce. The Scottish historian had been light on the details of how the poison affected the body, but he'd made no mention of convulsions. Indeed, his description made it clear that the soldiers had been immobilized by the draught and, unable to yield a weapon in their own defense, found themselves slain where they lay.

Aware that her options were rapidly dwindling, Bea tried to think of other poisons she had read about. Wasn't there one that was made from a lovely blue pigment called Prussian blue? It was mixed with water…

Prussic acid!

Yes, that was it, she thought, recalling it dimly from the biography of Carl Wilhelm Scheele, a Swedish apothecary who mixed the ingredients together to create the extremely toxic liquid. Did prussic acid create convulsions?

She truly had no idea.

Ah, but it *was* notorious for having the faint odor of bitter almonds.

Calmly, Bea contemplated Mr. Wilson and conceded the only way to discover if he smelled of almonds was to lower her head and inhale deeply. Inevitably, she found herself disinclined to proceed with such a plan, for there seemed to be something innately repulsive about getting that close to a dead body. But it would smell of things other than just almonds, would it not?

As repellant as it was, however, she had no choice, for what kind of investigator would she be if she allowed a little bit of squeamishness to stand between her and the acquisition of knowledge.

A very feeble one, she assured herself.

Slowly, cautiously, she bent her head forward, breathing in deeply as she drew closer and closer to his face. She did not detect almonds nor the vague stench of decay. Rather, she was struck by a disconcerting mix of lemon, bergamot, rosemary, mint and orange blossom—disconcerting because it was exactly the way her uncle smelled.

Startled, she looked over to the side table, searching for a snuffbox. Finding none, she examined the banyan for pockets.

Aha, she thought, locating the tobacco and promptly confirming that Mr. Wilson used the same sort as Uncle Horace: Lord Penwortham's mixture. It wasn't surprising, as its combination of fresh florals and piquant herbiness was pleasing if a little cloying.

Bea returned the enamel box to the banyan pocket and sighed heavily, for she was quickly running out of poisons. All that was left from her extensive reading was Cleopatra and the asp, and she could not believe an Egyptian cobra had been delivered to a residence in Mayfair.

Thoughtfully, she leaned forward and considered the possibility that Mrs. Otley had been correct in her insistence that Mr. Wilson had been felled by a medical problem. Although the violence of his struggle indicated that it could not have been a gallstone, it was possible that his contortions had been caused by something else. Apoplectic fits were often characterized by jerky, uncontrollable movements. Could he have suffered one of those?

Like Mrs. Otley, he appeared to be somewhere in the middle of his fifth decade, which made apoplexy possible but not very likely.

No, in this case, the obvious explanation was the correct one: Mr. Wilson had been poisoned. Now, if she could just identify the substance.

Scowling, she pressed closer to examine his face, which was not what she had been expecting. Emily's description of her father's business associate, given during a conversation in the Lake District, had included a large wart on his left cheek. Looking at him now, she saw nothing of the sort. Rather, he had an odd-shaped birthmark hardly larger than a fat drop of water. Perhaps it had been more pronounced before his sojourn in India, where he had been exposed to the relentless sun, which was no doubt responsible for the array of freckles across his nose and forehead.

The sun, however, could not account for the dried spittle edging his lips and dotting his chin.

Now that was interesting, she thought as she examined this new piece of evidence, which indicated the victim had foamed at the mouth like a dog suffering from hydrophobia.

It tickled something in her memory.

Had she read something about that—the frothing?

Yes, she had.

But where?

She stood up straight, closed her eyes and concentrated, trying to picture the words as they had appeared in the text. She saw it in the middle of a page about flora, for it had appeared directly below the image of a leafy tree with a short, crooked trunk and medium-sized fruit. What did the caption say?

Bea rested her head against her palm as she struggled to read the words.

And then she recalled the name of the book: *Travels in India: My Journey Through a Strange, Difficult and Wonderful Land.* It was a travelogue by the wife of the attaché to the second governor-general of Fort William, which she had used as a resource when looking for information about the country during her investigation at Lakeview House.

Now that she knew where the words in her head had come from, she could easily recall their context. In a section addressing native medicines, Mrs. Barlow mentioned the *Strychnos nux-vomica* tree, whose deadly seeds and bark were frequently confused with a local cure called *kurchi*. A common treatment, *kurchi* was used as a tonic, astringent and mild antiperiodic to no ill effect. But many people with evil intent mixed in nux vomica without anyone noticing, and when the victim died, they attributed the illness to tetanus, which had the same symptoms—symptoms that included convulsions and foaming at the mouth.

It was, Mrs. Barlow had written, a problem that the

local authorities had not yet figured out how to address.

Could Mr. Wilson's assailant have used nux vomica?

She thought about the people who might wish Mr. Wilson ill. Mrs. Otley's knowledge of his life had been frustratingly vague, but she felt that it was much more likely that the victim had made an enemy in India than in London. The seizure of the opium field by the East India Company must have been a fraught experience for the victim. Perhaps in the struggle he angered a company official. Or maybe he sought revenge against one of the perpetrators and failed to vanquish him. Even without the brutality of the takeover, his occupation as an opium smuggler was far from a genteel one. Perhaps he stepped on the toes of a competitor or betrayed an agreement with another merchant. Or it might have had nothing at all to do with the opium operation. Maybe Mr. Wilson seduced the wife or daughter of a local luminary. Having engaged in an affair with the spouse of his employer, he could hardly be considered inviolate in his principles.

Yes, Bea thought, it was quite possible Mr. Wilson's assailant used a poison indigenous to India. Did she think the killer followed him back to London?

No, the journey was far too long and costly to justify a vendetta.

The likelier circumstance was the villain bumped into Mr. Wilson in London and, realizing his propinquity, began to plan his attack.

She thought it was safe to assume the meeting happened sometime in the last few weeks. If only Mrs. Otley had any idea of his movements.

No matter, she thought, deciding there was no benefit to getting ahead of herself. At the moment, she had one responsibility and that was scrutinizing the body as carefully as possible.

His build, like his wart, defied her expectations, as Emily had described him as fat. Mr. Wilson, however, was not fat. His frame was solid, with broad shoulders and muscled forearms, which were perfectly in keeping with what she'd expect from someone who supervised an agriculture concern.

She reached down to examine his hands for signs of callouses and shivered when she noticed his skin was cool. Although hardly the missish type, she felt there was something particularly ghoulish about how quickly his lifeless corpse had lost its heat. Nevertheless, she ran her fingers over his hand and noted the roughness. As the overseer of the enterprise, he probably did not run the plow on a daily basis, but she assumed he had the knowledge and ability to operate it when necessary.

Having gathered all the information she could from the body, she turned her attention to the room itself. If Mr. Wilson was poisoned by nux vomica, then he would have had to have swallowed it sometime in the morning, for, according to Mrs. Barlow, it worked quickly once it entered the body. The authoress had not given the exact number of minutes from the moment of ingestion to the onset of symptoms, but she did relate that the poison typically killed its victim within a half hour, although sometimes, depending on the dose, it could take up to a full hour.

Bea recalled the sequence of events as described by Mrs. Otley. She'd woken up at eight o'clock and promptly retreated to her dressing room to indulge her usual morning routine of reading the newspaper and drinking tea. She heard the first indication that something was wrong with her lover about an hour later, which would put the clock at nine. By the time she responded to his cries of pain, his body had already begun convulsing severely, and although Bea did not know how long after that he expired, she felt it safe to conclude the interval was brief. According to Emily, he'd died very soon after she found him in her mother's room.

If Mrs. Otley discovered Mr. Wilson in pain at nine o'clock and the entire poisoning episode took thirty or forty minutes, then he must have ingested the poison at around eight-thirty. Given the hour, the most obvious assumption was he had consumed the deadly substance with his morning drink, which was either coffee or tea.

Examining the room carefully, she could not find any evidence of a beverage. There was no teacup on the bed, beneath it or beside it. The armoire had only clumps of dust under it, and the looking glass was pressed too close to the wall for anything to drop and roll behind it.

As far as the room revealed, Mr. Wilson had ingested nothing since waking up.

Patently, that was wrong, for if the victim had ingested the poison the evening before, then he would have expired the evening before. Something in this room killed him, Bea thought.

Unless it had already been removed from the room.

Quickly, Bea passed through the doorway to the left and entered Mrs. Otley's dressing room, a compact but comfortable space with the same pistache-colored paper on the walls and yellow curtains. As she'd suspected, there was no sign of a morning beverage in there either.

The staff had already cleared the trays.

Convinced this must be the correct explanation, Bea sought Emily's approval before visiting the kitchens to question the staff. Given the ruckus Mrs. Otley had described and the crowd that had gathered in response, she thought it was unlikely that anyone in the house was unaware of the events of that morning. Nevertheless, it seemed rude to raise the topic of murder with the servants without first gaining their employer's consent.

"By all means, yes, please do interview whomever you wish," Emily said with an enthusiastic nod. "I'm sure the servants are already talking about it, as they do so love to gossip. The sooner we can have this matter sorted out, the sooner we can get that dreadful man out of the house. As it is, I'm sure I won't be able to sleep a wink tonight knowing he's taken up residence in the cellars. Although would not know it from listening to my mother's tirade, I think delivering him to a medical school would be a very satisfactory solution to our troubles. Andrew insists, of course, that we alert his next of kin and that is why he went to call on the solicitor today, to begin the process of discovering who that is. Obviously, I, too, want to treat him with the decency he deserves. But at the same time, he *did* conduct an illicit affair with the wife of his employer and continued to do so in secret to hide the truth from his lover's daughter, so I'm not convinced disposal by his relatives *is* the decency he deserves."

Unsure how to respond to this observation, Bea withheld comment and asked Emily if she recalled seeing a teapot or tray in the vicinity of Mr. Wilson when she was inspecting him for signs of life.

She took a moment to think about it and then explained that her powers of observation, which she considered usually to be keen, had been compromised by her anger and shock at seeing Mr. Wilson in her mother's bed. She'd noticed nothing but his bare legs under his banyan and the defiant look on her mother's face. "As if daring me to criticize her for trying to find a little comfort after the tragic death of my father. And of course I would not had she not sought that comfort whilst he was still alive!"

Deciding the singular honor of soothing her anger, which was entirely justified given recent events, belonged to Mr. Skeffington, Bea nodded in a vague offer of understanding and closed the drawing room door behind her.

As Bea's last visit to the kitchens during an investigation had been less than successful, she was somewhat apprehensive as she climbed down the stairs at 112 Park Street. Her anxiety grew when she entered the room and found four members of the household gathered around the kitchen table. Among them was her own maid, Annie, who had no doubt heard every dreadful detail of that morning's proceedings.

How much easier it would be if she could simply interrogate her own servant.

As it was, she would now have to devote some of her

energy to convincing Annie not to mention her activities to the staff in Portman Square. As the girl had said nothing about her previous investigation into Lord Fazeley's death, Bea was hopeful she would hold her tongue now.

Regardless, she had no choice but to continue in her pursuit, for the murmur of conversation had halted the moment she'd appeared and several people started guiltily as if caught engaging in inappropriate behavior.

Their awkwardness made Bea's discomfort worse, and she struggled to appear composed as she approached the wary group.

"Good afternoon," she said, looking them each in the eye, one by one, even Annie. As a failed entrant in the Marriage Mart, she frequently felt invisible and always appreciated it when someone made a particular effort to acknowledge her presence. "I'm investigating the unfortunate death of Mr. Wilson and was hoping to ask a few questions. Would that be all right?"

Bea knew it was a bizarre statement coming from a young lady who had no connection to the family—indeed, it was a bizarre statement coming from any young lady, familiar or not—and she wasn't surprised to see the light of suspicion enter the housekeeper's eye. Yet she was relieved it was only mistrust that animated her, not scorn.

Cautiously, Mrs. Petrie said, "Yes, miss. What would ye like to know?"

"Well, as I'm sure you all know, Mr. Wilson fell sick and died this morning," she began cautiously, reluctant to speak too frankly lest someone among the group took offense.

Even with her restraint, Mrs. Petrie objected immediately. "No, miss, no. He didn't fall sick. He was made sick by something. And it wasn't the fault of anyone in this kitchen. We know how to prepare food without killing nobody."

Several heads around the table nodded in agreement, and one of the other servants, a dark-haired woman with angry eyes and a speckle of soot on her chin, said, "Yes, we do."

As Bea had never intended to blame the staff, the fact

that they would assume otherwise never occurred to her, and she felt the blush rise in her cheeks at the obvious oversight. "Of course not. I didn't mean to imply it was. Mr. Wilson was killed by—" She broke off midsentence, reluctant to share her conclusions before she knew them to be fact. Instead, she reaffirmed what the housekeeper said. "That is, he was made sick by something. I merely wanted to know more about Mr. Wilson's morning routine. Was he served tea or coffee this morning?"

"No, miss, not at all," Mrs. Petrie said. "As Mrs. Otley insists every time he stays here for the night that he's not actually here, on account of the miss not knowing about their relationship, she doesn't want us to bring him anything to eat or drink in the morning. She shares her tray with him. They drink out of the same cup in case the miss happens to see the tray when Lydia"—she gestured to the woman with the soot mark—"carries it up and down."

"The same cup?" Bea asked, unsure if this intelligence indicated a greater intimacy between the lovers than she'd previously suspected or a more developed capacity for stealth. It certainly complicated the poisoning of Mr. Wilson, for apparently it was impossible to gain access to his digestive system without first polluting Mrs. Otley's. The fact that the widow was alive and well indicated that her morning tea had been untainted. "When I looked in the dressing room for her tray a few minutes ago, I did not see it. May I ask when it was removed?"

"I removed it," Lydia said. "During the ruckus over Mr. Wilson."

Although Bea respected and appreciated the efficiency of a capable servant, she thought clearing a breakfast tray amid the frenzy of a shocking death went well beyond the bounds of duty. "I'm impressed with your presence of mind," she said honestly.

"Not mine," Lydia said with an emphatic shake of her head. "The missus insisted I take it away as soon as possible to make sure Miss Emily didn't see it."

"But it had only the one cup," Bea pointed out, confused.

"It's the teapot, you see," Mrs. Petrie rushed to explain. "She was afraid Miss Emily would spot the teapot or cup and realize her mother has chocolate every morning. The missus, you see, told her that chocolate is too dear for us to have right now. But she has a pot of it every morning, and she didn't want Miss Emily to find out. So she asked Lydia to take the tray away before she noticed."

Having already observed Mrs. Otley's contempt for her daughter, Bea should not have found this information shocking, and yet somehow the minor deprivation seemed worse than all the scorn she'd heaped on the Incomparable's head. She wondered if it really was a necessary economy or simply an opportunity to deny her daughter a small pleasure.

As surprised as Bea was by the widow's pettiness, she was more taken aback by the clarity of mind that allowed her to witness the horrifying spectacle of her lover's death and then immediately think of her own vulnerability. "She rang for you after Mr. Wilson had expired and requested that you remove it?" she asked, trying to get a better sense of the sequence of events.

"Ring her?" Mrs. Petrie said with a harsh laugh. "We were all there already. Oh, lordy, miss, the caterwauling that filled the house, what from Mr. Wilson's suffering and Miss Emily's yelling. She was irate when she saw the man in her mother's bed, for the missus had sworn to have nothing more to do with him. I was in the room when she made the promise, which she didn't keep for a single day. The racket was louder than a marching band, and everyone in the household came running. And even though everyone was there watching, Miss Emily kept screaming at her mother about betrayal and poor Mr. Wilson kept shrieking in pain, the poor lamb. And very calmly, as if she were having tea with Prinny, the missus leaned over to tell Lydia to take away the tray in her dressing room before her daughter noticed it."

Lydia nodded vehemently. "As calm as could be. She wasn't worried about Mr. Wilson at all."

"She said he was passing a gallstone," Mrs. Petrie added. "She said he would be fine just as soon as it came out."

Bea knew it was entirely possible that Mrs. Otley's underwhelming response to her lover's agony was due to a sublime indifference to the pain of dislodging a gallstone. The apathy was certainly in keeping with the woman she had interviewed only an hour before, who had seemed more annoyed by the inconvenience of Mr. Wilson's death than by the untimely passing itself.

But her detachment could also be attributed to something more nefarious, for Bea had only the widow's words that events unfolded in the way she'd described. With no method by which to confirm the veracity of Mrs. Otley's statements, she could not rule out the possibility that Mr. Wilson had risen much earlier than nine and partaken in a cup of poisoned chocolate. It would have been easy enough for her to contaminate the drink before passing it to her lover, who would have had no reason to suspect it had been tainted with nux vomica.

Could Mrs. Otley really be so wicked as to kill the man with whom she was having an affair? Undoubtedly, she felt some affection for him if she persisted in the connection after her daughter had demanded it be severed. And even if she was no longer enamored of him, there were less fraught ways of ending a relationship than murdering one's lover. If she had administered the poison, then it could have been only because she had either something to gain by his death or something to lose with his life.

The prospect of Mr. Wilson being in possession of a secret that would affect Mrs. Otley's comfort in either direction struck her as improbable until she recalled that her husband had swindled dozens of respectable people out of thousands of pounds and before that had trafficked in the illegal distribution of opium. Without question, the ground was rife with the potential for blackmail.

"Where is the chocolate now?" Bea asked, hoping that it remained untouched on a sideboard so that she may test its potency by feeding it to a rat or mouse.

"Gone," Mrs. Petrie said briskly. "Lydia brought the tray to the scullery, where it was immediately cleaned. I run a tight ship, miss, and would never let the morning dishes pile up until dinner."

Although she had been expecting some variation on this answer, Bea was nevertheless disappointed to hear it. She considered asking to visit the scullery to make sure the ship was as tight as the housekeeper said but decided it was futile when everyone around the table save Annie nodded their heads in confirmation.

The chocolate was gone and so was that avenue of investigation.

So much duplicity, she thought, regretfully.

"Do you think the teacup ruse was necessary?" Bea asked, recalling Emily's insistence that she could have no hand in his death, as she had no idea the victim was in the house. "Was Miss Otley truly ignorant of her mother's relationship or could she have figured it out?"

"Truly ignorant, miss," Mrs. Petrie insisted without hesitation. "I'd bet my life on it."

Lydia nodded, as did the two other servants at the table. "Miss Otley has a way of letting her feelings be known on any subject, you see, and if she had discovered the truth, everyone would have been made aware of it."

"Would've screamed the house down," the scullery maid muttered.

Grateful for their strong opinion, for it was a relief to be able to eliminate at least one suspect, Bea thanked the staff for their patience and help. Then she returned to Mrs. Otley's room to make a thorough search for a jar or canister of a suspicious-looking substance. It seemed unlikely to her that a woman who had never been to India would choose an obscure foreign poison over homegrown laudanum, which would have effectively settled the matter far more discreetly. Nevertheless, she could not dismiss the fact that the widow was capable of great acts of deception, and everything she had done since Mr. Wilson's death seemed designed to tamper with the evidence.

Determined to inspect every nook and cranny of Mrs. Otley's rooms, Bea began with the armoire, carefully examining each item of clothing for hidden pockets as well as the dark corners—top and bottom—of the wardrobe. She rifled through the escritoire, emptied the bedside tables, checked under the mattress and padded the curtains to make sure a small storage compartment had not been sewn into them. She gave the dressing room the same thorough scrutiny, and other than discovering that Mrs. Petrie's high standards did not extend to the living quarters, for there was dust on everything, including now Beatrice, there had been no revelations. She found nothing of interest, not even a packet of letters from Mr. Wilson. Perhaps she had burned the collection just as she'd said.

Brushing a hand down the front of her dress, she wondered if the lack of pristine cleanliness was a result of retrenchment. She had no idea what the family's financial situation was in the wake of Mr. Otley's death. She knew from reading his journal during her investigation in the Lake District that he had put the money from the hibiscus scheme into copper mining stocks. According to his reports, the stocks were doing quite well and before his murder he had made a notation to purchase more. Had his widow followed through on his intention? The fact that she remained in possession of the London house indicated that her finances were secure, for she did not have to sell the property to satisfy the creditors.

And yet a much-needed upstairs maid seemed to have been cut from the ranks.

It was impossible to tell the true state of affairs without talking to the lady, and Bea formulated her questions as she descended the stairs. Just as she was about to enter the front parlor, however, the clock within began to sound and she listened in horror as the chimes rose to six. Was it really so late?

Aunt Vera would be mortified that she'd lacked the circumspection to excuse herself earlier. Even if these hours in Bea's presence were the only moments of solace Miss Otley had experienced in five months, her aunt would still deem it indecent to have stayed so long. No doubt she would render the faux pas an egregious breach of etiquette and cite it as proof that her niece wasn't fit to return to society. At the last affair to which Bea had gone, her family had discovered her on the balcony tormenting a young nobleman who had information about the Earl of Fazeley's final days. Repulsed by his hypocrisy, she had sought to increase his discomfort by repeatedly and aggressively reminding him of his romantic entanglement with an older woman.

It was a little thing, a minor event, but watching him cringe had given her a modicum of satisfaction.

And then Aunt Vera ruined it all by screeching her name in horror and apologizing to Lord Duncan and dismissing the Duke of Kesgrave before he could provide some ameliorating explanation for her behavior.

Bea had been confined to the house ever since, the terrible bruises she had sustained in pursuit of his lordship's killer providing Aunt Vera with all the ammunition she needed to keep her inside.

But no more, Bea thought as she sought out Mr. Skeffington and requested he send her home in his carriage. No matter what her aunt contrived, it would prove insufficient in stopping her from attending the Pemberton ball that evening. She had passed three weeks without a glimpse of the duke and could bear it no more. She knew how weak it made her, pining for the sight of him, but there was nothing she could do to spare herself. She was a besotted idiot. So be it.

While Bea waited for her maid to appear, she apprised Emily of her progress, keeping her descriptions vague so as not to alarm the young lady with her suspicions. Although Mrs. Otley had been a perfect beast to the Incomparable, she was still her mother and necessarily the object of some affection.

"I cannot thank you enough for this effort," Mr. Skeffington said as he helped her into his carriage. "Emily is already calmer knowing you have taken the helm. She has tremendous respect for you."

At once, Bea recalled the girl's confession that she had told everyone about Mr. Davies because she thought it was vastly diverting that an aging spinster had developed a tendre for an inappropriate clerk and found it difficult to believe the girl had any respect for her at all. But she saw no reason to cavil and merely promised to do her best.

Mr. Skeffington nodded gravely, closed the carriage door and told his driver to see Miss Hyde-Clare and her maid to Portman Square safely. Alone with Annie, Bea contemplated how to proceed. Clearly, the matter of her unconventional habits had to be addressed, lest it become the topic on everyone's lips in the servants' quarters and slowly find its way to the drawing room.

Before she could figure out what to say, Annie commented on the quality of Mrs. Petrie's raisin scones. "They were delicious. Indeed, they were so delicious I don't think I will be able to talk about anything else for days."

Startled, Bea looked at her, unsure she was understanding the other woman correctly. "The scones?"

But she was, for Annie nodded firmly with a conspiratorial gleam in her eye. "Yes, ma'am, the scones. They have swept everything else from my mind."

Bea did not know what she had done to earn such loyalty, but she was far too grateful to call attention to it or question its origin. "How disappointing, then, that I was not served them in the drawing room during my visit."

CHAPTER SIX

Despite how thoroughly and consumingly Bea knew Damien Matlock, Duke of Kesgrave, was not smitten with her, she still felt something inside her shrivel and die the moment she observed him waltzing with Lady Victoria.

"Do they not make the most lovely pair?" Aunt Vera asked fondly, her eyes following their graceful figures across the dance floor. "It is quite a coup for her, as she is barely a month into her first season! His mother is quite pleased with the match. I believe she's the one who originally proposed it, for the Tavistock land marches along the Matlock estate's northern border. It would be the ideal marriage of elegance, prestige and property."

Unable to speak—indeed, barely able to breathe—Bea nodded in agreement, for what her aunt said was true. Kesgrave and the Tavistock heiress made a stunning couple. Of course they did. They were two beautiful people of breeding, wealth and status, and seeing them together now as they twirled in each other's arms, she understood the inevitability of their pairing. Both had been raised to be the best example of their kind, cultivated like orchids in a conservatory to possess only the finest traits of their species. Even their looks, which were opposite in every way, for she was dark and he was light, appeared calculated to promote the match, as if nature itself abhorred too much perfection.

"Mrs. Ralston says we should expect an announcement at any moment," Aunt Vera continued, "as they have been in each other's pocket almost continually for the past week."

Although this information did little to improve Bea's condition, it did nothing to harm it either. As shocked as she was to find herself staring at Kesgrave's future, she wasn't really surprised at all. From the moment she'd met him in the Lake District, she'd had a clear picture of his wife, and even if she hadn't known the particulars, such as Lady Victoria's raven hair and her wide-set black eyes, she'd had a firm grasp of the generalities.

He was always going to marry a diamond of the first water—the only question had been which one he would pick—and just because he seemed to get a perverse sort of pleasure out of Bea's company did not mean he would have reversed five hundred years of flawless domesticity to settle for a plain-faced spinster with little conversation and no grace.

Every step of the way she had known this: while fantasizing about throwing eels à la tartare at his pedantic and unbearably superior head during dinner at Lakeview Hall, while drawing up a list of suspects with him by the fire in her bedchamber, while sitting, battered and bruised, on a Strand sidewalk beside him while he confessed to having an inordinate pride in her astuteness.

No, there was nothing surprising here.

And yet her heart felt as if it had been crushed by a stampede of rampaging horses.

"I wonder if they will marry in London, at St. George's, or from the family estate in Cambridgeshire. I think country weddings are quite the loveliest," Aunt Vera said. "Your uncle and I were married from Welldale House by the same rector who had baptized him as a child, which was tremendously meaningful for all of us. It's about continuity, isn't it, and perpetuating the family line. Young people think marriage is about the present, about how they feel in the moment, but it's really about the past and the future."

On and on she went, happily speculating about the fecundity of the proposed union and the many ways Lady Victoria would uphold the proud history of the Matlock family.

Terrified that her aunt's thoughtless remarks might shatter what was left of her composure, Bea frantically searched the ballroom for an escape. The refreshment table was on the other side of the dance floor, so fetching a glass of ratafia would only give her a better view of Kesgrave and his intended. Was there a balcony? Assuredly, there was a balcony or a terrace. Yes, but the early-March weather was unseasonably warm and it might be crowded with other society matrons lauding the duke's sensible choice. As far as she could tell, it was the *on-dit* of the evening.

Did she have to go to the retiring room to get away from the chatter, she wondered in distress. And then her gaze settled on a fig tree in the corner.

Yes, she thought, that would do nicely.

During the last ball she'd attended, before offending the appalling Lord Duncan, her family had made every effort to bury her in a corner behind a fig tree. On that occasion she'd resisted their efforts, but today she would happily plant herself next to the shrubbery—the more abundant the vegetation the better.

Calmly, she turned to her aunt, whose conversation, while still centered on the duke, had shifted slightly to the many unfortunate ladies who had set their caps for him and were sure to be desolate at his removal from the Marriage Mart. Although she tried to sound genuinely mournful as she discussed Miss Carson's dashed hopes, she couldn't quite smother the hint of triumph, for she considered the girl a rival of her daughter and wished her only minor success. Obviously, Kesgrave would have been far too illustrious a feather in her cap.

"If you do not mind, Aunt Vera, I think I will sit down," Bea said, interrupting the other woman's monologue, as waiting for a natural pause was a futile project. "I will be over by that fig tree if you require anything."

The annoyed expression that had overtaken her aunt's face at this inconsideration was immediately supplanted by an almost comical look of relief. "Yes, yes, of course, my dear, do go sit in the corner. That is an excellent idea. You will be shown to advantage there, I think, as the blue color of the walls suits your wan complexion."

Although Aunt Vera frequently lamented her niece's pallid appearance, Bea was wryly amused to acknowledge that for once the description was overly optimistic. Standing there, next to the dance floor as Kesgrave and Lady Victoria swept by embodying perfection in every graceful line, she felt as if she'd been stripped of every ounce of color she'd ever possessed. All the satisfaction she'd gotten from figuring out the precise poison that felled Mr. Wilson drained from her body so quickly it might never have existed.

It will pass, she assured herself as she made her way to the corner with the fig tree. Although the prospect of an existence entirely free of Kesgrave felt like a tragedy now, the truth was she'd known him for less than six months, which was really only a meager fraction of her life. She'd passed twenty-six mostly content years before him and would no doubt pass twenty-six mostly content years after him.

For some reason, this thought, which had been calculated to put a little steel in her spine, deflated her completely, and as she crossed the floor, she had to resist the urge to drop to her knees and weep like a small child.

"By what yonder light, she emerges!" cried Lady Abercrombie excitedly as she beheld Beatrice for the first time in several weeks. "I had begun to think this day would never come, your aunt was so determined to keep you hidden. Of course I did not truly believe she had sold you to the Duke of Northumberland to do his bidding, but I was prepared to start that very rumor to induce her to display you as proof of its inaccuracy. My dear Miss Hyde-Clare, I'm quite pleased to see you again. Tell me, do, what has kept you from being abroad for so long? Vera's missives were so vague and spoke only of an 'unavoidable ailment,' which, naturally, struck me as bizarre, for what ailments are avoidable?"

Although Bea longed for nothing more than a quiet corner and the opportunity to nurse her wounded heart in silence, she knew trying to evade the Countess of Abercrombie was a futile proposition. And yet, even as she submitted resentfully to her eager attentions, she acknowledged some part of her was warmed by her ladyship's greeting, which seemed as sincere as it was effusive.

"Actually, this one," Bea said softly, forcing a smile as she quickly thought of a plausible explanation to excuse her absence. As her aunt had not given her any guidelines to follow, she felt free to come up with whatever explanation she wanted—although, recalling the unexpected consequences of the seemingly harmless Mr. Davies fiction, she knew it was best not to be too outlandish with one's details. "All I had to do was avoid the chair on the landing, but I was carrying a book and not paying attention so I walked right into it. Then I tripped and knocked my head against a table, which resulted in a pair of unflattering bruises around my eyes. It's all very mundane, as a matter of fact, but I suspect my aunt wanted to keep the contretemps, minor though it was, a secret because I embarrass her." That, at least, was true. "She would prefer that I were a little less clumsy and a lot more graceful."

"Nonsense," her ladyship said with emphatic dismissal. "Your awkwardness is part of your charm."

Bea laughed. Only minutes before—no, mere seconds—she could not have imagined being amused by anything ever again, and now she giggled so wildly at the countess's outrageous suggestion she drew the attention of several people around her. Although their startled looks did not concern her, the realization that Aunt Vera might be close enough to hear her caused her to abruptly stop. Alas, the sudden inhalation of air triggered a violent fit of coughing that threatened to attract more notice than the laughter.

As Bea struggled to regain control of her breathing, Lady Abercrombie looked at her fondly. "There, that's it exactly. Keep that up, my dear, and we'll have you married by June."

"With all due respect, my lady, I think this time you've overextended yourself," Bea said kindly. "No doubt you've turned so many sow's ears into silk purses you decided it was time to increase the level of difficulty by transforming a mouse's ear. While I appreciate the impulse, I'm afraid it was ill-considered and I suggest you return your attention to bringing a lion cub into fashion and leave me to my obscurity."

Although Bea intended many aspects of this speech to be insulting, her ladyship merely nodded with approval and moved her schedule up by a month. "Leg-shackled by May, I'm certain of it."

Bea felt an absurd desire to scream. There, while standing in the Duke of Pemberton's ballroom, surrounded by the finest members of the *ton,* as the last strains of the waltz faded to silence, she wanted to shriek at the top of her lungs with the same force and feeling Emily had displayed when she discovered her mother trysting with the forbidden Mr. Wilson, a visceral sound wrenched from the edges of her soul. It wasn't Lady Abercrombie's fault. It had nothing to do with the beautiful widow. She merely wanted to shriek at the world for being so astoundingly unfair, which was somehow even more absurd, for she had been orphaned at five and had never known anything but injustice.

But of course she didn't scream or yell or raise her voice to an injudicious level, for as awkward as her charm was, it certainly wasn't blundering. She knew what befit her station, and having just regained the freedom to leave the house, she would do nothing to endanger it again so quickly. Even so, she couldn't quite smother the nerves roiling her emotions, and she once again began to laugh with uncontained mirth. It was, she realized, a sort of surrender. She would submit to Lady Abercrombie's ministrations, whatever they were. Resisting them would get her nowhere, and it was better that someone took an interest in her than no one.

"Miss Hyde-Clare!"

Bea froze and watched in horror as the Duke of Kesgrave, his blue eyes glimmering with delight, walked toward her with the Tavistock heiress at his side. With her generous lips and thick lashes, Lady Victoria was even more exquisite up close.

"You are here," he said, stating the obvious with what appeared to be genuine pleasure. "How wonderful. I'm relieved to see you have suffered no lasting effects from your accident."

Bea knew she had to respond, but she couldn't think of anything to say that wasn't facile or nonsensical. She could not compliment him on the lovely curl of his blond locks, and she absolutely must not congratulate him on his impending nuptials. But that was all she could think: how handsome he looked and how attached he was.

Lady Abercrombie, of course, remained in full control of her faculties and did not hesitate to offer a cheerful greeting to the pair. She complimented Lady Victoria on her lovely gown, inquired about her mother and promised to visit just as soon as Henry, her lion cub, had recovered enough to pay social calls. He had acquired a nasty cut on his front paw from a shard of glass he stepped on while playing hide-and-seek with Groatson in the kitchens. Naturally, she blamed the butler for the mishap, as he seemed not to comprehend the fact that he was engaged in the game at the time, which was disappointing, for certainly he was at least as clever as any five-year-old child in a schoolroom.

Although Bea was still rattled by Kesgrave's sudden appearance, she felt some of her anxiety lessen as she watched the heiress struggle with how to respond to the countess's remarkable speech. It was not that she thought the girl was particularly idiotic—though, yes, Bea was petty enough to relish the prospect of the excessively articulate and intelligent duke bracketed to a goose cap for all of eternity—but rather that she welcomed the comforting reassurance that even poised, beautiful women were discombobulated from time to time.

Darting a confused glance at Kesgrave, Lady Victoria thanked the widow for her attention and suggested that perhaps she plan her visit *before* Henry recovered, as her mother had a strict no African animals policy.

She said the words so simply and sincerely, Bea could only assume she was teasing the widow for her aggressively exotic tastes, and finding herself in sympathy with the heiress, she asked what her mother's rule was vis-à-vis Asian animals.

Lady Victoria, however, did not comprehend the sentiment behind the question, and as she stared at Bea in confusion, Bea realized she had misunderstood her intention. The other woman had not been making a sally.

In that case: Did her mother truly have a policy against African animals?

Naturally, the possibility that such a rule was actually in place made Bea desperately curious to discover what event in particular had caused its adoption.

An awkward silence fell over the group as Bea tried to decide how one would word such a question without giving offense, and the Duke of Kesgrave, perceiving an oversight, stepped forward to make the introductions.

As befitted her reputation for elegance, Lady Victoria greeted her graciously and amiably, expressing hope that she was enjoying the ball and recommending the lemonade, which, in contrast with the variety usually served at assemblies, was pleasingly chilled.

Although polite banter about the quality of the refreshment table was precisely the sort of conversation Bea had been raised since childhood to engage in, it was also the type that left her feeling strangely inert. The inability to respond to mundane remarks with equally banal observations had undermined her confidence from her very first season and was largely responsible for her awkwardness, which, despite Lady Abercrombie's claims, was wholly deficient of charm.

Now she said yes several times and wondered if complimenting the voluminous fig tree in the corner would be an appropriate response. Did heiresses notice fig trees? Did they care about them? Perhaps she should remark on the flowers in the ballroom, which were also copious and beautiful, although she wasn't quite sure what type they were. There were roses, yes, but of what variety?

Lady Abercrombie spared her the obligation of identifying the genus, however, when she said to Kesgrave, "Isn't it delightful that Miss Hyde-Clare is finally recovered from her accident? I know it serves no purpose to be angry with an inanimate object, and yet I'm still out-of-account annoyed with the shoe that caused her fall."

Given that Bea had singled out a chair as the culprit only a few minutes before, she was surprised to hear the countess name a different obstacle. She saw no reason to correct, of course, for neither object was actually responsible and being a stickler for an untruth seemed needlessly churlish.

The duke, with whom Bea had had no contact since the afternoon he'd brought her home with a bruised face, glanced at her quickly as if to confirm that this was the story she'd put out and then agreed with Lady Abercrombie that the recalcitrant shoe had a lot to answer for.

Lady Victoria, who evidently believed in the cultivation of personal responsibility, particularly among the servants, rushed to point out the shoe itself was blameless and that the fault lay with the housemaid or footman who failed to remove the item from her path. She then observed how pernicious garden rakes could be and expressed her gratitude for the staff in Cambridgeshire, who always remembered to put them back in the shed when they were done clearing the lawn of leaves. "We have not had an accident with a rake in six and a half years."

Good lord, Bea realized, she's as pedantic as he!

She wanted to delight in the perfection of the match, for it served Kesgrave right to be riveted to such a plodding thinker, but all she felt was sadness at the prospect of his ossifying into a bore. He had such a wonderful ability to laugh at himself, and Lady Victoria would most likely give him no cause. No doubt she would hold him in as high regard as he held himself.

Uninterested in gardening equipment, Lady Abercrombie congratulated Lady Victoria on her staff's excellent work and promptly changed the subject by announcing her intention to launch a literary salon.

"It's Henry, you see," she explained. "His mishap with the glass shard has sobered him, and now he desires a more scholarly environment."

While Lady Victoria furled her brow as if trying to make sense of this ridiculousness, Kesgrave nodded sagely and said, "A literary lion, how droll."

While the widow preened, Lady Victoria reminded Kesgrave that he had been charged with introducing her to his grandmother. Called to his duty, he nodded abruptly and bid the two women good evening.

Although Bea had thought herself thoroughly resigned to the truth, the desolation she felt upon discovering Lady Victoria was about to meet the matriarch of the Matlock clan demonstrated that she somehow still needed convincing.

"Oh, no, dear, no," Lady Abercrombie said softly.

Pulled out of her misery by the distress in her ladyship's voice, Bea raised her head sharply to see what was the matter and was appalled to realize the countess was looking at her with concern.

No, not concern, Bea thought. Pity.

She knows.

Bea's heart raced frantically at the thought of this

woman—this collection of affectations and antics, this source of outlandish displays and elaborate bids for attention—knowing the truth. It was inconceivable to her that the aging widow with the Oriental fantasia for a drawing room would have any respect for the sanctity of a secret or the discipline required to hold her tongue. As soon as she saw a tactical advantage to sharing the information, the story of Miss Hyde-Clare's unrequited love for the Duke of Kesgrave would sweep across London like one of Mr. Rowlandson's caricatures, and she would be a laughingstock.

If Miss Otley had thought a woman of her advanced years finding love with a dreary law clerk was vastly diverting, it was nothing compared with the entertainment value of an ape leader developing a tendre for the most glittering prize of the season.

Truly, was there anything funnier than hopelessness on a grand scale?

"You mustn't look so stricken, my dear," Lady Abercrombie said in that same soft, soothing voice. "It's going to be all right. It will, I promise. You have nothing to fear from me. Despite how I might appear to you, I'm an excellent confidante. If your mother were here, she would tell you there was nobody she'd rather have in her corner during a heavyweight bout than me."

At the mention of her mother, Bea felt something break inside her, and she feared she might succumb to tears in the middle of the Pembertons' ballroom. Horrified by the shame and genuinely terrified of how her aunt would react, she took a deep breath, straightened her shoulders and raised her head until she was staring Lady Abercrombie in the eye. She expected to find more pity but instead saw only the light of approbation.

"Good girl," the countess said with satisfaction. "Just like your mother. I knew you were an out-and-outer the first time I met you, just like Clara. Now let's go have a coze over there by that plant in the corner. Everyone knows you are my protégé, so it will not raise eyebrows."

Lady Abercrombie, for all her insightfulness—and Bea was now prepared to concede the woman had more substance than she'd originally given her credit for—had no idea the harm she was doing with each mention of her mother. She was an orphan girl with only the faintest memory of her parents, and hearing that she resembled her mother in even the slightest way was a pain so exquisite it almost brought her to her knees.

Somehow, she managed to hold herself together until she sat down in the chair and then for a reason she couldn't possibly explain, she began to tremble. If anything, it felt as if she were shivering from the cold, but in actuality, she was quite warm. If Lady Victoria returned at that very moment to offer her a glass of cool lemonade, she would place it against her forehead.

"I won't ask how this happened," Lady Abercrombie said gently as soon as she was situated, "for the far better question to ask is how could it not happen. I'm sure half the room is in love with him right now, myself included."

Although the widow had already revealed herself to be a far more thoughtful person than she presented on first acquaintance, Bea was still taken aback by the gracious display of solidarity and resolved to be worthy of it. "I doubt it's no more than a third," she said, striving for cynical but sliding into dolefulness.

The countess nodded approvingly. "Yes, definitely an out-and-outer. Now, as I said before, you don't have to tell me the details, for I'm sure I can make a guess at them. Kesgrave can be devastatingly charming, which I don't think he realizes, and your situation in particular, where he was doing you a service, made you especially susceptible. I know it feels as though your heart is breaking into a million little pieces, but I swear to you it's not. It's merely bruised, and although this seems like the end of the world, it's only infatuation. Trust me, my dear, I speak from experience: It cannot be love if it's not returned. It's something else and it's just as painful, but it's not love and you will get through it," she said and reached over to grasp her hand.

The solemn intensity with which Lady Abercrombie spoke convinced Bea she believed every word she was saying. These were the truths of romantic relationships as she'd lived them, and given the breadth of her experience, Bea conceded that the other woman might know a few things she did not.

Alas, that ignorance cut both ways, for there were a few things Bea knew that Lady Abercrombie was wholly unaware of. The latter was under the mistaken impression that Bea's relationship with Kesgrave was based on a passing obligation he felt toward his father. That was a lie they had told her to hide the fact that they were investigating Lord Fazeley's death. She and the duke had been trying to locate the twin to the knife that had slain the earl, and to explain their interest in the blade, which Lady Abercrombie owned, Kesgrave hastily conceived a story about helping her purchase it as a birthday gift for her uncle as a favor to the late duke, who would expect him to assist the daughter of an old friend.

In actuality, Lady Abercrombie knew nothing of their true relationship and could not conceive the r bond.

Yet even as Beatrice tried to convince herself that her anguish varied greatly from the disappointments the beautiful widow had endured, she recognized the act as a futile attempt to elevate her own suffering to something greater. She wanted to believe her sorrow transcended ordinary misery, that it was in some way hallowed, but in reality it was just sadness, as common as dirt and as familiar as the sky.

"I know you don't believe me," Lady Abercrombie continued in a bracing tone as she gave Bea's hand a comforting squeeze. "It's the curse of the despondent to feel as though they are dropping from a high cliff and will never reach bottom. But you will reach bottom, and indeed I think you already have, as Lady Victoria is quite convincing terra firma. Now, I know this will seem contrary to your own intuition, but trust me when I say that the only remedy to a love affair gone awry is a new love affair. Naturally, you must take a little time to grieve and wallow in the sadness. How does a week sound?"

Although a week sounded like a grain of sand compared to a beach, Bea's sense of the ridiculous was far too well-developed not to appreciate the countess's matter-of-fact attitude. All of a sudden, she felt like a bill being negotiated with the milliner and wondered if she should counter with two weeks.

"One week to immerse yourself fully in the gloomy sensation that the world will never sparkle again. Then you will rise from your mourning couch and greet the new day," Lady Abercrombie said firmly. "Do you have a mourning couch? Most people assume it's merely a settee in a somber color, but it's really more like a divan, with an open side to accommodate the lethargy of dejection. If you don't have anything suitable, I can send one over. I keep several on hand, as I find it beneficial to my spirit to mourn the end of a relationship in a variety of environments."

The image of the Countess of Abercrombie going from room to room to lie languidly on each divan for a few minutes before rising to move on to the next one made her smile, which she assumed had been the widow's goal in describing the absurd scene. Slowly, the trembling in her limbs began to subside, and Bea felt grateful for her ladyship's tactics, for appealing to her sense of humor was by far the best way to calm her down.

"Thank you," Bea said brusquely, "but I'm sure I have something that will suffice."

Her ladyship nodded. "Very good. Then should we talk about diet? I recommend lots of sweets such as marzipan candies and chocolates. Your impulse will be to shun food, but there's no value in wasting away to nothing. It will only undermine your efforts when you are recovered and meticulously working your way through your list."

As Bea dutifully amended the picture of Lady Abercrombie in her head to include marchpane cakes and imagined her carrying a plate of brightly colored treats from couch to couch, she wondered what her ladyship meant by "your list."

"My list?" she asked.

"Of suitors," the countess explained. "For your new love affair. We will draw up a list of gentlemen who will do and then thoughtfully rank each one using a variety of criteria, including suitability, likeliness and what I've taken to calling the Lord Byron factor."

The creation of such a list appalled Bea, not in the least because she couldn't conceive of how any gentlemen would remain on it after likeliness was calculated into the equation.

Interpreting her stare of horror as surprise, Lady Abercrombie said with defensive heat, "Just because you're in the doldrums, there's no excuse to be scattershot about your future. We will be fastidious and thorough."

Her tone was confrontational, but her eyes twinkled with humor, and Bea knew she was merely teasing with her talk of a list. Suddenly overwhelmed with gratitude, she clasped the other woman's hands in her own and said, "Thank you."

Lady Abercrombie smiled and said, "Just wait until you see the catalog of suitors I compile, young lady, then you will know the true meaning of gratitude."

Bea's confidence that the list was merely a ruse to distract her slipped a little at this assurance, but she stayed focused on her intent. "Truly, my lady, I had been at risk of humiliating myself and you saved me. I don't know how to thank you enough."

Now Lady Abercrombie shook her head. "You don't have to, my dear. You are Clara Leighton's daughter, and it's my greatest pleasure to help you. I'm only sorry I did not seek you out sooner. I knew you'd been left with Richard's miserly brother and his wife, a more joyless person I have yet to meet, but I was too overcome by grief to do anything but be sad and mournful. Even all these years later, I still miss her. What a waste. They were so full of life and then…I will never understand how it could have happened. Your father was such an experienced yachtsman." She paused as if trying once again to make sense of an impossibility and then said with alacrity, "But I'm here now and we are going to get you bracketed by the end of the season. Yes, you are correct, I've pushed back our schedule by several weeks to account for this minor setback, but we will nevertheless succeed."

Discovering the depth and intensity of Lady Abercrombie's affection for her mother gave Bea a sort of solace she'd never expected to find. It also explained why she had taken a sudden interest in a twenty-six-year-old spinster. Knowing the widow hoped to expiate her guilt at not seeking out her dearest friend's daughter twenty years ago put Bea's mind at ease, for previously she had been unable to comprehend her attentions.

Hesitantly, Bea said, "I don't know much about either of my parents, as my aunt barely knew them and my uncle believes the quickest way to get over a loss is not to wallow in it. My mother had two brothers, as you may recall, but they both live in Boston and have shown little interest in me other than a card at Christmas. Would you mind very much if I called on you sometime in the near future and you could tell me about my mother?"

"Would I mind?" the Countess of Abercrombie repeated in a shocked voice. "My dear, I would love nothing more. I will gather her letters so you can read them and will reread my diaries from that time to remind myself more forcefully of the details. Oh, you poor darling, you have no idea what you're subjecting yourself to. A veritable orgy of remembrances. I will talk for so long, you will be glancing pointedly at the clock for several hours before I allow you to leave. Indeed, I will prattle about your remarkable mother to such an extent, you will beg me to stop."

"No," Bea said firmly, fully aware of how impossible that was, "I will not."

Delighted, Lady Abercrombie announced her spirits much restored and suggested they return to the company, which made Bea laugh, as it had not been her spirits that were in need of restoration. But of course she agreed, for she no longer felt quite so desolate herself. Yes, she was still miserable, and the thought of Kesgrave and Lady Victoria still caused her breath to hitch. Despite the countess's bracing certainty, she could not believe her heart would ever recover, let alone by the start of the following week. And yet she had things to be thankful for, and she found herself capable of counting her blessings: She had the widow's kindness and the prospect of learning about her mother and even the investigation into the untimely death of Mr. Wilson. Her life might have been absent of love, but it was rife with purpose, and as she rose to her feet, she decided the latter was a surprisingly satisfying consolation.

Her optimism was high, fueled by the belief that her future would be more interesting than her past, and when Lady Abercrombie pointed to Viscount Nuneaton and identified him as number six on her list of suitors ("Alas, his Lord Byron factor is much in need of improving"), Bea agreed to allow the countess to maneuver him into dancing with her.

CHAPTER SEVEN

Although Beatrice knew it was a gross mischaracterization to say the Duke of Kesgrave had waited in the shadows to ambush her, she did think it was striking how quickly he'd appeared at her side the moment she was alone. Flora had barely taken two steps toward the refreshment table before he'd materialized beside her and demanded that she apologize at once.

Having spent the past two hours meticulously and resentfully picking apart every aspect of Lady Victoria's appearance, from the vacant expression in her dark eyes to the awkward way she tapped her toe out of time with the orchestra, Bea felt a shot of terror at these words. Did Kesgrave have access to the deepest reaches of her mind now?

Aghast, she shrieked, "*What?*"

"For the letter," he said.

The intense stab of relief she felt when he didn't say Lady Victoria's name—of course he couldn't read her thoughts!—was immediately supplanted by confusion, as she tried to decipher what letter he was talking about. It was particularly vexing because her original and most persistent complaint against him was his pedantry. The Duke of Kesgrave loved nothing more than to pontificate on any number of topics for any length of time, and now, when the circumstance would be improved by a few details, he turned cryptic.

"What letter?" she asked.

"Exactly," he said with satisfaction.

Bea stared at him and wondered if he'd lost his mind in the interval since she'd last seen him. Was this what courting a diamond of the first water did to a man? "I cannot speak to what thoughts are actually forming in your head, your grace, but I wish to assure you that the ones coming out of your mouth make no sense at all. I cannot tell if this defect is a recent development or one you've been experiencing for a while and your peers were too overwhelmed by your importance to point it out. Perhaps they don't listen to your words because they are so content to bask in the glory of your presence. Regardless, you clearly need a few minutes to sort out the problem and I'm happy to wait here silently while you do so."

"No, Miss Hyde-Clare," he said with a firm shake of his head. "You will not cajole me out of my temper. You will apologize."

"Surely, even with your diminished capacity you understand that I can't possibly offer an apology until I know what it is for," she explained calmly.

If she thought this straightforward explanation of the problem would result in a sensical reply, she was sadly mistaken.

"Three weeks," he said maddeningly.

"Kesgrave!"

"It has been three weeks, Beatrice," he said, finally consenting to explain. "Three weeks. Your injuries, although certainly brutish to behold, were fairly benign and should have healed within a week, maybe two at the very most, and yet you were confined for three weeks. Every inquiry to your aunt was met with a vague explanation that you had yet to recover. She would provide me with no details, just the same assurances that you were on the mend. Naturally, this left me no recourse other than to

worry that your injuries were far more severe than I'd originally supposed. I began to fear that your eyes had been
permanently damaged or your brain had been injured. It
was very disconcerting and quite unpleasant, and all it
would have taken to relieve my anxiety was a letter from
you assuring me you were all right. Even if your bruises
hadn't taken an unusually long time to heal, a missive apprising me of your progress would not have been amiss. It
was, after all, my fault that you had been so abused, as it
was in my company that you suffered the attack. You had
always struck me as a decent woman, disrespectful of your
betters, of course, and far too curious for your own good,
but thoughtful and considerate and awake to your duty,
which in this case included a letter to put my mind at ease.
And yet I received nothing. So, yes, I'm fully expecting an
apology for your oversight, and I'm happy to wait here
silently while you figure out how you would like to word it.
I would advise starting with a timeless classic such as *I'm
sorry,* but you must do what feels right for you."

Beatrice got stuck at *Beatrice.*

She heard every word of the duke's impressively long
speech—the criticism of her aunt, the concern for her welfare, the objection to her silence—but she could not assimilate a single thing he said because she was too distracted by his use of her name. Beatrice, he'd said, with authori-
ty and familiarity, as if they were collaborators or conspirators. Beatrice, as if they had established a bond. Beatrice,
as if they were partners in an endeavor. Beatrice, as if they
would be partners for years to come.

Impatient, Kesgrave huffed irritably and took a step
forward, drawing her attention back to him, and she
looked at him, almost surprised that he was still there.

"I know you take exception to what you describe as
my fondness for pedantry," he said with a mix of exasperation and annoyance, "but I'm now compelled to explain
that my assertion that you should take all the time you
need to figure out how to apologize was sarcasm. I was

actually saying the opposite of what I meant, as I could not conceive it would take you long to formulate a response. All you have to say is 'I'm sorry.' In fact, I gave you the entire script."

"I'm sorry," Bea said at once.

But it wasn't the apology he sought, as the words had tumbled out of her automatically in response to his complaint. Now, however, she determined to dismiss her fixation on how he'd said her name and consider the validity of his argument. The core of his contention was accurate: She had not sent him a note apprising him of her progress. But his reasoning was off, for there had been nothing unintentional about it. Far from a thoughtless oversight, her lack of communication had been part of a deliberate effort to remove him entirely from her mind, an objective he undermined time and time again by calling on her aunt. Having discovered the depth of her feelings for him, all she had wanted was the opportunity to fortify her defenses so that the next time she saw him—in a ballroom dancing with a beautiful heiress, for example—she would not humiliate herself.

It was such a minor goal, and yet she had fallen well short of it.

As calculated as her decision not to send him a note was, it had not occurred to her to wonder if there might be a reason for him to expect one. Given the situation, she did not think she'd been obliged to, and although she wasn't sorry to have failed to consider the matter from his point of view, she did regret his worry. That Aunt Vera's manipulations had caused him genuine anxiety struck her as just as surprising as it was unfair.

He did indeed deserve an apology.

Believing he'd received it, Kesgrave dipped his head in acknowledgment.

"No, wait, that wasn't it," Bea insisted. "That 'I'm sorry' was for not replying to your request, which I felt required some consideration. You are no doubt accustomed to instantaneous replies and as such probably do not recognize the furrowed brow of deliberation. No matter. You are correct, your grace. My aunt, who still questions the stability of my mental faculties, saw an opportunity to keep me at home and did not hesitate to use it to her fullest advantage. As you said, the discoloration was entirely gone by the middle of the second week, but every time I claimed to be fully healed, Aunt Vera would detect evidence of bruising and insist I remain inside. It did not occur to me that you would interpret these events as a sign of significant damage, and for that I'm genuinely sorry."

"Thank you," the duke said with unexpected gravity. "And I'm sorry that I wasn't more suspicious of your aunt's motives. If I had been a little less concerned, I probably would have noticed how deviously imprecise her answers were. Truly, she's as evasive as a damned spy. If we had sent her to Elba, we would have known Napoleon's escape plan before he boarded the *Inconstant*."

Although the image of her aunt consorting with Napoleon's generals on the Mediterranean island to gather secret intelligence was without question amusing, Bea summoned instead the unpleasant memory of Lady Victoria twirling happily in Kesgrave's arms. She recalled the grace and elegance in every line of their beautifully matched forms.

Cultivated like orchids, she reminded herself.

This extreme measure was taken in a bid to smother the spark of hope that had flared when the duke admitted that his concern for her had clouded his ability to think. She knew it was only his sense of responsibility that had made her seemingly slow recovery feel dire—he'd even said so himself during his long speech—and she silently repeated, *Common decency, common decency,* a few times in her head until she was on firmer footing.

"And you will now, I trust, tell me the rest," Kesgrave said, throwing her once more into confusion. "Ah, I see you're furrowing your brow once more. Thanks to your earlier consideration, I know you are deliberating again. Do note, Miss Hyde-Clare, how quick I am to process new concepts and apply them to practical situations."

The glint of humor in his eyes revealed that he was enjoying one of his favorite pastimes: mocking himself as a way of teasing her. As charming as she found it, the tactic provided no elucidation and she remained puzzled. "Ah, but this is the wrinkled brow of bewilderment. I do not know what you mean by the 'rest.'"

"And now you are being deliberately obtuse," he said accusingly. "Recall, if you please, my last glimpse of you: bruised and swollen and wearing your cousin Russell's clothes as you stood on the top step waiting for the butler to open the door. How did you explain your appearance? I cannot believe you told your family the truth."

As much as Bea wanted to take his continued interest in the mundane details of her life as proof of his regard, she knew it was ordinary curiosity. Anyone who had seen her disappear into her aunt's house that day would want to know how she'd escaped punishment. "Mr. Davies," she said.

Kesgrave understood at once and nodded with approval. "An excellent fellow. Is there no end to his usefulness?"

"Presumably, his funeral is the decisive end," she said, "but if I find myself in another difficult position he may have to be exhumed."

"I gather his funeral was a rather unrestrained affair?" he asked, then immediately went on to answer his own question. "Let me guess, one of his brothers objected to your presence at what was a family event and inferred from your lewd glances at his sister-in-law that you intended to take advantage of a grieving widow."

"His father," she corrected, surprised by how closely his explanation mirrored the one she'd used. She didn't know if this resemblance was because their minds functioned in a similar way or because he knew how her mind worked, but it filled her with delight. Feeling the warmth of perfect accord, she smiled brilliantly at him.

No, Lady Victoria, she reminded herself forcefully.

Kesgrave drew his brows together—the wrinkled brow of confusion!—and she realized with horror that she had spoken aloud.

"Excuse me?" he asked.

The hot flush that covered her cheeks was instantaneous, and she felt a sudden, intense desire to run away. The only thing that kept her rooted to the spot was her conviction that fleeing would be tantamount to making an admission. Determinedly, she tried to think of a plausible reason for spouting the mortifying non sequitur. *No, Lady Victoria.*

"No Lady Victoria, I see," she announced a little too vehemently when inspiration struck. "She is absent from your side. I understand from my aunt that you live in each other's pockets. How did you manage to separate yourself?"

The question sounded slyly disparaging to her own ears, but Kesgrave noticed nothing amiss and simply said, "I have my ways."

Of all the possible responses he could have given, Bea thought this was the most damning, as it was informal and offhand, indicating a long-standing familiarity. She could hear him saying the exact same words to the heiress on their tenth wedding anniversary when she opened a gaily wrapped box to find the stunning sapphire necklace she'd long desired. "How did you know?" she would ask in coy surprise. Then he, with a mysterious smile and a shrug: "I have my ways."

The wrench of pain she felt was immediate, and fearful that she would succumb to a humiliating display after all, she frantically began to list the positive aspects of her life that had comforted her earlier: her mother, Lady Abercrombie, the list, the Lord Byron factor, Mr. Wilson in Mrs. Otley's bed with the yellow damask curtains and his remarkably pale skin and his snuffbox and his—

Hold on, she thought as she reviewed the scene in her head, the snuffbox.

The snuff!

It seemed so obvious now she could hardly believe it hadn't occurred to her the moment she'd seen the box. Of course the poison had been added to the tobacco. The scent of the sort would cover any smell naturally emitted by the nux vomica, and the likelihood of the wrong person ingesting it was very low.

You fool, she thought, annoyed that she had missed it.

Impatient now with her own obliviousness, she carefully reviewed everything about the snuff and the box it came in. From this vantage point, both seemed like unjustifiable extravagances for a former steward. The price of Lord Penwortham's mixture was very dear, she knew, for Aunt Vera frequently objected to her uncle's insistence on using it. Could he not find another type that cost less and didn't smell quite so much of bergamot?

Likewise, the box itself had been of excellent quality. Although it wasn't laden with jewels, its emerald-green cloisonné work was very fine and detailed and the enamel was inlaid with gold. It had not been bought from a stall in Spitalfields market.

Perhaps Mrs. Otley had given it to him as a gift? Could she have stumbled across it while going through her late husband's things and decided it made a wonderful lover's trinket?

Did that explanation make sense?

No, she thought slowly, recalling Mr. Otley's disgust of tobacco, which he had cataloged in detail in the journal he kept. The snuffbox had most certainly not been his.

So how had the valuable object come to be in the possession of a former opium smuggler?

Mrs. Otley mentioned that he had returned from India with several thousand pounds with which he intended to buy a farm. Would he have spent some of his precious savings on a vanity item like a snuffbox or would he—

"Miss Hyde-Clare," the duke said firmly, insisting on her attention, which had plainly wandered. "Despite your opinion of me, I actually do know the varied meanings of the furrowed brow, and right now yours is wrinkled in consternation. You are at once focused and distracted. I would like to know what the cause is."

Oh, wouldn't you just, Bea thought cynically, well aware of how strongly he would object to the information she was privately perusing. But it was none of his business, of course, for she was nothing to him but a baffling compulsion and she *had* complied with the promise she'd given. The dead body of Mr. Wilson did not happen to cross her path. It had been deliberately placed in it by Mr. Skeffington. If only the duke had been clever enough to include corpses of deliberate placement in their compact.

The fact of her investigation made her feel as though she had an advantage over the duke. He had his delightful Lady Victoria, with all her insipid perfection and preening beauty, and she had purpose, resolution and an interesting challenge.

Giving him the attention he'd requested, she answered honestly. "Snuff."

If he was particularly struck by the seemingly random subject, his expression revealed none of it. "Snuff?" he asked mildly.

"Yes, I'm thinking about snuff," she said slowly, examining him consideringly. He was a high-flying Corinthian who knew every aspect of male society intimately and would certainly know all the snuff dealers in London. But how to word the question without raising his suspicions?

The answer was obvious: her dear uncle.

Yes, of course.

"I would like to buy Uncle Horace a gift," she explained, pleased with her quick thinking, for the idea had several advantages, not the least of which would be to gain Kesgrave's help in the investigation without his knowledge. "It's his birthday soon, and I'm so grateful to him and my aunt for accepting my explanation for the bruises without asking any questions. If they had just pursued the matter even a tiny bit, my story would have fallen apart, but they remained almost willfully ignorant about the whole thing. So I'd like to buy my uncle a lovely gift for his birthday. I thought perhaps snuff. He is very fond of a particular type. I believe it's called Lord Penwortham's mixture. Are you familiar with it?"

"I know it," he said amiably. "Your uncle has luxurious taste in snuff. That sort can be bought from only one dealer, on Haymarket. It's quite extravagant. Are you sure you don't want to buy him something more reasonably set such as a sleeping cap?"

The idea of her buying her uncle something so drearily practical made her giggle. "A sleeping cap? He will think I'm punishing him for his interest rather than thanking him for his indifference. No, I am set on the snuff. I know the price is dear. My aunt frequently grumbles at the expense, which is what makes it the perfect gift, as it's ultimately for both of them. You say the dealer is on Haymarket?"

"Yes, Dupasquier and Morny. It's an old established house at number thirty-three," he said.

As she committed the information to memory, she pondered what her tactic should be to discover the information she needed. If the duke's estimation was accurate and the snuff was indeed an indulgence, then perhaps it would not have a wide distribution but rather a small group of habitual users, which would supply her with a compact catalog of suspects to consider.

It was, she conceded, an unlikely avenue of investigation, but she felt confident it would bear fruit. It had to, for at the moment she had no other theory for how the victim ingested the poison, and she knew it wasn't outlandish to suppose Mr. Wilson had taken the snuff soon after waking. Her uncle frequently partook first thing in the morning, and if for some reason he did not, her aunt would grumble about his crankiness. The compulsion of tobacco users worked to her advantage, for it meant that Mr. Wilson had not had the snuffbox long in his possession. He had probably gotten it yesterday or the day before. If only Mrs. Otley had been some help in accounting for his daily movements. Then she would be able to re-create his last few days and pinpoint the most likely source of the poisoned tobacco. Hopefully, searching his rooms at the Melbourne would provide some insight into how he spent his time.

And the buyers, she thought. If Monsieurs Dupasquier and Morny could be convinced to reveal the names of their clients who had recently purchased Lord Penwortham's mixture, she would know exactly whom to investigate next.

But how to persuade them?

She would need a compelling story, of course, something heart wrenching to earn their sympathy.

"Miss Hyde-Clare," Kesgrave said sharply.

Yet again, she forced herself to focus on the man before her, who seemed at once annoyed and expectant. What was he expecting from her? Once she had understood the reasoning behind his request for an apology, she had given it immediately. What else could he want?

And then she recalled that he had very helpfully provided her with important information. "Oh, yes, your grace. Thank you. I will visit Monsieurs Dupasquier and Morny posthaste to buy my uncle his gift. I very much appreciate your help."

A faint smile appeared on his lips as he shook his head. "You have accused me many times of having too high an opinion of myself, and I must congratulate you on discovering the most effective tactic to cut me down to size. No, brat, I was not demanding that you thank me for the information about snuff dealers. I was requesting an answer to my question: Would you do me the honor of the next dance?"

"Dance with you?" she said, staring at him in astonishment.

After all of Lady Abercrombie's excellent work to keep her standing upright and her own monumental effort not to collapse into a mound of self-pity, he wanted her to now place herself in his arms? He had paraded Lady Victoria's perfection before her, admitted with aggressive familiarity to having ways of dealing with the young heiress and made no indication that their expected announcement was not in fact imminent.

Did he think she was impervious to all emotion?

It was some consolation, she supposed, that he didn't consider her susceptible to his charms or himself vulnerable to her schemes. She recalled the duke she'd first met at Lakeview Hall, seemingly fixated on the idea that conscienceless harpies were constantly trying to trap him into marriage. Clearly, she was in a different category, and although it was flattering to be thought of as something resembling a friend, the treatment was still what she had feared the most when she'd said goodbye after the resolution of the Fazeley investigation. To be treated like just another person in his life when he was in fact the most important person in hers was simply unbearable.

"No, I can't dance with you," Bea said frankly. "It's out of the question."

Despite his claim to wounded vanity, Kesgrave seemed only amused by her rejection and calmly asked her why it could not be considered.

Since the true answer could not be given, Bea found herself at a loss to explain. Again, she took comfort in the fact that he seemed genuinely confused by her response, for it meant he had no idea of the turmoil roiling inside her. To keep it that way, she said, "My ankle."

He raised an eyebrow skeptically. "Your ankle?"

"Yes, my ankle. I twisted it"—the secret to a successful lie, she reminded herself, was to keep it vague— "earlier. I've been limping around the ballroom quite dreadfully. It's the reason I stayed here while Flora went to the refreshment table to get us lemonade. I'm surprised you haven't noticed. It's really quite embarrassing how awkwardly I've been lumbering around."

That, at least, was true, she thought. She'd been lumbering awkwardly all evening.

"I've noticed only your usual grace," he said softly.

It was just flattery, Spanish coin tossed to a peasant, but her heart fluttered and her mind emptied of thought. While the orchestra started the first notes of a waltz, she gazed at him blankly, unable to make her usual objection to insincere praise. Apparently in no rush to find another partner, he lingered there, his eyes focused on her, amused and watchful.

Bea thought it was likely they both would have stood there all night if Flora's sudden appearance hadn't disconcerted them both.

"Good evening, your grace. I did not expect to see you talking to Bea," she said, darting a smug glance at her cousin. Obviously, she wasn't at all surprised to find him there and had been intentionally slow in procuring their lemonade.

Kesgrave greeted Flora cheerfully and assured her that he could not in all good conscience abandon her cousin until she'd come back. "Not with her ankle," he added.

"Her what?" Flora asked, baffled.

"Her twisted ankle, which has forced her to limp around the ballroom quite dreadfully," the duke said seriously. "I'm sure you've noticed. It is, after all, the reason you went to the refreshment table on her behalf."

"Oh, her *ankle*," Flora said with needlessly exaggerated emphasis. "I thought you said rankle, and I was confused, as I don't believe Bea has made anyone angry this evening. As far as I can tell she'd been the perfect guest. But, yes, her *ankle* has been a problem. It's a wonder she can walk at all. But I'm here to support her with"—she held up the two glasses—"lemonade and whatever else she might need."

As accomplished a performance as this was, the duke didn't even pretend to be swayed. "You are delightful," he said to Flora before making his goodbyes. He bowed over Bea's hand. "A pleasure as always, Miss Hyde-Clare. I'm sure I will see you very soon."

Bea, however, very much doubted it, for now that he had Lady Victoria and she had Mr. Wilson, she intended to stay as far away from him as possible. Nevertheless, she nodded at his comment as she bid him good night.

Satisfied, he walked away, and as soon as he was well clear of earshot, Flora turned to her cousin and chortled with delight. "Now tell me he isn't smitten."

Although Bea could tell her and offer convincing evidence in support, she drank her lemonade and held her tongue. It would be only a matter of days before the Duke of Kesgrave announced his engagement to the Tavistock heiress. Then she would not have to say a thing.

CHAPTER EIGHT

The old established firm of Dupasquier and Morny had a simple, elegant shop front, with a pair of bow windows beneath the rasp and crown—the mark of a snuff dealer—and a sign declaring itself a purveyor of fine tobacco. Beatrice, who felt uncomfortable dressed as a lady's maid, particularly because Annie's dress was a little too tight on her, especially around the bosom, appreciated its restrained design and felt positive she would find a practical and sympathetic merchant inside.

Well, not exactly positive, she conceded silently as she approached the door. Her mood was closer to optimistic. She would get nowhere with her ploy if the vendor turned out to be a tyrannical and apathetic businessman more concerned with protecting his clients than saving a wretched serving girl from poverty and deprivation. Then she would be at a loss as to how to proceed other than wait until nightfall and break into the shop to examine its books.

Given how awkward she was in the bright light of day, she could only imagine how clumsy she would be in the dark gloom of night.

Hopefully, it wouldn't come to that.

It had already been a difficult morning of disappointments, as her second interview with Mrs. Otley had yielded few results. The widow bristled at questions about her finances, which Bea considered vital to understanding her current situation, and professed complete ignorance of the cloisonné snuffbox. Upon discovering that her lover had been in possession of something of significant value, however, she insisted it was hers and accompanied Bea down to the dank wine cellar to assume immediate custody of it. Unwilling to give up the item without first testing its contents for poison, Bea held fast, and a minor tussle ensued. In the struggle the enamel box fell and emptied its contents onto the dirt floor. Both women reached for it at the same time, but the widow swung out with her right arm to block Bea's progress while her left arm swooped down to grab the item, inadvertently scattering what was left of the tobacco across a wide swath of floor.

But was it inadvertent?

Awake to the possibility that the widow's actions had in fact been carefully calculated to obscure the collection of information, Bea accused Mrs. Otley of intentionally thwarting her investigation. "It's as though you don't even *want* to know who killed your lover."

Mrs. Otley opened her eyes in surprise at the charge as she hid the snuffbox in the folds of her dress. "Can there be any doubt? I thought for sure I'd made myself clear on the matter. Very well, let me speak plainly: I didn't care who killed Otley then, and I don't care who killed Charles now. There seems to be no point in investigating all of these dead men other than to subject me to impertinent questions. I cannot see the point, for dead is dead is dead."

Swallowing a growl of frustration, Bea had bounded up the stairs and out of the house.

Now, however, as she opened the door to the snuff shop, she wondered if the spill had been intentional. Perhaps the real reason Mrs. Otley didn't want her to discover the name of the culprit was she already knew it. The only pause that theory gave her was the overwhelming brutality of the death. Although Bea could imagine the widow dosing her lover to remove the complication of his existence from her life with alarming ease, she could not conceive of her going about it in such a violent manner. Unless Mrs. Otley wanted him to suffer, she would have used laudanum and put him to gentle, everlasting sleep.

What cause could she have had to want him to suffer? The servants had reported no discord, and they seemed well abreast of most household drama.

As she stepped into the shop, Bea put these thoughts from her head and focused on the matter at hand, namely ingratiating herself with a pair of snuff dealers. She noted at once the refined interior, with its wooden screen in the style of the Adams brothers dividing the front section from the back and its walls lined with oak shelves filled with canisters of tobacco.

Although her steps were measured as she crossed the threshold, as soon as her eyes alighted on the gentleman behind the counter, she adopted a frenzied manner. The distance to where he stood was minor, but she ran across the floor as if traversing a great field. Then she pressed herself against the wood and begged him to help her in her best French accent, which was, she readily admitted, a little less than horrible.

"Monsieur, monsieur, you must," she said breathily. "You must 'elp me or I will be tossed on ze street like ze littlest urchin child, unloved and forsaken."

The man behind the counter—white-haired and dignified with a key that hung around his neck from a chain and a narrow scar above his lip—held himself rigidly still as she agitatedly drummed her fingers against his counter. "Please calm yourself, mademoiselle. This is a respectable business establishment."

"I know, I know, it is ze finest snuff shop in all of London," Bea said, grateful for the dim lighting because it hid her blush. With every melodramatic word she uttered, she grew more and more mortified by her own performance. "This is why I'm here. Because this is ze business that provided this." From her reticule she produced a small square canister that she'd borrowed from her uncle's study and placed it on the counter with a heavy thump. "It was delivered to my mistress with a card, but I lost ze card, you see. It blew away in the wind. Flut, floot, gone! I try to chase it but it goes places I cannot, under carriages and horses' hoofs. Then it stops and it lands in horse extract—how do you say, manure—and I cannot read ze card anymore. My mistress finds out ze card is ruined, she turns very cross. She fires me. Please, monsieur…"

She trailed off expectantly and he obligingly supplied his name. "Dupasquier," he said.

"Ah, Monsieur Dupasquier, you are French like me," Bea said with satisfaction as she let her shoulders sag with relief. Then, realizing the movement made the already revealing dress a little more indecent, she straightened her back. "You are sympathetic to ze cause. You don't want to see a fellow countrywoman tossed out on ze street like ze littlest urchin child, unloved and forsaken. 'Ow will you sleep at night knowing I am ze cold and starving?"

"Really, mademoiselle, I hardly think your plight is my—"

"No!" she screeched, making the snuff dealer jump, "don't think. If you think, you will turn cold and rigidly indifferent like all zeez Englishmen around me. It is as if they care nothing for love! How heartless they are. But you aren't like that, are you?" The cajoling, she noted, made him particularly uncomfortable, which was a good thing. The more uneasy he felt, the more inclined he would be to acquiesce to her request just to free himself of her presence. "No, you are kind and ze French. You understand 'ow the 'eart works. You will 'elp me find the man who gave my mistress ze gift. It is a little thing. Just provide me with ze names of all ze gentlemen who bought this snuff in the past two weeks and I will recognize ze name of her suitor." She snapped her fingers as if to demonstrate how easily her problem could be resolved. "You will do it, no? Zen it will not matter that ze card is in the horse extract."

Fiddling with the key that hung from his neck, Dupasquier coughed nervously and stared fiercely at the canister of snuff on the counter, as if fearful of making eye contact. "I do not think…" He trailed off as the sound of the door opened and seemed visibly relieved by the presence of another shopper, as if that would force her to be more circumspect. "It is against my store's policy to provide that information. I cannot help you."

Bea, who felt sufficiently disguised both because she was dressed as a maid and because she was a nonentity in society, had no reservations about making a scene. The prospect of embarrassing him in front of one of his loyal customers emboldened her, and she raised her voice as she said, "You dare speak of policies when my life it at stake? You are a most unfeeling creature." Now more than ever, she regretted her inability to produce tears upon demand, for she felt positive a little waterworks before the paying customer would convince Monsieur Dupasquier to help her in any way possible. "But you cannot be, for you are ze French, like me. I cannot believe—"

"All right, then, Miss Hyde-Clare," said a cool voice behind her. "I think you've tortured poor Mr. Dupasquier enough for the day."

As strong as the desire was to whip her head around and confront the Duke of Kesgrave with sneering anger, Bea held her position against the counter. She took several deep breaths, hurled a few silent insults at his head, and clenched her hands into fists for several irate seconds. Then smoothly, as if only minorly interested in what he had to say, she turned to look at him, his amused expression already seared into her brain before she even encountered it. Determined to meet his nonchalant omniscience with her own, she said calmly, "It took you long enough, your grace. I expected you to be here ten minutes ago."

He laughed with delight, which was even more galling, and shook his head, so unimpressed with her empty boast he didn't even feel the need to refute it. Rather, he walked up to the counter and laid a slip of paper on the darkened wood. "Here you go, Mr. Dupasquier, an order from Prinny, just as I promised. It is, I assure you, entirely on the level and you may feel free to amend your sign to say 'purveyors of snuff to the royal family.' I trust you will hold to your end of the bargain, as well, and say nothing of this encounter to anyone?"

As Kesgrave smugly and complacently settled the details of his arrangement with the shop owner, Bea tried to piece together what had happened. The most obvious fact was undeniable: The duke knew that she was engaged in an investigation. Unless Mr. Skeffington bizarrely and inexplicably confessed everything to him, he could not know the particulars of the situation. Rather, he had figured out the broad outline of her scheme last night when she had questioned him about tobacco dealers.

Naturally, she was offended by his suspicion, for it was not entirely outside the realm of possibility that she would want to buy a birthday gift for Uncle Horace. Kesgrave could not know that his birthday was in fact eight months away, and it would have served him right if he had walked in on a scene of quiet, dignified commerce.

She would have loved to have seen the expression on his face then.

Not so smug, are we? she thought.

But of course that wasn't the scene he'd walked in on, and no doubt he felt very clever at how well he'd arranged the affair. She could not have possibly done anything more mortifying than dressing in her maid's dress and affecting an outrageously bad French accent to argue with a snuff dealer over the release of his private records. It was the epitome of humiliation.

And yet Bea did not feel humiliated. She was too angry to feel anything but fury at the supercilious and maddeningly superior Duke of Kesgrave.

How dare he move her around London as if she were a piece on a chessboard!

Either as part of his original deal with the merchant or as an additional act of generosity, Kesgrave placed a personal order of snuff and asked that it be delivered to his town house later that day. Then he thanked the man again for his discretion and turned to leave.

Although Bea wanted to snarl at the shopkeeper, who had shown no reaction whatsoever to the strange events unfolding in his store, she would give neither him nor the duke the satisfaction of seeing a strong reaction. Instead, she picked up the canister, dipped her head in acknowledgment and said, "There are many vulnerable young women in this city who are at the mercy of their employers' whim, and I hope to God none of them ever has cause to walk into your shop to plead for help, for all they will meet is the cruel, hard visage of a businessman with policies. Good day, sir!"

Bea strode to the door, stepped outside and walked several feet down Haymarket in hopes of soothing her anger. But the temerity and arrogance of the duke's presumption was more than she could bear and she spun around, marched up to him until they were toe to toe and said, "You lied to me!"

Astoundingly, Kesgrave's audacity knowing no bounds, he said the same words to her at the same moment.

Even more outraged, she tried again. "No, *you* lied to *me*."

But the duke, feeling himself to be the injured party, made that claim too.

Bea was so frustrated she wanted to scream.

Kesgrave appeared merely amused by the circumstance and calmly suggested that they have a quiet, reasonable discussion somewhere private.

Oh, how she loathed that air of condescending equanimity he wore like a suit of armor, impervious to the opinions of other people and wholly confident in the quality of his own. This was what he had been like in the dining room at Lakeview Hall in the fall when she fantasized about throwing fish patties and stuffed tomatoes and fillets of salmon at his head.

Monstrously arrogant!

"I don't want to go anywhere with you," Bea declared peevishly. "If you would like to discuss the matter of how you lied to me, I'm happy to do so here. If you are not amenable to that arrangement, then we will have to take this up at another time, for I cannot linger. As you apparently know, I have an investigation to attend, which is now half a day behind schedule, thanks to your interference."

"We cannot talk here, on a public street," he said as if explaining the obvious to a particularly dense child.

But Bea was not so easily maneuvered. "Why not? Only a few weeks ago, we spoke quite freely on a public street. And the Strand was far more crowded than this," she said as she gestured to the dozens of pedestrians who strolled by.

"On that occasion you were dressed like your cousin Russell. Now, however, you are dressed like a woman," he explained. "It's not appropriate for me to be seen arguing with a woman on a public street—and a servant, at that!"

The fact that he was arguing with her on a public street about arguing with her on a public street appealed to her sense of the absurd and she started to laugh.

This sound—perhaps because it was so unexpected, perhaps because it was inappropriate for a public street as well—startled him, and he stared at her with an arrested look.

"We must talk," he said, his voice surprisingly deep.

Bea sighed with annoyance and looked around for his carriage, which she knew had to be somewhere nearby. She spotted it across the road. "Oh, very well," she said with an impatient huff.

The duke's groom rushed to open the door to the coach and congratulated Bea on recovering fully from her bruises. "They were mighty nasty, but ye look as fresh as a parcel of spring flowers, miss."

"All right, Jenkins," Kesgrave said. "Stop your courting and drive us to Clarges Street."

"No, Jenkins," Bea said firmly. "We will stay right here. Our conversation will be brief."

As much respect as the groom had for her, she was in no way his employer and he merely shook his head. A few moments later, the carriage lurched and pulled into the road.

Bea gave the duke several minutes to say something and when he remained determined to look out the window, she said with admirable calm, "Very well, I will go first. You lied to me."

Kesgrave shook his head and said, "No, Bea, no."

Although she was angry and it could make no difference, she allowed herself a moment to enjoy the maudlin pleasure of hearing the sound of her name on his lips. He'd called her Beatrice before but never Bea, and even as her heart fluttered accordingly, she cursed the constraints of her situation. The whole point of investigating Mr. Wilson's death was to have an occupation that had nothing to do with the Duke of Kesgrave. And yet somehow it had landed her in his own carriage en route to Clarges Street.

'Twas not fair.

The drive to Clarges was short, and less than ten minutes later they arrived at an imposing white town house with a portico. Uncertain where they were, Bea climbed out of the carriage with great reluctance and followed the duke up the stairs. It could not be his home, for he lived in Berkeley Square, and it was far too fashionable a neighborhood for it to be the house where a gentleman would keep his mistress.

Kesgrave rapped on the door, which was opened immediately by a light-haired butler with a welcoming expression, and entered the house with curt familiarity.

"Tell my grandmother we're in the drawing room," he

added briskly, strolling down the hallway without checking to see if Bea followed, "and do bring tea. Thank you!"

Although Bea faltered slightly on discovering where they were, she trailed closely on Kesgrave's heels, and as soon as the door to the room was shut, she shrieked with all the anxiety and confusion she felt, "*Your grandmother!*"

But in the seclusion of the private home, the duke felt free to give unrestricted rein to his anger, as well, and bit out angrily, "You have betrayed my trust!"

"Why are we here at your grandmother's house?" she asked, unable to smother her apprehension. She was nothing to him, a slight agitation at best, a thing that bothered him every once in a while like a pebble in his shoe, and yet she was standing in the middle of his grandmother's drawing room, the grandmother his soon-to-be-affianced bride had met only the night before.

It made no sense.

"You gave me your word you would stop investigating murders," he said with alarming heat, as he stalked across the room to the mantel.

"What will your grandmother think?" she asked with a wild glance around, as if afraid the esteemed personage was somehow already there, hiding behind the elegant settee or the beautifully tailored velvet curtains.

"You *promised*," he said forcefully.

"What will we tell her?" she said more softly now, as her mind began to focus on the challenging task of concocting a believable story that would account for her presence. Last night, she'd invented a twisted ankle. Perhaps she could use that now. After all, she was dressed like a maid and—

By all that was holy, she thought, her face going white. *She was dressed like a maid.* She couldn't meet the Dowager Duchess of Kesgrave wearing Annie's frock. Her gaze flew to the curtains as she wondered if she could slip through the window and escape.

Suddenly, the duke was in front of her, his hands on her shoulders and his blue eyes blazing with fury. "For

God's sake, Bea, tell me what you are doing! I swear, you will drive me mad."

Truly taken aback by his vehemence and unnervingly aware of his closeness, she said, "I was trying to ascertain if I could climb through the window before your grandmother came in."

His look of astonishment was decidedly comical, and as if perceiving that fact himself, he began to laugh. At once, his face lightened and his blue eyes sparkled and a blond curl fell onto his forehead, adding an element of endearing boyishness to his already handsome visage. Bea, who was only a few inches away and could feel the heat from his hands through the fabric on her dress, stared at him in bemusement, for it seemed impossible to her that someone, anyone, could be so appealing. He already had everything—wealth, status, intelligence—and yet if he had only this, his open demeanor, his amiable appearance, it would have been more than enough.

Gradually, his mirth subsided and he shook his head as he regarded her regarding him. "Bea," he said deeply, "you are—"

But he didn't finish his thought, merely shaking his head again, as if in wonder, and continuing to look at her intently.

Bea's heart began to race.

She had no experience with romantic liaisons, had never stood so close to a man that she could fell his breath on her skin, but she knew what it was. She could *feel* what it was, and she was surprised to discover how much she craved what it was. It was powerful and unsettling, and its ferocity made her feel like someone else. Beatrice Hyde-Clare had certainly never felt the blindingly overwhelming desire to kiss a man. Dizzy with it, she bent her head forward only a fraction of an inch, as if to see what he would do.

Ah, he liked that, she noted, for his eyes seemed to flash and he pressed closer. Slowly, she closed her eyes and, blooding pounding, allowed herself to succumb to the unbearable anticipation of feeling the duke's lips against hers....

CHAPTER NINE

The door banged as a petulant voice growled, "I said I've got it, Sutton!"

Gasping in horror, Bea dashed to the other side of the room, to the window she had so recently contemplated squeezing through, and watched the Dowager Duchess of Kesgrave walk in carrying a tea tray.

Kesgrave, recovering his wits so quickly Bea wondered if she'd imagined the kiss that had almost happened, sauntered—oh, yes, he *sauntered* while she had scurried—over to the entry to relieve his grandmother of her burden. She promptly twisted away and said testily, "Did you not just hear me tell Sutton I can do it? I may be closer to cocking up my toes than kicking up my heels, but I can still manage a tray with a few cups on it."

"I did not come over here to assist you, my dear, because you are feeble," the duke said mildly, "but because you are female. I believe the last time you berated me was for letting my cousin Josephine hold a parcel while I remained empty-handed."

"That's because your cousin Josephine is blunderous and bumbling. I wouldn't let her hold my hat if I had any desire to ever wear it again," the dowager said as she crossed to the table. "The lesson there was don't let clumsy people carry parcels, not women. You are a fool, Kesgrave, and I'm not sure why I put up with you."

Although her tone was just as harsh as her words, the duke took no offense at this criticism and even bowed as if receiving a compliment. "A weakness I'm sure you'll over-come soon enough. In the meantime, do put the tray down before you drop it. I know you like to boast of your strength and Sutton and I are agog at your impressive vigor, but you suffer from the rheumatic complaint and your doctor strictly advised against unnecessarily straining your joints."

At the mention of her doctor, her grace let forth a string of invectives, and Bea, standing by the window, re-gretted the fact that she was in no state to appreciate the scene. How heartily ridiculous it all was—the august Duke of Kesgrave getting his ear cuffed like a schoolboy and she too horrified to do anything but stare blankly, her mind trying to understand exactly what had happened before the septuagenarian had burst into the room.

He had intended to kiss her, that much was clear, even if his insouciance immediately after belied the intensi-ty of the moment. She even thought she understood why, for she had felt the same tug of attraction as he, the same undeniable awareness as he, the same inability to break the connection. It was as if they were magnets, drawn together by an incontrovertible force, and what she didn't know was if that was what happened when all women and men stood too close together or just she and the duke.

On one hand, the answer didn't matter, for it would change nothing about the circumstance. Even if the power of their attraction spoke to the depth of their bond, it wouldn't have any bearing on his future. She was no hot-house orchid and never would be.

And yet knowing it was endemic to them would alter everything, for it would justify the intensity of her feelings and make her feel less like a gullible schoolgirl. Lady Aber-crombie said it couldn't be love if it wasn't requited, and maybe she was right. But maybe she was wrong as well.

As engrossing as her confusion was, Bea never for a moment forgot where she was and how she was dressed and the unlikeliness of sneaking out without anyone in the room noticing. Although Kesgrave continued to bicker with the dowager, energetically detailing the many accomplishments of her insufferably qualified doctor—because, of course, he had a list at the ready; 'twas his raison d'être—he knew exactly where she was.

Apparently, his grandmother did too, for she interrupted his exceedingly dull catalog ("patched up Wellington's knee after he suffered a musket ball at the Battle of Seringapatam") to castigate him for failing to introduce his guest.

"You are Miss Hyde-Clare, I trust," she said, raising her voice as she turned to address Bea across the room. "Get away from that window. At six and twenty you are far too old to place yourself in the path of natural daylight."

"Grandmother…" Kesgrave growled warningly.

"That sound you hear is my grandson ordering me to be polite," she explained. "Very well, I shall. Miss Hyde-Clare, *please* get away from that window exposing you to unflattering sunlight. There, I hope you are satisfied."

"No," he said. "Are you?"

The dowager echoed his negative answer but spoke in such a gratified tone one could only believe the opposite to be true. Even in her state of heightened anxiety, Bea found it impossible not to smile at the older woman's antics.

"That damn fool Sutton, bringing three teacups when I specifically told him you would need only two," her grace said peevishly, as she reached down to remove one from the tray. "He is an unrepentant profligate."

Startled, Bea darted a glance at Kesgrave, who didn't seem at all surprised by her intention not to join them. She opened her mouth to protest, for she dreaded the prospect of being alone with the duke, but realizing she feared his grandmother more, promptly shut it again.

Although Bea did not say a word, the dowager responded as if she'd spoken. "No, no, I can't stay. I'm not invited," she explained with a cross look at her grandson. "In fact, I've been given strict instructions not to linger. You've got Damien all worked up with your lying and he's eager to light into you."

"I did not lie," Bea said.

"Yes, you did," Kesgrave said.

Her grace laughed with genuine amusement, and Bea marveled at how much younger she appeared. "I'll leave you to work it out. Damien brought you here because I have a reputation as a stickler and no one would dare imply anything untoward had happened under my chaperonage. Added to that, I trust my grandson implicitly. Nevertheless, this door will remain open. I wish you the best of luck in sorting out your difference of opinion, and if either one of you is compelled to throw something at the other—and here I am thinking mostly of you, Miss Hyde-Clare, as I know the Matlock men can be singularly immune to reason—do stay away from the blue vase by the window. It's worth very little but has great sentimental value to me."

Bea watched her leave with a mixture of relief and disappointment. She was grateful to be free of the older woman's discerning eye, for surely she had noticed her absurd outfit and would have said something cutting about it sooner or later. But she also regretted the lost opportunity to find out more about the duke, for watching him interact with his relative had been a revelation.

As intriguing as his relationship with the dowager was, gathering notes on the Matlock family dynamic was not the reason she was there.

Purposefully, she turned to him. "I did not lie."

"You did," he said, more calmly. "In exchange for my returning you to the Sylvan Press to interview Mr. Cornyn, you gave your word that you would cease investigating the horrible deaths that keep crossing your path. And do not trot out the meaningless semantical distinction that this particular corpse did not *cross your path*."

"Ah, but it isn't meaningless, your grace," Bea said lightly, for she was on firm footing with her argument and felt confident in her reasoning. He may be impervious to logic, as his grandmother had observed, but that didn't mean her logic was flawed. "Words matter. Specificity of ideas matters. Perhaps grasping the significance of that will be a salutary lesson for you. The next time you try to limit a woman's movements, be more precise in your restrictions. Take care in outlining the boundaries. Do not expect that she will fill in the blank spaces for you. Verily, I could argue with myself that when you said *corpses that cross your path,* you really meant any method by which a corpse entered my life, but I really don't see why I should have to do the hard work of interpretation. Indeed, I'm already working hard, as I have to maneuver from under your restrictions. If you are displeased with the bargain you made, that is your responsibility, not mine. Now, if that is all, I shall return to my day and let you carry on with yours. Do thank your grandmother for her hospitality and please express my regret that we did not have a chance to chat further."

Bea turned to walk to the door as if she were about to leave, but she was too clever to believe the matter had actually been settled. Kesgrave would now make his long speech explaining why her reasoning was fallible and insist that she comply with the original compact. Given his penchant for pedantry, she imagined he would cite legal precedent and local statutes and Broughton's rules for boxing.

She sighed wearily, for she did not have time for such a long and pointless address. Her promising investigative lead had gone nowhere, thanks to Kesgrave's machinations, and she needed to go home, change into a respectable walking grown, figure out how to finagle information about his stuff dealer from her uncle without raising his suspicions, change back into Annie's dress and sneak out of the house for the second time that day. To minimize the likelihood of being intercepted on the way to the door, she'd utilized the servants' entrance, which came with its own hazards. Now she would have to slip past Mrs. Emerson and Dawson three more times.

"You confirm it, then?" the duke said.

Surprised by the comment, Bea halted only a few feet from the door and looked at him. "That I outwitted you? Yes, your grace, I readily confirm it."

He shook his head dismissively. "Your interest in Lord Penwortham's mixture—it's in pursuit of a murderer. Despite your promise to me, you've embroiled yourself in another investigation."

"On the contrary, I did not promise to callously refuse a plea for help from a distraught source who did not know where else to turn," she said calmly. "Once again, if you had thought to include such a provision in our agreement, I would have of course turned this person away."

"Someone *asked* you to investigate a murder?" he said, thoroughly appalled. "Please assure me you did not advertise your services."

Advertise, Bea thought speculatively. That option hadn't occurred to her when she was trying to devise ways to locate another mystery in need of solving.

"No, Miss Hyde-Clare, no," he said firmly, responding to the expression on her face, which indicated he had given her an idea worthy of consideration. "I was not making a suggestion. Please, sit down. Let me pour the tea and we will discuss this rationally."

Although the offer was everything gracious, she eyed him suspiciously. "If by 'discuss this rationally' you mean talk me out of my current course of action, then, no, thank you, I'd rather not. And you will note, I hope, how I'm not assuming your words are limited to their surface meaning. I'm digging deeper to examine all possible interpretations. I say this as a way of demonstrating how you might approach all your negotiations in the future," she explained with meticulous condescension. "It's shocking to me that you're a member of the House of Lords and don't understand how slippery oaths can be."

"*Bea!*"

She sat down.

Kesgrave took the chair adjacent to the settee, filled two teacups and handed one to her. "The brew will be tepid because my grandmother's grasp is uncertain and the housekeeper does not want her to scald herself. I trust you will not mind."

"Of course not," she said amicably.

After taking a sip of tea, he leaned back in the chair and said with deceptive mildness, "I could tell your aunt and uncle."

So much for a rational discussion, she thought, feeling far less affable now that his opening maneuver was to issue threats. But her demeanor revealed none of her anger as she answered matter-of-factly. "You could, yes, but it would be a betrayal of such cruelty I could never forgive it."

His calm nod gave no indication if such an outcome would be problematic for him. "At least you would be unharmed."

Bea laughed without amusement. "Would I, your grace? Would I truly be unharmed?"

As with many things, the question contained the answer, and she watched the expression on his face as he considered how her family might respond to the news of her investigative activities. They would not beat her or physically abuse her—in that way, he was correct, she would not be harmed—but they would react in anger and deny her freedom. And that was to say nothing of the damage it would do to her spirit and heart.

Raising her teacup, Bea made a quick calculation and said with straightforward candor, "I do not think my French maid story is quite as irresistible as I supposed when I came up with it this morning. It's impossible to say, though, as your interference ensured that it did not get the proper trial run it deserves. I suspect Monsieur Dupasquier would have been more sympathetic to my plight if he did not know you were waiting in the wings to relieve him of my desperate presence. Am I right, by the way, in assuming you sent me to the wrong place?"

He confirmed her supposition with an abrupt nod.

"What gave me away?" she asked.

"You said it was a birthday gift for your uncle," he explained. "And while I find that in itself highly suspect, the fact is we gave Lady Abercrombie the same excuse when we asked her about the jade dagger."

Bea shook her head, slightly amused by how the mind worked. "No wonder it had come to me so quickly."

"No wonder."

"Well, regardless of how it was contrived, this morning's exchange at the old established firm of Dupasquier and Morny makes me less than sanguine about my gambit's success in the future. With that in mind, I'd like to suggest a partnership."

Ah, he wasn't expecting that, Bea thought with satisfaction as surprise overcame his features.

"A partnership?"

"Your grace," she said, leaning forward while balancing the teacup delicately on her knee, "it has long been my goal to pursue and identify the perpetrators of these crimes in private. On all three occasions I have examined the evidence on my own and neither sought nor requested your assistance, and yet here we are, implausibly, in your grandmother's drawing room. For reasons neither you nor I can understand, you keep inserting yourself into matters that have nothing to do with you. Undoubtedly, you are operating under some sort of compulsion, and I would never seek to deny you something you need. Indeed, it seems much more sensible to make use of it, so, yes, I propose a partnership. We solve the matter of who killed Mr. Wilson together."

The word *together* echoed in her head as Bea wondered if what she was proposing would do her further harm. Having never been in love before, she could not properly estimate the damage yet to be done, but it seemed to her that the system itself must be finite. There could not be degrees of misery. She was already devastated. What else was left?

Giving the matter additional thought, she conceded that watching Kesgrave court Lady Victoria would provide her with a new and different sort of pain. But would it be a larger pain?

That she couldn't say.

Nevertheless, she felt fairly certain that identifying Mr. Wilson's murderer together would not increase the likelihood of her having to spend more time with the beautiful heiress. If anything, it would ensure that she spent less.

Having made her bold offer, the last thing Bea expected from the duke was amusement, but he smiled brightly at her, as if relieved, and said, "Mr. Wilson?"

"Yes," she said definitively.

"The same Mr. Wilson you were so convinced had secretly infiltrated the Skeffington household, you found yourself unceremoniously locked in a shed by our hosts' son?" he asked. "The one who was almost assuredly on a ship home from India, if not still in that country, the whole time you were placing him at the top of your list of suspects? Is that the Mr. Wilson you mean?"

Ah, so that explained his attitude—he was convinced she was investigating the murder of a phantom. She knew she should not take offense, but his conclusion was as insulting as her aunt's conviction that exposure to Mr. Otley's corpse and Mr. Davies's death had corrupted her ability to think clearly. Nevertheless, she told herself she should be relieved, for her original plan to stay out of the duke's path still seemed like the most sensible one.

"I did not expect you to make light of my suffering, but, yes, that Mr. Wilson. To be clear, then, you are declining to lend your assistance to my investigation? I trust this is the end of it, your grace. You will stay out of my path when I, employing a different ruse, hopefully one more successful than fear of being cast out by a cruel mistress, attempt to persuade another shopkeeper to give me access to his list of clients?" she asked, not entirely sure if she was trying to be provoking or merely expressing a sincere hope. "Naturally, I will stay out of your way, as well, although I trust it goes without saying that I would never stand in the way of any man in his pursuit of insipid children. After all, dull progeny are the birthright of the ruling class."

And there it was, she thought sardonically as she observed herself coming down decisively on the side of provoking.

Alas, Kesgrave didn't rise to the bait. Rather, he calmly explained that he'd assumed she had been mocking him by naming Mr. Wilson as the victim. "You will own that you enjoy teasing me."

Bea stared at him with her eyes wide and innocent, but she couldn't quite smother the smirk that rose to her lips. To hide it, she dipped her head into the teacup.

"Is he truly dead?" Kesgrave asked, leaning forward. "How did he die? How did you become involved? Was Mrs. Otley the distraught source who was so desperate she requested your help?"

"Not at all," she said, recalling how little the widow had welcomed her assistance. "It was Mr. Skeffington."

Unaware that the young heir had been courting the Incomparable Miss Otley, let alone that their relationship had progressed so far as sanctioning murder investigation requests on the other's behalf, the duke tilted his head at this apparent non sequitur. "Mr. Skeffington?"

Bea refreshed her cup of tea, noting that it had progressed from tepid to cool, and settled in to give him a full explanation of recent events. She left nothing out, starting with Mr. Skeffington's wish to make amends for his behavior at Lakeview Hall and ending with her realization that the snuffbox in the pocket of Mr. Wilson's banyan was far too expensive to have been purchased by him.

As Kesgrave was unable to contain his shock at several developments, the narration took far longer than she'd expected.

His first interruption came immediately after she explained that she'd examined Mr. Wilson while he was still in bed.

"In his *nightclothes*?" the duke gasped.

Although he did not turn pink at the notion, his discomfort was plain and Bea had to squelch the laughter that rose in her throat. It was so impossibly funny that she, a spinster of advancing years, was less prudish than a duke who must have had several if not dozens of mistresses. "Yes, in his nightclothes. It didn't strike me as prudent to have the butler dress him in his afternoon attire and arrange him in the sitting room. For one thing, it would have been ghoulish to see a dead man with the affect of an alive one. Furthermore, it would have ruined any opportunity for me to gather useful information from the scene itself. But that is just my opinion and you should of course feel free to attire and arrange the next corpse you examine in whatever way is least offensive to your sensibilities."

She'd meant to make him feel ridiculous for his scruples, but he merely thanked her for the suggestion and promised he would indeed keep it in mind should the situation arise.

He gasped again, this time in awe, when she explained how she had settled on nux vomica as the poison that felled the former opium smuggler.

"Even if I were half as well-read as you, I would never have been able to sort through so much information to arrive at the correct conclusion," he said admiringly.

Now she *did* blush.

"To be fair, we don't know if my conclusion is accurate," she felt compelled to admit. "However, I think the best course is to assume I'm correct until new evidence surfaces to refute it."

"Why do you think the poison was delivered via snuff?" he asked.

"The snuffbox was elaborate and well-made, with gold filigree, and the materials and craftsmanship were far too refined to be the possession of a man of his standing," she explained. "The snuff itself was quite expensive as well, as you yourself pointed out. It seems more likely that Mr. Wilson received both as a gift. Discovering who had purchased the sort recently would give us a list of names of suspects to be examined further. As you are determined to thrust yourself into my investigation—"

"I'm reasonably sure your suggestion of a partnership is what is generally called an invitation by everyone else," he murmured.

"—you can peer imperiously down at the snuff dealer, presumably the correct one this time, from your great ducal height and intimidate him into providing us with the information we seek," she said.

"I'm merely an inch above six feet, which is hardly towering," he said mildly.

"Naturally, you would feel compelled to point out the distinction," she allowed graciously, "but I was speaking figuratively in my description. If I'd meant to be literal, I would have said 'peered down from your slightly-taller-than-the-average-gentleman ducal height.'"

Kesgrave's lips twitched at the rebuke. "Of course. Lord Penwortham's sort is actually mixed and distributed by the Mercer Brothers, which is on Clifford Street. Although I'm not a customer, I'm familiar with the establishment and am confident the proprietor will respond positively to my request for information. I suppose it's too much to ask that you trust me to make this inquiry on my own and report back on my progress? Yes?" he said, reading her expression. "I thought so. As the long-suffering French maid did not prosper in the way you'd hoped, I assume you will be going as Mr. Wright, my steward."

During her last investigation, she had availed herself of her cousin's wardrobe and her uncle's steward's spectacles and presented herself at Lord Fazeley's residence as an employee of the duke's. The ruse had afforded her all the time she needed to rummage through the deceased earl's things and had provided coverage when she insisted on interviewing the publisher of his memoir.

It was immediately following those events that she returned home sporting two black eyes and falsely confessed to attending the funeral of her dead former beau. Her aunt, more appalled by her brazenness than the abuse she'd suffered, promptly confiscated her clothes and threw them into the trash, much to the displeasure of Russell, who recognized his shoes and thought it was grossly unfair that he be deprived of his favorite pair of pumps just because his cousin had secretly commandeered them. His mother, alas, was too irate to listen to reason.

Although her cousin had grumblingly accepted defeat, Beatrice had snuck downstairs late at night and reclaimed the items.

For this reason, she was able give this query a positive reply. Yes, she said, she would go as Mr. Wright. In the best possible arrangement, they would pay their visit immediately after she'd changed, but the truth was, she'd been gone from the house for too long already. Over breakfast that morning, she'd professed herself exhausted from the previous evening's festivities and announced she would spend the day in quiet pursuits. As a bulwark against her aunt's interest, she invited the other woman to sit with her in the parlor and read. To no one's surprise, Aunt Vera declined the pleasure and insisted her niece find somewhere else to indulge the activity, as the drawing room might be needed at any moment to host social calls. Flora, ever her staunch defender, argued that her cousin was still young enough to respond quickly and could absent herself from the drawing room in less than a minute if it were necessary. This argument held no sway with Aunt Vera, and Bea, fighting a grin, apologized for the presumption and announced she would read in her room.

That scene had taken place hours ago now, and sooner or later someone would knock on her door to see how she fared. When that happened, it would be better for everyone if she was at least in the house.

But it was not just her schedule that needed to be consulted, she reminded herself as she proposed a visit to Clifford Street for the next morning. The Duke of Kesgrave was an important personage with many responsibilities, and surely the obligations that claimed his time were as restrictive of his movements as a house full of family members was of hers.

Nevertheless, he agreed easily to an eleven o'clock visit to the Mercer Brothers and even allowed that she seemed more than capable of getting to the establishment on her own.

Congenially, they shook hands on it, and then Kesgrave, knowing his grandmother would expect nothing less, insisted on returning Beatrice to her home. She protested, fearful that his coach might accidentally be spotted by a curious inhabitant looking out of a window, and after much wrangling, which occupied the whole of the carriage ride, settled on a compromise. Bea was dropped off at the corner of her street by a disapproving Jenkins, who, having not been consulted on the matter, felt her dress was far too revealing for such an arrangement. He escorted her to the residence and watched as she cautiously snuck into the house through the servants' entrance.

Bea spared him a brief wave and darted quickly through the hallways until she reached her room. She had barely closed the door behind her before Flora knocked on it to see if she felt well rested enough to join her for a pot of tea. Dashing to her bedside table, Bea grabbed the book she'd been reading the day before and rushed back to the door to open it, freezing in place with her hand on the knob as she realized she was still wearing her maid's dress. Frantically, she made up a lie about her formerly bruised eyes paining her again and requested that a tray with tea be left by her door.

Confused but sympathetic, her cousin agreed.

CHAPTER TEN

The Duke of Kesgrave was so accustomed to the deference owed his station that he did not immediately understand that his request was being denied by the proprietor of the Mercer Brothers. Given a lifetime of acquiescence that ensured his path always remained as smooth as it was straight, he naturally assumed it was Mr. Hamish who failed to comprehend the situation.

"I would like to know the names of the customers who recently purchased Lord Penwortham's *mixture* from you," he explained for a third time, stressing a different term as he spoke, as if the emphasis he put on particular words was at the root of the problem rather than the merchant's inviolate code of ethics.

An anxious fellow who had bought the establishment from the elder Mr. Mercer after his younger sibling died unexpectedly, Mr. Hamish colored slightly as it became clear he was going to have to be more plainspoken in his refusal. "You must see, your grace, why it's untenable," he said, then immediately tried to soften his language. "I mean, I beg you to see the matter from my perspective. That is, from *another* perspective. I am the proprietor of this establishment, and as such I have a certain responsibility to my customers. The sanctity of the client list must remain intact. If somehow word spread that I'd shared information with you, I could stand to lose a significant portion of my business. I've worked very hard this past year to earn the trust of the Mercer Brothers' clients."

As Mr. Hamish was so impertinent as to stand at the same height as the duke, Kesgrave was unable to peer down at him, but sneering across at him served the same function. "Do you dare to suggest that I would not keep my word to tell no one about this exchange?"

Bea rather thought a reminder that he was the Duke of Kesgrave would not have gone amiss in the derisively asked question, but she also knew it would have been for naught. Mr. Hamish was resolute.

Terrified, she noted, observing how Mr. Hamish's nose, a not inconsiderable appendage, jumped up and down like a scared rabbit's, and yet he held his ground.

Although the apprehensive shopkeeper stood between Bea and the information she sought, she'd been the focus of Kesgrave's contempt enough times to recognize the bravery it took to stand firm. Even as she wished he would succumb to the duke's pressure, she wanted to leave him with his courage intact.

As irreconcilable as the two goals seemed, Bea, spotting Mr. Hamish's sales ledger on the counter behind him, realized it was possible to achieve both aims. All she needed was for Kesgrave to distract the proprietor long enough for her to examine the book's pages.

But how to apprise the duke of the change in plans?

Mr. Hamish's flush deepened as he rushed to assure Kesgrave that he did not mean to imply he wasn't to be trusted. "Obviously, you're a man of honor, and as such I implore you to understand the policy of circumspection that I must adhere to for the sake of my clients and my business. I know you would expect nothing less from Monsieurs Dupasquier and Morny, to whom you give your custom. They are quite renowned and understandably achieved their reputation through discretion and providing their clients with a superior product. I, too, provide my clients with a superior product," he said, his nose ceasing to jump so wildly as he seemed to grow less agitated. "Indeed, I think you might find our morning blend with attar of roses to your liking. While you are here, I could give you a sample."

Bea, who had been trying to figure out how to arrange subtle communication with the duke, stared at Mr. Hamish with newfound respect, for he'd hardly seemed bold enough to seize the opportunity to attain an impressive new client. And yet there he was, audaciously making a bid for the duke's custom.

"Are you proposing a bargain? If I purchase your morning blend, you will provide me with the information I seek?" Kesgrave asked consideringly. He didn't sound at all opposed to the idea, which made sense to Bea. Wealth, after all, was just another component of his prestige, and he would accept genuflection to his net worth as much as to his title.

Mr. Hamish, however, turned white at the suggestion that he was receptive to bribery and began to stammer an apology, explaining through painful starts and stops that he had never meant to give the impression that he was proposing an exchange. He'd simply been making a feeble attempt to advertise his wares in a respectable fashion, which he could see, in retrospect, had been a poorly thought out decision on his part.

On and on he rambled, and while Bea found it difficult to listen to him talk with such apparent discomfort, she was grateful for the extra time it gave her to come up with a plan to distract him. The sales ledger was so close she felt as if she could almost extend her arm just far enough to reach it. And yet it was on the other side of the counter, so any attempt to retrieve it would require leaping over the wooden barrier, an action that was sure to attract attention.

"I don't know how…this misunderstanding is entirely my fault," he continued as the color slowly returned to his face. "But I must assure you...my policy of circumspection...I would never—"

And then suddenly Bea had it, the idea she needed, and she interrupted his apology to ask where it was posted.

Mr. Hamish, who, in his agitation, had forgotten the Duke of Kesgrave had been accompanied by his steward, looked at Bea in surprise. "Excuse me?"

"Your policy of circumspection," she explained in Mr. Wright's bright tenor. "I don't see a sign."

The snuff dealer stared at her as if she were mad, but Kesgrave, to his credit, merely drew his eyebrows in curiosity and waited to see what she would do next.

"If circumspection is the store's policy, should there not be a sign posted to that effect?" she asked sensibly. "How do I know it's the store's policy? Must I take your word for it?"

"Must you take..." Mr. Hamish trailed off as he looked to the duke, uncertain if he could really be expected to answer such an absurd question.

"If you don't have a sign outlining your policy, then you must make one," Bea said firmly with a speaking glance at Kesgrave. Then she tilted her head and shifted her eyes meaningfully to the book on the counter behind Mr. Hamish. She could not tell if he understood the pantomime entirely, but he grasped enough of her plan to second her statement.

"My steward is correct," he announced. "You should have a sign stating the store's policy. That is, I believe, standard procedure for the best London shops. Is yours posted somewhere private where the public cannot read it? Perhaps in your office?"

"I don't have a sign, your grace," Mr. Hamish admitted with a strange mix of confusion and shame.

"Then Mr. Wright is correct. You must write one," Kesgrave said.

"At once," Bea said forcefully. "You must write a sign at once explaining your store's policy with clarity and simplicity for all your customers to see."

"I must write a sign that explains my store's policy is circumspection?" Mr. Hamish asked, bewildered by the assignment.

"Yes," Kesgrave said. "Go fetch a sheet of paper and a pen for writing the sign. I will wait."

Somehow, this development was even more difficult for him to reconcile. "You, the Duke of Kesgrave, will wait here while I fetch paper and a pen to write a sign that says my store's policy is circumspection?"

"Yes, but do hurry," Kesgrave said impatiently. "I don't have all day."

Mr. Hamish's whole body jerked in response to this command, and darting another perplexed look over his shoulder, he scurried toward the small office that occupied the back corner of the shop.

As soon as the snuff dealer's back was turned, Kesgrave took three steps to Bea, leaned over and said quietly, "The ledger?"

"The ledger," she affirmed. "I'll look at it while he writes the sign. You hold his attention."

He barely had time to nod before the proprietor was back with a sheet of paper, pen and inkwell. He placed all three items on the counter and said to the duke. "To be clear, I'm writing a sign that says: 'My policy is circumspection'?"

Kesgrave picked up the sheet of paper and walked several feet away from where the ledger sat on the back shelf. "Yes, but do it here," he said, "by the window. The light is better."

"Yes, yes, of course," Mr. Hamish said, skipping to the window so as not to keep his esteemed visitor waiting.

Silently, Bea hopped onto the counter, slid across it and lowered her legs to the floor, grateful for the ease and maneuverability of her cousin's trousers. She seized the book, and as she opened it to that day's date, she heard Kesgrave question Mr. Hamish on the actual wording of the sign.

"*Should* it say 'my policy?'" he asked.

Mr. Hamish tittered anxiously, uncertain what the duke was implying with his query. Nevertheless, he gamely made a suggestion. "Perhaps '*our* policy'?"

"Is that correct?" Kesgrave said. "Are there other proprietors here who share your stance on the policy?"

The tobacco dealer admitted there were not, and after a moment of silence wondered if the policy should be positioned as one that represents the store itself. "It could say, 'The Mercer Brothers' policy is circumspection.'"

"My good man, that sounds like the ideal solution," the duke said approvingly. "Now write that, but very carefully, please, as I don't want you to make a mess of it and have to start over."

While Kesgrave exhorted Mr. Hamish to write with precision, Bea searched the ledger for all references to Lord Penwortham's mixture. The task was more difficult than she'd anticipated, thanks to the sheer number of entries on each page. When she'd first opened the book, she'd felt a fleeting moment of panic, as she'd had no idea that snuff dealing could be such a prosperous business.

But once she'd grown accustomed to Mr. Hamish's handwriting—his needlessly extravagant letter *S* that looked almost interchangeable with his *G*, the dots of his *I*'s, which were a little too far to the left—she could read the record of his sales easily and found five orders for Lord Penwortham's mixture in the previous week. She quietly murmured the names once to commit them to memory, then flipped to an earlier date and searched for additional buyers. She went back another week and found three more names.

Satisfied, she closed the book just as she heard Mr. Hamish assure the duke for the second time that the sign was precisely as it should be.

"I really think it represents the policy of the Mercer Brothers," he said, beginning to swivel his shoulders to look toward the back of his store.

A split second from discovery, Bea stood on the wrong side of the counter, frozen in panic, her eyes meeting Kesgrave's as he flashed a look at her. For one humming moment they stared at each other in dread.

Then Kesgrave smiled, winked, wrapped an arm around the shopkeeper's shoulder and said, "Ah, but where will you post it? May I suggest here?" He pointed to a spot above the front door. "Or is that too high? Perhaps your customers will not think to look up to discover your policy. Maybe next to the door would be better? Or near the window?"

While Mr. Hamish agreed with each and every suggestion, Bea climbed over the counter and landed on the other side with a soft thud. Kesgrave swiveled his head at the sound, but the snuff dealer continued to examine the various options the duke had proposed. She nodded firmly to communicate that her mission had been a success, and he smiled again.

"Ah, there, you see, Hamish, now that your policy is posted," Kesgrave said amiably, "I understand it entirely. As the proprietor of the Mercer Brothers you are fully committed to circumspection in all your dealings, and you can't possibly provide me with the names, as it would be a violation of your policy. How much easier everything is to understand when it's written out and clearly posted. Now, if you don't mind, I would like to purchase that morning blend you described. You said it had hints of attar of roses? It sounds charming."

"I do see, your grace, I do," Mr. Hamish said eagerly. He had been well convinced of the efficacy of useful signs, and Bea imagined that after he posted the one he'd composed under the duke's aegis, he would write half a dozen more. If she came back in a week or a month, she felt confidant she would find the entire interior of the shop covered with signs explaining policies and codes of conduct.

Although it was common for gentlemen to buy snuff by the quarter or half pound, Kesgrave, perhaps hoping to expunge his guilt over the needless sign, purchased an entire pound.

"Thank you, your grace," Mr. Hamish said as he took the order. "I will have a canister delivered to Berkeley Square by the end of the day."

"I do not doubt it," Kesgrave said, "knowing your circumspection."

Mr. Hamish preened happily.

Their transaction complete, Bea and the duke had no reason to linger, and thanking the proprietor once again, they left the shop.

As soon as they were several feet away from the store, Kesgrave turned to her and said, "I do not think I can properly explain the strange sensation I feel at having impelled poor Mr. Hamish to hang the sign. There's an odd stirring of guilt and an equally strong sense of immateriality. The sign not only does no harm but clearly and precisely states a position that is laudable. I should feel satisfaction at having helped a tradesman better articulate his business stance, and yet I feel as though I've undermined him."

Bea laughed at the confusion in his tone and rushed to assure him that overseeing the posting of one minor sign was a peccadillo at best. "Your conscience will quiet soon enough. And if it doesn't, you can always return next week and tell Mr. Hamish you have reconsidered your position and now advise him to remove the sign. In the meantime, I found eight customers who purchased Lord Penwortham's mixture in the past two weeks. They are: Kirkham, Erskine, Mowbray, Coleman, Summersmith, Parton, Taunton, and my uncle."

Kesgrave acknowledged the list with an abrupt nod and tilted his head thoughtfully. "We do not need to consider Kirkham. He's a confirmed recluse and hasn't left his home in Lincolnshire in over a decade. Erskine, as well, can be safely eliminated. He suffers from an infection of the lungs and has been abed these past two weeks. Additionally, I've had some dealings with him and have found him to be nothing but honest and forthright. I would not believe him capable of murder."

As much as Bea respected and admired the duke, his endorsement of a subject increased her interest, for in her limited experience it was always the least likely suspect who turned out to be the guiltiest.

But would Erskine have been devious enough to take to his bed two weeks prior in order to provide himself with a believable story should anyone manage to trace the poison in the snuffbox back to him?

Forget devious, she thought, as she considered the amount of effort constructing such an alibi would require. Would he have been so concerned about discovery as to confine himself to his home for a fortnight? She rather thought he wouldn't, for it was only due to an unlikely series of events that the list of Lord Penwortham's mixture buyers had been sought and attained.

"Very well," Bea said. "We may dismiss Kirkham and Erskine. And my uncle, of course. Is there anyone else you consider not worthy of investigation?"

"I would argue that Summersmith is not a good use of our time," Kesgrave said as they approached his carriage. "He's seventy-five if he's a day and given to fits of incoherency, usually on the floor of the House of Lords. Judging by the increasing length of his disjointed speeches, the affliction has worsened in recent years. I'm not sure he has the mental clarity necessary for deciding to kill someone, let alone actually following through on the impulse."

Again, Bea pondered the possibility of an elderly peer affecting senility as a way to evade suspicion of murder and decided it was far too improbable.

Nodding her approval of the duke's ability to cut their list of suspects in half, she said, "That leaves us with Taunton, Parton, Mowbray and Coleman. What do you know of them?"

Before he could answer, Jenkins jumped down from the driver's seat of the coach and opened the carriage door.

"Where to next, your grace?" he asked.

Without allowing Kesgrave an opportunity to answer, Bea announced their destination as Houghton Street in St. Clement Danes and then swallowed her annoyance when Jenkins looked at the duke for approval. It was irrational, of course, to mind his seeking confirmation, as he was in Kesgrave's employ and she was just an overly curious spinster who had somehow become a presence in his life. If the groom marveled at the development, he was no more surprised than she.

Displaying no resentment at her presumption, the duke repeated the address and climbed into the carriage after Bea. As soon as they were settled, he said, "Houghton Street?"

"The Melbourne, which is the boarding house where Mr. Wilson took rooms. In my experience, there's much information to be gained by examining the private quarters of the victim," she explained.

Kesgrave smiled at this prim response. "And your experience is vast, is it?"

The comment wasn't without its merit, as only two murders in six and twenty years was hardly the sort of high rate of involvement that made one an expert, but she didn't let his cynicism undermine her confidence. "It is sufficient," she said. "Before we interview our suspects, I believe it behooves us to find out all we can about our victim. Or do you have a better method of investigation? I am, of course, open to suggestions."

"Because we are partners," he said, visibly entertained by the concept.

It was, she knew, a radical notion for a man and a woman to consider themselves equal participants in a venture, and she fully understood his amusement. It was certainly not an idea that Lady Victoria would expose him to, and she could only assume he took comfort in that knowledge.

Although thoughts of Lady Victoria and the duke caused her spirits to dip, the drop wasn't as steep as she would have expected. If Kesgrave was foolish enough to embrace the dull and tedious future that awaited him, then he deserved all the tedium and dullness he was sure to get. Indeed, the image of him bored out of his mind while sitting across from his impeccable wife at the dinner table caused no end to her delight.

It was sour grapes, of course, but all she had.

"No suggestions," he said in response to her query. "I'm happy to follow your lead. You appear to know what you're doing."

It was a high compliment indeed, indicative of a deep well of respect, and determined to deprive herself of the satisfaction it produced, she asked if the meeting between Lady Victoria and his grandmother had been happy. "The momentous occasion was quite the *on-dit* at the Pemberton ball. My aunt could barely breathe for the excitement."

Kesgrave found nothing untoward about the question, which at once comforted and distressed Bea, for it demonstrated how widely off the mark she was. Nowhere in this philosophy did he allow for the possibility of someone like her as a rival who could experience jealousy. "It went well, thank you. It was a mere formality, as the two families are close and Victoria has always been away during my grandmother's visits."

Bea had no idea how to take such a remark, for it presented the occasion in quite an ambiguous light. The mere formality could refer to the meeting itself, which had long been sought and yet never arranged due to timing issues of one or both of the parties, or it could apply to the event it was mean to mark—that was, the engagement between the couple.

Thinking of the former option, she wondered if perhaps her aunt and Lady Abercrombie and the whole of the beau monde had misunderstood his intentions. For years, the Duke of Kesgrave had resisted the parson's mousetrap, and it struck her as deeply out of character that he would succumb now simply to facilitate a land deal. Would not a man of his mettle consider marrying to enlarge the Matlock estate to be craven and dishonest?

How else to explain what had almost happened yesterday in his grandmother's drawing room? A man who was truly contemplating marriage to one young lady wouldn't find himself on the verge of kissing another woman, particularly not the Duke of Kesgrave. He had far too much respect for what he owed his own dignity.

But even as she had these encouraging thoughts, Bea recognized their desperate futility. The fact that she was still able to find some speck of hope demonstrated how very far gone she was, and embarrassed yet again by her foolishness, she titled her eyes down and kept her gaze firmly fixed on the floor for the rest of the ride to the Melbourne.

CHAPTER ELEVEN

Bea and the duke alighted from the carriage in front of the gentlemen's residence, a three-story mansion near Piccadilly that was formerly the home of Viscount Sidsmouth. The building, with its generous windows and pleasing symmetry, had been divided into apartments two decades before, and as Kesgrave escorted her down the front path he commented on the poor condition of the courtyard, which was riddled with pot-shaped holes.

"I'm sure what the Melbourne lacks in rigorous maintenance, it makes up for in reasonably priced accommodations," Bea observed, climbing the steps. "His rooms are on the first floor. I suggest we walk directly to the staircase as if paying a visit to a tenant upstairs and not stop to consult the clerk at the lobby, as he might impede our progress."

"Of course we will consult him," Kesgrave said imperiously, "as we are in need of the key. Or do you propose we damage the door to gain entry?"

Bea ardently decried the charge of vandalism, but in fact she had been imagining some variation on his proposal that would have left the premises a little less pristine than when they'd arrived. Breaking down the door was far more dignified, she thought a few minutes later, than receiving assistance from an obsequious clerk who could not wait to invade his resident's privacy at the bidding of a duke.

"He won't mind, Mr. Wilson won't," the man said as he eagerly handed over the tenant's key without asking a single question. Whatever the duke's purpose was, he was unmistakably confident it was correct and appropriate by virtue of being the purpose of a duke. "He'd be honored by your interest. Honored, I'm sure. Like me, Mr. Wilson respects his betters. If he were here, he'd give you the key himself, I'm sure of it. Top of the stairs, first door on your left."

Kesgrave thanked the clerk and even went so far as to call him "my good man."

Mr. Dodd simpered.

As they climbed the stairs, Bea said, "You must be relieved."

"I must?" he asked curiously.

"To have your self-worth restored by Mr. Dodd's enthusiastic toadying," she explained. "After Mr. Hamish's implacable circumspection, I mean."

"Have I truly not demonstrated by now that my self-worth is impervious to the treatment of others?" he replied with exquisite disdain as they reached the landing. He turned left, identified Mr. Wilson's rooms and unlocked the door with smooth efficiency. "After you, my dear."

Bea swept into the space, which was compact but orderly, with only three small rooms: a parlor with a book-case to the left of the fireplace and a table with chairs to the right, a bedchamber with barely enough space to walk around its most prominent feature and a dressing room.

"He lived simply," Bea said, peering into the dressing room, which was mostly bare. Four shirts were neatly fold-ed on the bottom shelf, and two pairs of trousers rested on the one above it. A single coat hung from an exposed rod, and a handkerchief sat on the top of the clothespress.

Kesgrave examined the bookshelf, which was as

sparsely populated as the closet, and selected a slim volume with a brown leather binding. "He wasn't an avid reader."

"Perhaps the majority of his possessions have yet to return from India," Bea suggested as she opened the top drawer of the clothespress. She found a nightshirt, two nightcaps and stockings. The next drawer contained under-things and a dark-blue waistcoat that should have been hung to preserve its shape. The bottom drawer was empty. She sighed and rested one shoulder against the large piece of furniture. Thoughtfully, she fingered the handkerchief, appreciating the superior quality of the smooth silk, which had the initials JBW. "The expense incurred in shipping a trunk from one continent to the other must be great. May-be he was still acquiring the funds."

"His father was steward to the fifth Marquess of Taunton," Kesgrave announced.

Surprised that the duke had gathered such an interest-ing piece of information so quickly, she put down the handkerchief and walked into the parlor. "Was he now?" she murmured.

He handed her a book of the first canto of the *Faerie Queene* opened to the title page, opposite of which there was an inscription dated a decade before and addressed to Mr. Wilson: "For your years of service as a faithful stew-ard, with gratitude and respect, Taunton."

"That aligns with something Mrs. Otley said, for she vaguely recalled that Wilson had inherited his position af-ter his father had died. She couldn't be sure but thought the estate somewhere in Yorkshire," she said.

"Bestlemore Castle is in Norfolk, near the coast," he explained. "The old earl died about five years ago and his son inherited. Taunton turned forty a few years ago, which would make him about the same age as Mr. Wilson. That means they most likely grew up together."

"Plenty of opportunity for resentments to form," Bea said as she put the book back on the shelf and examined another. As Kesgrave had noted, the selection was thin, and she chose *A Tale of a Tub* by Swift. She flipped quickly through it, looking for another revealing dedication, but all she saw was the bookplate with the Taunton family crest. Although she hardly expected to find an accusatory inscription detailing a young Taunton's dissatisfaction with the son of his father's steward, she was still disappointed to find nothing of note. She replaced the book on the shelf with a sigh. "I believe that moves him to the top of our list."

"I do not believe that an old childhood resentment would serve as a plausible motive for murder, but I agree the connection requires further investigation," Kesgrave said. "An interview with Taunton is certainly in order."

Bea nodded and inspected the other items on the shelf, most of which consisted of a seemingly random assortment: a gold-trimmed teacup with a pink thistle design, a pair of scissors, a silver locket with the inscription "*vous seule*" from a man named George, another snuffbox, this one far less ornate than the last, with its humble coral exterior and brass interior. Finding nothing of interest among the collection, she turned her attention to the table, which was small and square and could accommodate no more than two people comfortably. It seemed logical to conclude that Mr. Wilson had few visitors.

On its surface were two packets of letters wrapped in neat ribbons as well as a worn copy of *The Book of Common Prayer*. Suspecting that it, too, was a gift from the library at Bestlemore Castle, she turned first to the inside cover. In place of a bookplate was a note from his father wishing him wisdom and prosperity at university. Mr. Wilson had studied at Cambridge.

Bea closed the book and turned to the first packet of letters, which were carefully folded in their original envelopes. She opened the first one, which was dated July 1814, and immediately scrolled down to the bottom to read the name of the author: Mr. Erasmus Robinson.

As Kesgrave disappeared into the bedchamber to examine its contents, she wondered if Mrs. Otley would have any insight into Erasmus Robinson. The letter was sent to Mr. Wilson in India and, she realized once she started reading, from India as well. Mr. Robinson was a clerk in the employ of the East India Company and worked for an administrator who reported directly to the governor-in-council for Bombay. He expressed gratitude to Mr. Wilson for sending the introduction from a mutual acquaintance in London and felt confident they could come to a business arrangement that would suit them both. He looked forward to hearing more.

Bea did too and immediately read the next letter and the next. There were, she noted, five letters in all, and taken together they detailed a devious scheme to deprive Mr. Otley of his poppy fields and his income from smuggling the illicit drug into China. The plan itself was relatively simple and required only the passing of information from one person to another. Mr. Otley had managed to preserve the autonomy of his little agricultural concern in the midst of John Company's vast empire by paying a bribe every month to the local administrator, who, in exchange for the generous stipend, ensured that his presence remained unknown. Determined to leave India and fill his coffers in a single stroke, Mr. Wilson arranged for Mr. Robinson to reveal the particulars of this illegal compact to his superiors. The clerk in Bombay was handsomely rewarded for the information, which was doubly valuable, as it revealed both an untrustworthy employee and an unknown drain on the company's income.

For betraying his employer's trust and destroying the livelihood of his lover's husband, he was paid a sum of three thousand pounds.

It was not a princely amount, but it was certainly significant and would easily cover the purchase of a small farm and maintain it until it turned a healthy profit. Mrs. Otley knew of her lover's plans, but did she know the source of his windfall? Had she discovered his devious scheme that had deprived her family of income and exposed them to ruin? If she had somehow found out, she would have undoubtedly resented his coldhearted betrayal. Would that bitterness and anger not account for the violence of Mr. Wilson's death? How grievously she must have wanted him to suffer when she learned the truth.

But how did she know of nux vomica and where would she get it?

It was naïve, Bea realized, to believe Mrs. Otley had gleaned nothing about India during her years of marriage. Despite her claims to indifference to business matters, the country was the source of her family's wealth and the focus of her husband's attention. He must have discussed some aspects of it with her and could have easily revealed the information.

Just because the widow appeared not to listen to anyone did not mean she heard nothing.

Reentering the parlor, Kesgrave announced that there was nothing of interest in the bedchamber. "And the dressing room is an embarrassment. In order to avoid thinking ill of the dead, I've decided to assume your original assessment was accurate and the majority of his possessions are still in transit. What do you have there?" he asked, his tone rising with interest as he spotted the letters.

"A detailed accounting of Mr. Wilson's underhanded plot to destroy his employer's livelihood and return himself to England," she said, sliding the packet across the table for his perusal. "Reading it makes for a strange experience, for I find myself in sympathy with poor Mr. Otley, for he had no idea his trusted associate and Mr. Robinson were conspiring behind his back to destroy his business, and yet I know him to be a dyed-in-the-wool villain undeserving of my compassion."

"Mr. Robinson?" he asked, looking up from the letter he was unfolding.

"Yes, clerk to the chief administrator of the governor-in-council for Bombay."

At once, Kesgrave stiffened in surprise. "*Erasmus Robinson?*"

"Yes," Bea said, considering him with astonishment. "How did you know?"

He sat down in the chair opposite her and explained that Erasmus Robinson was the new Earl of Mowbray. "He had no expectation of inheriting when he left for India, for he was not directly in line for the title. But the old earl died in a freakish coach accident along with his two sons, which left him the title and the estates. Naturally, he returned immediately from India to claim both. That was about six months ago now. What do you mean 'conspiring behind his back'? Was he involved with Otley's losing the poppy fields?"

"Oh, yes, he was quite instrumental," she said before laying out the details of the scheme as revealed by the letter. "Now what did you mean by 'freakish coach accident'?

"The horse threw a shoe while a drunk farmer careened around a bend just as the axle on the carriage broke," he said. "Each misfortune on its own would cause difficulties, but all together they were a fatal combination and the occupants of the carriage as well as its driver perished. By all accounts it was quite gruesome."

Although Bea appreciated his evenhanded approach, for it would not serve her interest to investigate alongside an excitable partner, she felt he was far too accepting of the explanation, especially given recent developments.

Before she could point that out, Kesgrave said, "And I know what you are thinking, but you are wide off the mark. The countess readily admitted their groom's maintenance was lax, something her husband despaired of weekly, and an accident of some sort was bound to happen."

"If that information was widely known—" she began.

Kesgrave shook his head. "A comprehensive examination of the family's other conveyances revealed the same slipshod treatment."

"Even so—"

"Miss Hyde-Clare, I admire your ability to concoct a theory of guilt out of a ball of yarn and a misplaced kitchen spoon, but I assure you that you're digging for a bone in the wrong graveyard. The former Mr. Robinson did not hire a confederate to compromise every vehicle Mowbray possessed from thousands of miles away in India. It is too ridiculous, and I won't allow you to entertain the notion. You are, of course, welcome to suspect him all you want in the matter of Mr. Wilson's murder. And, no," he said when she opened her mouth to speak, "before you ask, I don't think you need my permission to suspect anyone."

As she had indeed been about to ask that very thing, she couldn't help but smile at his presumption. "You will concede that he has a potentially convincing motive. If Mr. Wilson was threatening to reveal the dishonesty of the new earl's dealings in India, he might have moved to silence him permanently. You haven't read them yet, but trust me when I tell you the letters are persuasive and could be embarrassing for a newly titled lord."

"I don't doubt it," the duke said firmly, "as the newly titled lord is still struggling to adjust to his position. Having come into a sudden, unexpectedly large sum of money, he seems determined to lose it just as quickly by gambling every night at the Red Corner House."

"Struggling to adjust or consumed with guilt for how he rose to such heights?" she asked thoughtfully. "No matter. We do not have to figure it all out now. We'll simply move Mowbray to the top of the suspects list and put a little star next to his name denoting he might be responsible for four other deaths as well. In the meantime, we should finish our examination of Mr. Wilson's rooms. It has been so fruitful already. I'm confident we will find evidence of an association with the two other buyers of Lord Penwortham's mixture."

Despite her assurance, however, they found nothing to connect the victim with Coleman and Parton. The letters in the second packet, while informative, were far less interesting than the first, containing sundry business matters such as the renting of his rooms at the Melbourne and the purchase of his passage home from Madras.

After a second perusal of the bedchamber, during which she confirmed the duke's initial estimation that it contained nothing of interest, she announced herself ready to leave. Kesgrave, who had been standing at the door for at least five minutes, nodded gratefully and followed her into the hallway. They returned the key to the clerk in the lobby and found Jenkins waiting by the coach immediately outside the front door.

"This has been a very productive day," Bea said with satisfaction as the coach began to move. "Although one doesn't want to be accused of seeking the easier path, I'm relieved to have whittled our list of suspects down to three."

"You believe Mrs. Otley knew about Wilson's betrayal?" he asked, his brow furrowed as he considered the possibility.

"I cannot dismiss it," she replied. "I've been operating under the assumption that she would know nothing about obscure Indian poisons because she has never been to the country and is not literate enough to have read about it in Mrs. Barlow's excellent *Travels in India: My Journey Through a Strange, Difficult and Wonderful Land*. But perhaps I am being too narrow in my opinions. She might be more clever than she lets on, and she did spend all those years with Mr. Otley. It's entirely possible she learned things through no fault of her own. Furthermore, she has thwarted my investigation from the very beginning. I cannot find a connection, however, between her and Lord Penwortham's mixture. If she did introduce the poison to the snuffbox, how and when did she acquire the tobacco? I also find the former Mr. Robinson to be quite an intriguing prospect. We need to arrange an interview with him as soon as possible. And Lord Taunton too, as you said."

"How do you propose to do that?" he asked, his tone smooth as he calmly raised a curious eyebrow. "Mowbray is often pin-brained from drink and might believe I'd make morning calls in the company of my steward. Lord Taunton, I assure you, will be harder to persuade."

Knowing this to be true, Bea assumed the duke's solution was for him to conduct the interview on his own. Obviously, she would not agree to that, for she couldn't rely on him to ask the right questions or display the appropriate amount of suspicion. He was clever, of course, and certainly had a devious mind, but he wasn't cynical enough—to wit, he believed a freakish accident had cleared the way to an earldom.

Additionally, this was her inquiry, not his. She had proposed their alliance as a partnership, yes, but she really considered him more of an assistant. Every great investigator needed a second in command, and it had soothed her ego to think of Lady Victoria's dignified fiancé as her underling.

It was, she thought, an aspect of him that the wealthy beauty would never see, let alone possess.

'Twas cold comfort, she knew, but comfort nonetheless.

Working with the duke had provided other advantages as well, for his name and position opened many doors. Gaining entry to the Earl of Fazeley's residence had been as easy as his steward—his real one, that was—requesting access from the managing agent.

But now his ducal rank was a liability, and Bea asked herself how she would have tried to elicit answers from the Marquess of Taunton if Kesgrave were not part of her investigation. In that situation, she would have employed a ruse like the French maid persona she had adopted to wrangle the customer list from Monsieurs Dupasquier and Morny. Although that pose had not achieved any of its aims, her failure had been ensured in advance by the duke. Who knew what feats of deception she might have been able to achieve without his machinations.

All she needed, then, was to come up with a convincing pretext, and as the carriage rolled through the streets, she considered the matter. The most likely gambit would utilize what she knew about Lord Taunton, which was, admittedly, very little. His family seat was in Norfolk, it had a seemingly excellent library, and the elder Mr. Wilson served as his father's steward for decades. But as thin as her knowledge was, it was more than enough to concoct a believable story about a deceased man's desire to return a pair of beloved books to the estate from which they had come. Naturally, it fell to Bea, his solicitor, to make sure that happened, and accompanying her on the important call would be…

"My law clerk," she said evenly.

Kesgrave was understandably confused, as it had been almost a minute since he had spoken and the prospect of impersonating a law clerk was not one that would occur to him. "Excuse me?"

"You asked how I propose to arrange an interview for us with Lord Taunton tomorrow," she reminded him, "and that is my answer. I will present myself as the solicitor overseeing the affairs of the deceased Charles Wilson, whose last wish was that his father's books be returned to the library from which they had come. And you may pose as my law clerk."

It was a provoking suggestion, to be sure, and Bea expected him to respond with the full force of his rank. A man who respected order so much he felt compelled to correct the sequence of warships mentioned in casual conversation—HMS *Goliath*, HMS *Audacious*, HMS *Majestic*—would not easily accept the idea of being anyone's lackey, let alone an upstart spinster's.

Bea waited for him to stiffen his shoulders and stare down at her as if she were an ant daring to step onto his picnic blanket. It was, she knew, the definitive Duke of Kesgrave look, full of imperial displeasure and impatience, and although it had caused her to tremble the first time she'd encountered it, now it only made her smile. Indeed, being able to draw it out of him at will felt almost like power.

She was astonished, then, when all he did was laugh and ask if he may borrow Mr. Wright's spectacles.

Too surprised to think clearly, she removed the eyeglasses from her face and handed them to him with the cautionary note to treat them carefully. "They are in fact the real Mr. Wright's, and I would like to return them in the pristine condition in which I borrowed them."

Surely, this addendum would elicit a glare of irritated condescension, for he certainly knew how to have a care with other people's possessions and as the Duke of Kesgrave it was his privilege not to care at all. But he merely let out an amused chuckle.

His response confounded Bea, and she wondered if he was mocking her with his laughter. It wouldn't be unprecedented, as he'd taunted Mr. Skeffington with sarcastic approval after the young man had accused her of having an affair with Mr. Otley during their sojourn in the Lake District. But on that occasion Kesgrave had seethed with anger, and now his eyes seemed to twinkle with humor.

Could he really not mind the reduction in his rank?

Although she did not believe the matter truly to be settled, she decided to proceed as if it were and proposed they meet at Taunton's town house, which was located in Edward Street, at eleven. Kesgrave agreed to the arrangement with one slight alteration, insisting that he accompany her to their destination rather than allow her to arrive alone in a hack. She immediately pointed out the utter ridiculousness of a lowly solicitor and his even lowlier clerk arriving in such high style, and now, finally, the duke straightened his shoulders in offense.

"I am not a turnip wiping dew from my ears," he said stiffly. "I will of course hire a hack to drive us there."

Although Bea felt the impish desire to point out that turnips were not cobs of corn to have ears, she squelched the impulse and moved on to their second suspect. "And Mowbray is always drunk, you say, and will easily be deceived by us. Shall we visit him after Taunton? That would be noon at the latest. Will he be sober then or already into his cups?"

"Recovering from the night before, I imagine," he said,

"and in a wretched mood. He will answer our questions just so that we may leave him in peace. The timing is ideal."

"And his faculties will be corrupted by the aftereffects of alcohol, which is also perfect for our ends," she said, nodding with approval. "The only thing better would be if we could interview him while he was still foxed."

"We cannot," Kesgrave said sharply. "It's a violation of the most basic civility to ply a man for information when he is a trifle disguised, let alone when he's fully sprung. I cannot allow it."

Although Bea did not have contempt for all the rules governing society, she considered many to be without merit and the idea that she could not interrogate a possible killer while he was drunk because it was rude struck her as particularly worthless. Undoubtedly, the greater social ill was the ruthless taking of an innocent life.

Nevertheless, she smiled placidly and said, "Yes, of course."

Kesgrave, however, did not believe her ready acceptance and immediately demanded that she promise not to visit the Red Corner House by herself. "First of all, you will not get anything sensical out of him while he is in his cups. Second, it's a hell with a particularly unsavory reputation and is no place for a young unmarried woman, even one who makes a somewhat convincing young man."

As Bea would never consider such a reckless course, she promptly agreed. Obviously, she would take someone with her. The question, of course, was who. "You have my word."

Although he nodded with approval, he was far from satisfied. "You will also promise that you won't visit the Red Corner House in the company of your cousin Russell."

Bea smiled as she imagined her cousin's excitement if she proposed such an outing and had little doubt that his eagerness would be her undoing. Either he would unintentionally reveal the plan to his parents or say something indiscreet to Mowbray. "Again, you have my word."

"Thank you," he said graciously. "You will also promise not to go with your cousin Flora."

It was just as easy to guess Flora's reaction to such a proposal, and picturing the look of horror on her cousin's pretty face made her laugh. If she was seeking a proper conspirator who would help her gain entry into the gaming hell and blend in with the company, she would do well to look elsewhere. With no compunction at all, she gave her promise.

Kesgrave dipped his head, then added another request. "You will also promise not to go with Miss Otley or Mr. Skeffington."

Although she could see the latter lending some gravity to the situation with his fortune and pending title, he was too inexperienced. The person she had in mind knew every aspect of society like the back of her hand and could stare down any ogre who took an interest in them. For this reason, she easily gave her assurances that she would not go with Miss Otley or Mr. Skeffington.

"And Nuneaton," he added. "You must promise not to go to the Red Corner House in the company of Nuneaton either."

The idea of her asking a lord whom she had met only a handful of times to accompany her to a gaming hell to interrogate another lord with whom she had no association was preposterous, and she dissolved into laughter so intense she almost slid off the seat. "Why on earth would I ask Nuneaton?" she said a full minute later when she finally regained her breath.

Kesgrave's expression was inscrutable, but his tone was stiff. "You appear to be on quite close terms."

This information was news to Bea, who considered the handsome dandy with the practiced affect of ennui to be an acquaintance at best. As with Kesgrave, she had met him at the Skeffingtons' house party in the Lake District, where he had made up one of their number. Although she had scarcely spoken to him while at Lakeview Hall, they had conversed a few times since the start of the season. The viscount was curious to know all that had transpired during their stay—the stealthy dealings that led to the stunning denouement in the drawing room—and considered her to be the most promising source of information. While resisting his entreaties, Bea had discovered him to be far more engaging than his affectations would indicate, but that was the extent of their association. If she did reveal the details of her investigation into Mr. Otley's death, she imagined his lordship would lose all interest in her.

"All right, then," she said agreeably because there was no reason to cavil. "I promise not to go to the Red Corner House in the company of Nuneaton either. May I ask why you are making such a thorough catalog of whose escort I might seek? It seems needlessly piecemeal. Would not a blanket request serve your purpose more efficiently? We are rapidly approaching our destination."

He pressed his lips together, as if smothering a grin, and shook his head. "Ah, no, Miss Hyde-Clare, no. You will not get me that way."

"Get you?" she asked in confusion.

"That is, get around me," he clarified. "You advised me to be more precise in my restrictions the next time I tried to limit a woman's movements. With your advice in mind, I'm methodically listing one by one every person to whom you might apply for company."

He was teasing her, of course, for his face was alight with amusement as he explained his intention, and yet the moment felt profoundly somber to Bea. It was not often that a man of his stature—a wealthy nobleman with every advantage of birth and breeding—actually listened to a woman's words and made a point of remembering them. He was, she decided, a fundamentally decent man, and for the first time ever, she thought Lady Victoria did not deserve him. Yes, he was raised in a hothouse to be beautiful just like she, but somehow he had transcended the limitations of his garden.

"To that end," he continued, "you will promise not to go with Jenkins."

The absurdity of the demand freed her from the sudden turn her thoughts had taken. "No," she said at once, firmly shaking her head. "He is in far too much awe of you to risk your displeasure by consenting to such a scheme, and I won't insult him by implying otherwise. Move on to your next candidate, please. I trust my aunt and uncle are on that list. They are family, of course, and yet somehow less likely than your groom. Mrs. Otley is also implausible, but we should include her just to be thorough. I believe that's it. Oh, wait, no, let's throw in my maid, Annie, since we are considering servants as possible accomplices. Very well, I ardently swear not to go to the Red Corner House in the company of Aunt Vera, Uncle Horace, Mrs. Otley or Annie. I do believe that's everyone I know. We are lucky I'm so socially awkward and unpopular or we'd be here for hours listing possible conspirators."

Bea had ended her speech on a purposefully self-pitying note in hopes of discomforting him so much he would find a new topic, but Kesgrave remained focused on his goal. "No, we are not done. First you must swear not to go in the company of Lady Abercrombie. Then we may be grateful for your unpopularity."

But Bea could not make that promise, for her ladyship was precisely the person she had in mind for the excursion. The daring widow was far too experienced to be a stranger to gaming hells, particularly ones with unsavory reputations, and she certainly relished a good lark. Why else keep a poor lion cub as a pet?

"Well done, Kesgrave," she said approvingly. "Very well done. You have the ability to learn from past mistakes, which is a very attractive and rare quality in a man. I believe there is hope for you yet."

Although she meant the comment merely as a distraction from his efforts to restrict her movements, she could not smother the admiration she felt for him, and whatever ruse he was expecting, he appeared too struck by the warmth and sincerity of her tone to recall it. Nonplussed, he stared at her for several long seconds before murmuring, "Is there? I think I might be too far gone."

It was, Bea thought, a cryptic thing to say, and she puzzled at its meaning during the rest of the ride to Portman Square. The most obvious explanation was the most likely, which meant that he merely considered himself, at two and thirty, too set in his ways to change. As logical as it was, however, it did not account for the thoughtful, slightly bewildered expression on his face. That look, that confusion, suggested something more intense and more disconcerting than simply the ingrained habits of age. Wondering what he had been thinking of when he said it only bolstered a dream that she already knew to be hopeless, but the idea, once sprouted, immediately took root.

Annoyed with herself and with him, she lapsed into silence and bid him an absentminded goodbye when Jenkins stopped the coach on the corner of her street.

CHAPTER TWELVE

If Beatrice had realized that the Red Corner House's unsavory reputation meant the gaming hell was brimming with tap-hackled lords and long-limbed incognitas, she would have tried harder to resist Lady Abercrombie's efforts to improve her appearance. As it was, she'd voiced only a single protest.

"Is this really necessary?" she'd asked as the countess held up a blue silk dress edged in lace and beautifully tailored. It was far more delicate than anything she'd ever worn, and she began to worry about the damage she might do to it. She wasn't particularly clumsy or given to spills, but the shade of cerulean was so beautiful, so pure and untainted by green, it almost demanded protection.

"I have a reputation for fastidiousness and perfection, which you know, as you've sat in my drawing room and admired its stylish precision," Lady Abercrombie had replied, referring to the Oriental fantasia of lotus-shaped chandeliers, gilded serpents and bamboo stalks where she accepted visitors. "I will not risk it by appearing in the company of a young lady dressed as an impoverished governess whose employer let her go because she couldn't conjugate French verbs properly. Standards, Miss Hyde-Clare! I have standards, and if you are to be graced with my presence, then you must aspire to meet them too. I

cannot be the only one propping up all of Western civiliza-
tion. Now change into this dress and allow Marie to do
your hair, and then we will discuss how to secure the information you seek from Mowbray. I trust it goes without
saying that you are free to retain your look of studious
penury, as I have nothing but respect for the principles of
other people, even the ones with which I disagree, but I
will of course be forced to decline your invitation to join
you at the Red Corner House."

Bea had been unwilling to argue, as submitting to her
ladyship's maid's ministrations had been the only condition
the countess had set for her participation. Indeed, she had
agreed to accompany her with disconcerting speed after
ascertaining that Lord Mowbray was not on Bea's list.

"My list?" Bea had asked in confusion.

"Your list of gentlemen suitors," the widow had explained. "For the new love affair that will help you forget
your feelings for the duke. Is Mowbray on your list?"

That the beautiful widow had intended to compile
such a list herself had completely slipped Bea's mind, and
she had rushed to assure the other woman that she didn't
have a list at all. She'd intended to add that she didn't think
it was necessary for anyone to compile lists, but her ladyship spoke before she had the chance.

"Good," Lady Abercrombie had said, nodding with
approval. "I do not mean to discourage initiative and you
should have some say as it's ultimately your future, but
competing lists could get quite complicated. Do change
and we shall leave as soon as Marie finishes making you
presentable."

Now, as Bea stood in the Red Corner House's hazard
room next to a jug-bitten gamester who peered down at
her décolletage from his superior height without embarrassment or self-consciousness, she understood the advantage of looking unpresentable and longed for her out-
moded green gown, with its spinsterish high collar.

If only she had a fichu or a chemisette or even a small

tablecloth that she could fold up and insert over her bosom.

Resigned, she turned her shoulders slightly to remove her chest from the leering gambler's line of sight. This maneuver did little to improve her situation, for now her revealing neckline was thrust under the nose of a red-faced gentleman who smiled with lascivious delight and winked.

Behind her, a fashionable impure in a pistache gown cut so low it made Bea's dress seem modest in comparison, laughed huskily and drove her elbow into Bea's back. Bea tried to take a step forward to provide the woman with additional space to ply her wares, but there was nowhere to move. Although the room itself was of a reasonable size to house a large hazard table, the swelling group of hopefuls eagerly calling out bets had quickly made it feel cramped.

Bea found it increasingly difficult to breathe.

"Perhaps we should approach him now," Bea said, after the room erupted in disappointed jeers as the caster rolled the main. Previously, when she'd suggested they have their consultation with Mowbray, Lady Abercrombie had objected on the grounds that no young man would stop his play whilst winning. Now he had lost three bets in a row, which marked the end of his streak.

Her ladyship turned around and said, "Mowbray is next as caster. We will request a conference with him after he rolls."

"Assuming he's losing then," Bea said.

"You mustn't despair, my dear," the widow said, smiling. "Ultimately, they all lose. That's why gambling is so deliciously pointless."

Pointless indeed, Bea thought as Mowbray specified the main and tossed the dice onto the table. Having recently learned vingt-et-un from her cousin Russell, she understood the pleasures of mastering a game of skill. Keeping track of which cards had been played and calculating their likelihood of appearing was an enjoyable challenge and one that required a good memory. Hazard demanded nothing at all of its players, not even a strong throwing arm, for even a paltry toss resulted in an out-come. Every aspect of the game was left entirely to chance, and Bea could not understand the appeal of playing some-thing at which you had no hope of improving.

What was the point of doing anything if not to get better at it over time?

If only Mowbray had devoted himself to losing his fortune at whist or another card game that needed concen-tration and strategy, then she could respect the endeavor and wait patiently while the game played out.

"Ah, there you are," a voice said.

Taken aback, Bea turned to find herself looking into the warm, amused gaze of Viscount Nuneaton. It was clear from his expression that he was not at all surprised to find her in the unsavory gambling house. "What are you doing here?" she asked, astonished to pose the question politely.

"I requested his company," Lady Abercrombie said. "Obviously, a pair of ladies could not come to a den of iniquity such as this without an escort. Good evening, my lord, and thank you for joining us."

Bea darted him a smile that she hoped was graciously welcoming, then leaned close to the countess's ear. "Why would you do that?"

"He's number six on my list," she explained softly before raising her voice to address the newcomer. "You have arrived at precisely the right moment, as my protégé is growing tired of hazard. Perhaps you could return her to the other room for another game or perhaps to get a little something to eat. I believe the sideboard has a nice as-sortment of meats and cheeses."

Ah, so it was the opportunity to promote the match that had led the widow to agree so quickly to her request, Bea thought wryly. She'd naïvely assumed the other wom-an said yes out of a sense of adventure.

"My pleasure," Nuneaton said with a slight bow. "Miss Hyde-Clare, I hope you will allow me the honor?"

Bea hesitated before responding, although it was not

because she was surprised to discover Lady Abercrombie's list was an actual thing and not merely a diversion to alleviate her heartbreak. No, the pause was due to the fact that he was on Kesgrave's list. She had expressly promised not to visit the Red Corner House in the viscount's company.

And she hadn't, she reminded herself.

Keeping her word, she had requested the escort of the one person about whom she had made no promise, intentionally and subtly slipping that bond when it had been sought.

No vow had been broken. Indisputably, the duke would allow the truth of that statement and agree the distinction this time was sharp and clear, not merely a semantical discrepancy.

"Yes, of course," she said agreeably. "I'm grateful for the opportunity to leave this room, which is far too crowded for my comfort."

The gaming hell's main hall was far more hospitable, with navy blue curtains trimmed in gold, Greek statuary and a large chandelier swathed in ormolu wreaths of oak leaves and glittering crystals. Along the far wall, between a pair of windows, was a table covered with serving platters, and Nuneaton directed her there as soon as they entered the room.

"I must warn you that Lady Abercrombie's estimation of the repast provided was wildly optimistic," he said as they threaded their way through the crowd, which was thinner and more sedate than in the hazard room. "As you can see for yourself, it's an indifferent assortment of boiled items such as meats, vegetables and puddings. As you are in my care for the moment, I would suggest you give it a wide berth unless you are particularly hungry. Culinary excellence is not an area in which the Red Corner excels, as its patrons come here to lose their money, not dine at leisure. The blue ruin on offer is a much higher quality, but I would advise you to give that a miss as well."

Unable to distinguish one joint of gray meat from the

other joints of gray meat, Bea quickly assured him she was far from hungry, which was true. She had partaken of dinner with her relatives before leaving to spend the evening in Lady Abercrombie's company. Although her aunt had been quite suspicious of the invitation, which said little more than the countess longed for the youthful presence of her protégé, she could say nothing in protest. The family had no plans other than to pass a few hours reading or playing cards, and Bea's so-called youthful presence was not required for either activity.

"Come, then," Nuneaton said, "let us find a quiet corner to talk while we wait for Lady Abercrombie to emerge and you can tell me why we are here in this unusual spot. Her ladyship's message said only that you are on a mission. I find the idea of a young lady with a mission to be a very appealing notion. Speaking of appealing, I'm compelled to observe that you look very well tonight. Either that shade of blue or having a mission is remarkably becoming on you."

Although she couldn't resist a smile, Bea looked at his handsome face—brown hair closely cropped, brown eyes glittering with warmth, the cheeks rounded and the bottom lip full—and tried to assume an austere expression. "We have already had this conversation, my lord. If we are to be acquaintances, then you must dispense with the flattery. Spanish coin is strictly forbidden."

Nuneaton indicated a chair for Bea and waited until she was seated before sitting down himself. "The last time it was friends, Miss Hyde-Clare. You said if we are to be friends, then I must refrain from flattery."

Bea recalled the occasion to which he referred and knew that she had indeed suggested the more familiar connection. She had altered it because *acquaintance* was the word she had thought in the presence of the duke and to amend it now felt oddly dishonest.

"Although the distinction might seem minor, it's of particular importance to me," he continued, "as I know you would never share the secrets of your Lakeview Hall investigation with a mere acquaintance. But as a friend, I believe there is cause to have hope."

The eagerness on his face delighted Bea as did the simple honesty with which he spoke. "Aha!" she said with a wide grin.

Nuneaton smiled back, and Bea marveled that a man who had appeared bored by everything in the Lake District could be so engaging now. She genuinely liked him and thought she would enjoy his friendship if it was truly on offer.

Just then Kesgrave hailed the viscount from several steps away, and Bea started guiltily. She hadn't done anything untoward, of course. Her actions since leaving his coach that afternoon had complied strictly and wholly with every one of his dictates.

And yet her heart pounded fitfully as she considered how damning the situation looked.

It was patently unfair!

"Good evening, Nuneaton," Kesgrave said, his tone everything amiable and kind as he greeted his friend, who stood to receive him. "I'm surprised to see you here. I thought you were attending the opera with your uncle."

"I am. Indeed, I will be heading there soon," Nuneaton said. "But first I had to discharge a favor for a lady."

"Did you?" he asked softly and darted a fleeting look at Bea. It was only a glance, a glimpse and then gone, but it burned hot and angry. And yet somehow his voice remained cordial. "Your consideration is inspiring."

Nuneaton rushed to assure him his consideration was nothing of the sort, and Bea opened her mouth to insist it was not she for whom the viscount was showing consideration. Before she could speak, however, Lady Abercrombie, who had finally emerged from the hazard room with Mowbray in tow, called out a greeting to Kesgrave. "Now this is most unexpected. I would not have thought the Red Corner House would be the sort of establishment you would frequent. What about you, Miss Hyde-Clare? Would you have expected to see the duke here?" she asked, looking at her protégé with marked disappointment.

Her ladyship's expression confounded Bea but only for a moment. Then she realized that the countess thought that she had invited the duke there in some desperate bid to gain his attention that would only prolong her suffering.

"No!" she said, denying the unspoken charge with more vigor than the spoken one required. She took a deep breath and calmly explained that she had not expected Kesgrave. "I'm as surprised to see him as you are. Just as I was surprised to see Lord Nuneaton. The only person here whom I expected to see this evening is you."

"And Mowbray," Lady Abercrombie reminded Bea as she gestured to the young, disheveled man standing beside her. He was slim, of ordinary height, with heavy-lidded blue eyes clouded by drink and loss. "I have persuaded him to indulge a hand of cribbage with me by assuring him I'm not very good. Come, Miss Hyde-Clare, I've arranged a room so that we may play in private. Nuneaton, you may join us. Kesgrave, it was a pleasure as always. I will see you again soon, I'm sure."

Although it was a clear dismissal, the duke refused to take it as such and instead expressed concern for Nuneaton, whose uncle was waiting for him in Covent Garden. "You mustn't tarry as the opening curtain waits for no man. I shall accompany the ladies in cribbage."

Lady Abercrombie, whose confusion at this maneuver was apparent to anyone who looked at her, thanked Kesgrave for his generous offer but insisted it was not necessary. "The overture is deadly dull and Nuneaton won't mind missing it. He will accompany us."

"The overture to *The Marriage of Figaro* is only six and a half minutes long," Kesgrave pointed out, "and comprises some of the best music in the opera. Nuneaton would be loath to miss it. He will go. I will stay."

Bea could not say what she felt watching Lady Abercrombie wrangle with Kesgrave over who would join them in conference with Mowbray. She knew it was unkind to be amused by the situation, for her ladyship had generously lent her support without knowing anything more than the most general details of the excursion, and yet the tussle was comical. Nuneaton, who seemed content to remain above the fray, even though it was the quality of his theater experience that was under increasingly passionate discussion, plainly felt the same way, for he caught her eye and smiled.

"Well, this is dashed odd fish," said Mowbray with sudden and surprising coherence. "Why don't you both stay and I'll go. Cribbage don't appeal to me anyway. It hurts my head. I like a game with an element of *je ne sais quoi*. Throwing dice. Spinning wheels. Games that keep you guessing like EO."

Having watched the young man guess erratically while playing hazard, Bea rather thought that wild conjecture would be his undoing. Nevertheless, she said, "An excellent suggestion, my lord. Let's play EO. First, however, a brief conversation. I believe Lady Abercrombie has arranged a quiet room for us to talk, yes? Truly, it won't take a minute. Perhaps you would like another glass of port? I'm sure Nuneaton would be happy to fetch it for you."

"I would?" his lordship asked with a wry expression before agreeing. "But I have a feeling I'm about to miss out on a story as interesting as the one at Lakeview Hall. Be warned, Miss Hyde-Clare, I will redouble my efforts to discover every grisly detail."

At this startling admission, Lady Abercrombie looked from Nuneaton to Beatrice to Kesgrave and then back to Nuneaton again. "Lakeview Hall? What happened at Lakeview Hall?"

The viscount revealed his ignorance by shrugging his shoulders and said, "That's exactly what I'm trying to find out. These two have a secret and neither will reveal it. I do hope you will tell me if you have more luck eliciting information from either of them than I."

As he walked away, the countess turned to Bea with narrowed eyes and accused her of grossly violating the code of ethics that governed the protégé relationship. "You are supposed to disclose all relevant information so that I may decide the best path forward with my mentorship. I could choose to hold this against you and withdraw my support, but I'm not given to pettiness and spite. Rather, I will graciously forgive you and adjust my plans accordingly. You may express your gratitude now."

Although Bea wasn't sure she was grateful for her ladyship's generosity, she realized now was not the time to debate the matter. "Thank you."

Lady Abercrombie's nod exemplified noblesse oblige so perfectly Bea thought the duke could take lessons. "Of course," she said.

Mowbray, who seemed just drunk enough to be thoroughly baffled by the proceedings, muttered about dashed odd fish again before politely excusing himself from the company. The countess, however, refused to let him slide off the hook and threaded her arm through his so forcefully it caused him to stumble. "Do tread carefully, my lord. The floor is uneven and I would hate for you to trip. Let's find that quiet room so that you may sit down and enjoy your port."

As soon as Lady Abercrombie and the earl were a few steps away, Bea turned to the duke and said with insulted outrage, "How dare you not trust me!"

Whatever charge Kesgrave had been about to level at her, it was forgotten in his amusement at her daring to accuse him of distrust. "I'm not sure indignation is your best strategy in this situation, my dear Bea. You surrendered the high ground the moment you entered the establishment."

But she would not be put off by his humor. "You thought I came here with Nuneaton. Despite the fact that I gave you my word. Deny it if you can."

He could not. "What else could I possibly think when I arrive to find you alone with him in a corner having a tête-à-tête?"

"That my word is inviolate," she suggested heatedly. "That I'm worthy of trust. That we are partners, more or less, in this investigation and if it appeared as if I'd somehow broken my word then there must be some other explanation such as Lady Abercrombie invited the gentleman."

Although her catalog was comprehensive, it was far from reasonable and he made no attempt to hide his exasperation with her belief that it made complete sense. "Why would Lady Abercrombie invite him? As Mowbray would say, it's dashed odd fish."

"Because he's on her list," Bea said.

He sighed with aggravation. "What list?"

"Of potential suitors. The countess was a friend of my mother's and is determined to marry me off to expiate her guilt for not saving me from Aunt Vera," she explained impatiently. "But that's neither here nor there. The issue is you didn't trust me to keep my word, and I absolutely did. I specifically did not promise not to come with Lady Abercrombie because I wanted to retain the option."

But Kesgrave was too aghast at the idea of anyone wanting to marry her, let alone a dandy who sought perfection, to hear her words. He simply stared at her as if unable to even understand the concept, which was mortifying for her, and just as she feared the embarrassment was so intense she would burst into flames, Lady Abercrombie called for her to follow.

"I must tell you, Miss Hyde-Clare," the widow said peevishly, "your mother would be most displeased with your making me wait. She was always efficient and punctual. Now do please begin your interview of Mowbray so that I may feel as though I am mentoring you properly."

"Yes, of course," Bea said, turning away from Kesgrave and entering the room. Although she worried what the countess would think of her questions, she knew it would be churlish to request her assistance and then deny her access.

Flinching slightly as Kesgrave closed the door behind

him, Mowbray strode back and forth in the small room, peering at them with a trapped look in his eye. As Bea watched him awkwardly steer around the green-baize table, with its set of four cushioned chairs, she became convinced of his guilt. Now all she had to do was surprise him into confessing.

After observing him a full minute in silence to increase his anxiety, she said, "Tell me about the snuffbox you gave Mr. Wilson."

Mowbray's agitation, however, had risen to such a high degree, he couldn't take the suspense any longer and he spoke at the exact same time. "Deuced awkward to admit, your grace, but I don't recall how much I owe you. I've racked my brain but still cannot come up with anything. Is it a very large amount? The thing is, I can't even recall wagering against you. Was it at Musgrove's place? You know, his hunting box in Somerset? Didn't think you were there. I thought our third was Quorn, as he had a rather large mustache, but perhaps I consumed a little too much of Musgrove's claret—he keeps an impeccable cellar—and mistook a stain on your upper lip for a mustache. The goose had a particularly thick sauce. Dark, too, if I'm remembering it correctly. Could the sauce be the source of the confusion?" he added softly, before mumbling softly under his breath "the sauce be the source, the source be the sauce" a few times. Then he shook his head, as if trying to banish a great conundrum. "The answer, I suppose, would depend on how slovenly you eat your dinner. But if that's the case, then Quorn owes me several hundred pounds, as I settled the debt with the wrong person. If that was the situation, then he should not have taken the money. Or did *he* confuse *me* with someone else? I wonder if—"

"Lord Mowbray!" Bea called with some insistence, unable to bear his rambling one second more. She'd thought for sure Kesgrave would put an end to it, especially when the young man had taken to impugning his tidiness as an eater, but he seemed only amused by the nonsense. "You owe the Duke of Kesgrave nothing."

Heartily relieved, the earl brightened at once and let out a huge sigh, only to immediately inhale sharply and resume his anxious pacing. "Oh, dear, do I owe you money? Could you have been at Musgrove's hunting box? I truly thought that was Quorn, as the mustache, you see, was so fulsome. But I suppose you could—"

"You owe me nothing either," Bea said firmly, fearing another pointless digression. When his eyes shifted to Lady Abercrombie, she added her ladyship's name to the list of people to whom he was not indebted. "We are not here to hold you to account. We are merely seeking information about the snuffbox you gave Mr. Wilson."

His cloudy eyes, already so confused, went blank. "Mr. Wilson?"

"Yes, Charles Wilson," she reminded him. "You had dealings with him in India."

Mowbray repeated the name under his breath several times before illumination struck. "Ah, yes, Charlie! An excellent fellow. Why are you asking? Does he have some complaint about me? I hope not, for I dealt with him with the same honesty with which I dealt with all my associates in India. I split the profits from our scheme evenly in half. After I deducted my service fee, of course," he explained, as if the need for this surcharge were readily obvious. "And my clerical fee. Oh, and I mustn't forget the implementation fee. But these were all minimal, I assure you, and nothing to complain about if discovered, for I'm a very honest fellow. Honest to a fault, aren't I, your grace. Now remind me, how much do I owe you?"

Kesgrave quirked an eyebrow at Bea, as if smugly asserting that he had warned her of the hazards of interrogating an intoxicated person.

She refused to believe no useful information could be gotten from the earl. In the midst of his drunken rambles, some truths would certainly fall. In vino veritas! "Indeed, yes, Lord Mowbray, you are quite the honest gentleman. So fine and upstanding. That is why it would be such a shame if stories about your nefarious dealings in India were to circulate among the *ton*."

At once, the young earl raised an outraged hand to his lips as if to shush her. "The devil you say! My dealings were perfectly respectable. Perfectly respectable. Not a hint of nefarious…nefarious…" He struggled for the right word and in his cups came close. "Nefariousity! Not a hint of nefariousity about them. Told you, I split the profit evenly with Wilson after taking various administrative fees. Entirely aboveboard, I assure you. No one would say otherwise. I'm a regular out-and-outer, you know. Bang up to the mark and a whipster as well. Might try for Four-in-Hand. Or maybe Gentleman Jackson's instead. I haven't quite made up my mind. What do you think, your grace? Quorn said I would never make a boxer. Too gangly by half, he said. Or was that you?"

Struggling to hold on to her patience, Bea wondered by what method could one increase the sobriety of an intoxicated lord. Would a cup of tea help clear his mind? Would stepping on his foot? Shouting loudly in his ear? Unsettling him with mention of the snuffbox failed miserably, as he'd reacted to neither reference.

"But your agreement with Mr. Wilson was not aboveboard," she pointed out, still hopeful of unnerving him and gaining access to the truth. "He gave you secret information that you then passed off as your own to your employer."

"Yes, precisely," Mowbray said with a slovenly smile, "for it was my job to report any information to my boss that would enrich or benefit the company. Why do you bring this up? Is Wilson claiming I behaved dishonorably? Is he? I cannot believe he would indulge in such disreputable behavior! Where is he? Let me talk to him. I should like to persuade him to desist with these charges. It's unbecoming of a gentleman. Is he here? It would be the best of all things, as I must ask him about my ring, my talisman ring. I lost it moments after we met. Or days. Perhaps weeks? Regardless, it felt like an ominous turn, and yet I came into my inheritance almost immediately after so perhaps the thing wasn't working correctly. Maybe rather than warding off bad luck it was warding off good luck. Is it possible I had a broken talisman? What do you think, your grace? To whom should I lodge my complaint?"

Kesgrave laughed at the question, and even Lady Abercrombie chuckled. Frustrated, Bea glared at both of them, indicating that their amusement was not helping the situation.

But what *would* help it, she wondered. Would informing Lord Mowbray of Mr. Wilson's death cut through his dull-witted inebriation or merely confound him further? She could easily imagine him going off on a nonsensical digression about funerals in India or ask if Wilson was to be buried with his talisman ring.

Surely, nobody was that much of a fool.

Of course not, she thought, wondering for the first time if his drunken stupor was merely an act to distract her from getting the answers she sought. Could he really be that diabolical?

If so, she would deliver him a surprise he would never expect.

"Where do you get nux vomica?" she asked.

Mowbray darted an angry scowl at her, and observing the show of temper as it crossed his face, she felt a flash of satisfaction that something had finally penetrated his facade. Clearly, he'd assumed nobody would figure out the type of poison he used, and he wasn't prepared to hear its name spoken in the Red Corner House or anywhere else in the kingdom.

Just let him try to befuddle his way out of that one, she thought.

But when Mowbray spoke, it was to accuse her of trickery. "You will not get away with that. No, you will not! *Ut profluenter Latine loqui et non cadere in plures!*"

Dumbfounded, Bea looked at the duke, who grinned

with unrestrained glee and translated: "I speak Latin fluently and won't fall for your tricks."

"Tricks?" she asked, baffled.

"He thinks you made up a phrase that sounds like Latin but is in fact nonsense," he explained.

He's toying with me, she thought, unable to believe anyone's thinking could be so tangled and snarled. Mowbray was a man of superior intellect pretending to be a buffoon of staggering proportion.

She appreciated the deviousness even as she seethed over the results.

Before she could accuse him of evading the truth with his intentionally idiotic responses, Lord Mowbray announced that he would tolerate no further questions. "I understand now what you hope to accomplish with this interview, and it is to humiliate me. I do not know why you would settle on such a goal, though I assume Quorn is somehow involved, for it is impossible to fully trust a man who has swindled me with sauce. Your grace, I think this scene is unworthy of you and hope you will seek more honorable company in the future. Lady Abercrombie," he said, turning to face the countess, "I do not know why you are here, but it has been a pleasure nonetheless. You must not think for a moment that I hold you responsible for the glass of port that has failed to appear."

At that moment, the door opened and Nuneaton swept into the room with a glass of port held aloft. "Ah, there you are, Mowbray. I did not mean to tarry, but I had a devil of a time finding the right room. Harper-Smith and Carvin are playing casino next door and objected quite strongly to the interruption. And that is nothing compared with what is going on in the room next to theirs. Spillikins," he said with relish, "for a pound a stick."

Mowbray received his drink and thanked the other man for procuring it. Then he bowed at the duke, bobbed at Lady Abercrombie and left.

As soon as he was gone, Nuneaton turned to Beatrice

and said, "It would be futile to pretend I wasn't listening at the door, but my sense of what is going on could be no less acute than if I'd spent the entire time playing spillikins with Hathmore, Simpson and Warnock. I truly hope, Miss Hyde-Clare, that one day you will be kind enough to explain."

Recalling again the finely honed disinterest on display in the Lake District, she said, "Be careful, my lord, not to exert yourself too much or society will discover that your studied pose of ennui hides a curious mind. Then what will you do? Engage with people? Laugh at their sallies? Inquire after their health? Imagine the horror."

He shuddered on cue.

Kesgrave stepped forward and reminded the viscount of his theater obligation. "The curtain has most certainly risen by now."

"And the overture begun," Nuneaton agreed. "I must leave, as my uncle will be wondering where I am. Kesgrave, I trust you will escort the ladies safely to their carriage."

The duke dipped his head in response.

Despite concern for his uncle, Nuneaton stayed to receive Lady Abercrombie's gratitude for his willingness to serve. He assured her he had been unable to resist from the moment he'd read her note. When the door was closed behind him, Bea looked at Lady Abercrombie and thanked her in turn for being so ready to lend her assistance to a worthwhile and productive cause.

"Productive?" Kesgrave said scornfully. "You did not get a single satisfying answer out of him. He was incoherent from beginning to last." He turned to the countess and smiled with superiority. "Do note, Tilly, I tried to warn her of the limited efficacy of interviewing a man whose faculties had been impaired by drink, but she would not listen."

"Did you now?" the widow said thoughtfully.

Although Bea bristled at the smug expression on the duke's face, she forced herself to remain calm as she replied. "Respectfully, your grace, I disagree. I learned a tremendous amount of pertinent information, which I will now sift through. Lady Abercrombie, shall we leave or would you like to linger in the hazard room? Having obtained my goal, I'm confident I can be a more patient observer."

"Continue to tease me, Miss Hyde-Clare, and we *will* return to the hazard room," Lady Abercrombie said firmly.

Bea lowered her head in contrition.

True to his word, Kesgrave escorted them to their carriage, and as they passed through the gaming hell's main hall, he conversed exclusively with the beautiful widow. His tone was light and flirtatious as he peppered his chatter with excessive compliments and blithe observations about people they knew. It was exactly the way he had spoken to Lady Abercrombie on the afternoon she and Beatrice first met. At that time, Bea had found his ability to effortlessly adopt the mannerisms of a Bond Street beau both intimidating and disappointing, but now she felt nothing. Her original response had been based on an anxiety about their future interactions and a fear that having seen the Duke of Kesgrave in his proper milieu—the London drawing room—she would never feel comfortable in his presence again. Now, of course, there could be no worry of future dealings, as the advent of Lady Victoria had demonstrated just how unnecessary those concerns had been. As soon as she discovered who poisoned Mr. Wilson, her association with the duke would be firmly and irrefutably at an end.

Bea realized she'd had that very thought only a few weeks before when she and Kesgrave worked together to identify Fazeley's killer, but this time she knew it would hold. Her mistake then had been in assuming she could solicit information from him without raising his suspicions. Obviously, he was too clever for that. Going forward, she would limit their exchanges to trivial matters such as the weather and their host's excellent choice in flowers.

Her resolution set, Bea turned her attention to the far more interesting matter of Lord Mowbray. Pondering the interrogation, she became convinced every word he had spoken had been calculated to make himself appear too stupid for consideration. From the moment she had uttered Mr. Wilson's name, he had known her objective and devoted himself to outwitting—or, rather, underwitting—her. Kesgrave, for all his intelligence and pedantic attention to detail, had missed it entirely. He had been too busy gloating over Mowbray's imbecility to realize it was diabolical, not drunken.

But not she.

Oh, no, Beatrice Hyde-Clare knew true inconsequential prattle, for she had been living with one of its masters for most of her life, and his nonsense fell well short of many of Aunt Vera's towering achievements. If anything, his rambling had been too disjointed as he jumped from one topic to another. The genuine blatherer followed a general through line, with each thought building on top of the other.

Lord Mowbray, whose connection to India had already given him an edge over the other candidates, firmly jumped to the top of the suspects list and deserved a deeper look. The next step would be to search his quarters for evidence of his guilt, such as the poison itself or a receipt for the snuffbox.

She would propose the matter to the duke tomorrow after they met with Taunton. Naturally, he would have some objection about invading the private residence of a fellow peer, but she felt confident she could either overcome his scruples or ignore them entirely.

At Lady Abercrombie's coach, Kesgrave bid them good night. As he turned to leave Bea coughed discreetly and looked him pointedly in the eye. Her intent was to confirm their appointment for the next day, and perceiving her meaning, he nodded abruptly.

As subtle as the exchange was, the countess observed it and wasted no time in taking her protégé to task for the many falsehoods she had told her, starting with the knife. "It wasn't a gift for your uncle at all, was it? It was the weapon that killed Fazeley. You were investigating his death just as you investigated the death of that spice trader. What was his name? Ostler? Olsen?"

"Otley," Bea supplied.

"Otley, yes," she said, nodding. "Until Nuneaton mentioned the Lake District, I hadn't realized you were at Lakeview Hall when Lady Skeffington murdered her lover. That must have been quite awful for everyone involved. Most house parties are deadly enough without someone getting bashed to death with a candlestick."

Although Bea knew the countess to be more than a beautiful pea widgeon, she was still surprised by this level of deduction. It was a tremendous amount to piece together based on an offhand remark from a London dandy.

Noting her surprise, Lady Abercrombie laughed lightly. "Yes, my dear, I'm clever. I thought for sure you knew that by now. Your mother did not suffer fools gladly. Now, I don't know who this Mr. Wilson is, but given your interest in his life, I can only assume he is dead. And you believe Mowbray is responsible, yes? What I can't figure out is Kesgrave's part in all this," she continued thoughtfully. "You misled me there, didn't you, allowing me to believe that you were like the dozens of foolish school misses who lose their heart to him every season. But I can see now that you've had encouragement—indeed, a fair amount, which is even harder for me to make sense of. You are not at all in his usual style."

No comment was necessary, and yet Bea felt compelled to say, "I'm well aware of that." Although she'd intended to affect the sublime indifference of Lord Nuneaton, her tone was peevish and annoyed.

In the darkness of the carriage, Lady Abercrombie smiled. "You think that's a criticism of you, but it's not. It's a criticism of him. Your looks are plain, to be sure, even in that gown, which is highly flattering of your complexion, but you are lively and clever and difficult to intimidate. Kesgrave usually values only one of those qualities in a woman, and as lively as Lady Victoria is, she is oxen-like in her thinking. I feel bad saying that, for it's not her fault. Her parents raised her to be a beautiful ninny and succeeded beyond their expectations. Despite this preference, Kesgrave has taken an interest in you. And yet he continues to further the connection with the Tavistocks. I have no idea what it means and find myself curiously unsure of what actions to advise. I'm sorry for that, for I feel positive your mother would have had something helpful to offer."

Her regret was sincere, and Bea, feeling the unexpected desire to comfort *her,* laughed at the absurdity. "It is a muddle from every direction, but it is invaluable to me to hear another opinion on the matter. For weeks I've been unable to decide if the bond I feel with Kesgrave is real or entirely one-sided. Your observations confirm that I haven't invented it out of whole cloth. And you do not need to advise me on the correct course of action. I know what I must do, and as soon as the mystery regarding Mr. Wilson's tragic death is solved, I will end my association with him. I cannot spend so much time with him without hurting myself."

The widow nodded with approval. "Brava, my dear. We shall proceed with the list, which already has several interesting names on it. I have nothing but respect for a broken heart, so I won't say this now, but I believe Nuneaton is a genuine prospect. You made him laugh, which I know from personal experience is not easy to accomplish."

"And I have nothing but appreciation for your willingness to help me tonight, so I won't protest the list right now," Bea said generously.

"You will, of course, concede in the end, but I welcome a spirited debate on the merits," her ladyship said. "But tell me, regarding your investigations, do you take referrals?"

As Bea could only assume the countess sought to discourage her unsavory interest in murder victims, she answered evasively. "Given the extreme unlikeliness of such a thing happening, I'm not sure it's worth the effort to address the question."

"Oh, but it is very likely," Lady Abercrombie said matter-of-factly, "as I'm the one who would make the referral."

That the beautiful widow could be genuinely nonchalant about her gruesome activity struck Bea as implausible, and sensing a trick, she said, "But don't you think it's ghastly, what I do? Aren't you horrified? Doesn't the thought of my examining a corpse offend your sensibilities?"

"I assure you, my dear, I've entertained my own share of lifeless men," Lady Abercrombie said wryly, causing Bea to giggle in startled amusement. "Every woman must have a hobby or expire from boredom. Why do you think my drawing room is an orgy of Oriental perfection? Is it because I like arguing with artisans over the thickness of a bamboo chair leg?" Although her tone was rhetorical, indicating the answer was so obvious it need not be stated, she smiled deprecatingly and admitted that she was *somewhat* motivated by the prospect of a satisfyingly vigorous quarrel with a craftsman. "But it's the design itself that interests me, creating a vision and working to see it fulfilled. The whole town house is just as elaborate, as is my home in Essex, and when I ran out of my own rooms to decorate, I borrowed a friend's. If you think my drawing room is excessive, you should see poor Lady Marshall's facsimile of an African village. The only reason she agreed to let me have my way was I promised to stand the expense. Your hobby is a little more macabre than mine, to be sure, but that is probably for the best, as you don't have the funds to support an interest in decorating."

Shocked by Lady Abercrombie's calm acceptance of her investigative pursuit, Bea felt the hot flush of shame creep over her cheeks. How judgmental she had been the first time they'd met! Stepping into the overdone splendor of her Oriental drawing room, Bea had dismissed the countess as silly, vain, shallow and desperate for attention. No doubt she was all of those things, but she was much more besides. She was a remarkably beautiful woman, yes, but she had cultivated other, more interesting traits.

Did she owe her an apology? Should she explain and say she was sorry?

"You did not answer my question," Lady Abercrombie said, seemingly unaware of Bea's embarrassment. "Do you take referrals? I'm not sure how an unmarried woman with an unpleasant fish like Vera Hyde-Clare for a guardian would find new murders to investigate. Do you seek them out or do concerned friends and family members come to you? If it's the latter, then there's something I'd like to discuss with you."

Although this development was certainly unexpected, Bea had lost the ability to be surprised by anything the countess said and agreed to the consultation without a moment's hesitation. Of course she wanted another assignment, her next assignment, all ready to go when she resolved the problem of Mr. Wilson's death. Without a distraction, she would pine for the duke and that would be miserable.

"The investigation I'm working on now came as a referral," Bea said. "To be completely honest, other than dressing up in a uniform and pretending to be a Bow Street Runner, I don't know how one would find murder victims."

"I respect the fact that you've given it thought and trust you've realized the disadvantages of the Runner scheme without my having to list them," Lady Abercrombie observed mildly. "I admire pluck, of course, which you seem to have to the backbone, but there's nothing commendable in being reckless. Recklessness is just stupidity pretending to be bravery. No one is fooled."

Although Bea nodded in agreement, she thought it was a particularly strange thing for a woman who owned a lion cub as a pet to say. She could think of few things more reckless than trying to tame a wild animal. "May I ask who the victim is?"

"Let's hold off on discussing it for the moment. You

are already investigating Mr. Wilson's death, and I don't want to distract you with my concern," her ladyship said. "After you have identified the culprit, we'll talk. You will come for tea. Until then, don't give it another thought."

"Yes, of course," Bea said affably as if she had immediately dismissed the matter from her mind. But if there was one thing in the world calculated to ensure that she would give something plenty of thought it was the exhortation not to think about it. Now her brain buzzed with the strangeness of Lady Abercrombie's so-called concern, for how could she be in need of an investigator but display no urgency? Was there not a corpse slowly rotting in the wine cellars? Had nobody noticed that a particular dead person was missing? Was the victim or target not dead? Was the countess attempting to distract her from her ghoulish course by inventing a mystery because she was secretly horrified and felt she owed it to Bea's mother to return her to the track of marriage and domestic happiness? Would the investigation turn out to be an elaborate fiction that paired her with the gentleman Lady Abercrombie deemed most suitable? Perhaps the real reason she refused to discuss the matter was she had just devised the idea and needed time to figure out the specifics.

As if determined to validate Bea's worst suspicions, Lady Abercrombie returned her attention to the list of suitors she had compiled and devoted the rest of the ride to Portman Square reviewing the various prospects. True to her word, she did not mention Nuneaton at all, although when she got to his name she conspicuously skipped over it while lauding herself for being so thoughtful.

Apparently, her respect for a broken heart went only so far.

Bea listened to the list silently and wondered how strenuously she should object to the countess's plan. Viscerally, she felt a need to make it clear that she would never go along with a plot so patently desperate in its goals it could only humiliate her further. If there was any consolation in being a plain-faced spinster of six and twenty, it was that the *ton* barely knew she existed. If Lady Abercrombie had her way, that would change.

At the same time, it hardly seemed worth the effort to protest, for it wasn't as if the men on the list would simply fall in line with her ladyship's plan either. To be fair, the group she had assembled was a varied mix, with prospects from every stratum of society, including second sons and minor peers from families of modest circumstances. There were a few highfliers, of course, such as Nuneaton and Lord Davison, but by and large, it was a reasonable assortment, and Bea felt a surge of respect for Lady Abercrombie's clear-eyed pragmatism. Nevertheless, even the most humble candidate had dozens of options available to him, and like Kesgrave, every one of the gentlemen on the countess's list would be delighted with a lively affect and an oxen-like mind.

Given how much she enjoyed teasing the duke, Bea could not blame them for seeking the comfort of an unchallenging companion.

On and on her ladyship went, thoughtfully outlining why she had added each particular gentleman to the list and explaining her cause for optimism. Lord Davidson had been jilted by an Incomparable seeking richer quarry. Mr. Walker was studious and appreciated thoughtful responses.

Unswayed, Bea nonetheless held her tongue, for there was no reason to vex the widow with her intractability. The scheme would fail on its own merits, and the truth was, Bea wouldn't altogether mind the distraction from her own romantic misfortunes. Unable to conceive how the other woman would implement her ambitious scheme, Bea could imagine only comedic results. Perhaps a hearty laugh was worth a little mortification.

A half hour later, she was describing for Aunt Vera and Flora an uneventful evening of playing speculation with the countess and two of her friends whose names were thankfully not sought by either of her relatives. Indeed, her aunt was far too distressed at the idea of Bea playing cards for money, even a farthing ante, to wonder about her companions and chastised her at length for succumbing to the family illness. Although Bea thought it was unfair that her uncle's beloved pastime was described as an illness only when it pertained to her, she listened patiently as the older woman lectured on the compulsion to gamble—a tirade that was abruptly cut off as she realized her niece was wearing an unfamiliar dress.

"Good lord, never say Lady Abercrombie loaned you something so fine and elegant," Aunt Vera exclaimed, aghast at the excellent quality of the silk. "I cannot imagine what in the world warranted such an extravagant gown. You were just playing cards with her cronies. And what must you have done to your own dress. Did you set it on fire? Do go change out of it at once before you destroy it and be sure to hang it up immediately. I'm sure we could never afford to reimburse her if you caused it damage. Go, go, go."

Despite the urgency with which her aunt instructed her to remove the dress, she would not let Bea leave the room until she had fully impressed upon her the egregiousness of her actions.

It was a full twenty minutes before Bea was allowed to retire to her bedchamber.

CHAPTER THIRTEEN

The sixth Marquess of Taunton was singularly unimpressed with Mr. Wright and even more dismissive of his clerk, who, unused to being a lowly subordinate, had commanded his attention by saying, "Now, see here——" before Bea ruthlessly cut him off with an apology.

"He's never mixed with gentry before, my lord," Bea explained with a pointed look at the duke, who, in his outrage over being treated with contempt and disdain, hadn't thought to disguise his voice. She was agog that the marquess hadn't instantly recognized Kesgrave's deep baritone. "It's my fault, my lord. I should have prepared him better or left him at the office. Do forgive me. We won't take up much of your time. It's an important topic, my lord, but one easily dispensed with. We would never presume to disturb you if it wasn't necessary. Please, my lord."

Bea adopted her most contrite expression, perfected over years of apologizing to her aunt for her very presence. Next to her, Kesgrave, dressed in the plain gray trousers and coat of his own steward, with Mr. Wright's spectacles perched on his nose, looked as imposing as ever. He stood at his full height, his shoulders back, as if the concept of obsequiousness did not exist for him.

Indeed, it appeared it did not.

She'd realized the moment she'd climbed into the carriage twenty minutes before that he would never be able to affect servility. On him, the humble clothes of Mr. Stephens looked oddly regal, and she'd insisted at once that he rumple himself up so as to seem properly poor and blighted. He had complied with alacrity, tousling his hair, mussing his cravat and rubbing dirt from the floor of the hack onto the hem of his trousers.

It was a valiant effort, and yet when she looked at him, his face half hidden by a monstrous false mustache a full shade darker than his blond hair, all she saw was a man born to wealth and privilege.

Now, as Lord Taunton frowned in impatience, she worried that Kesgrave's noble bearing would ruin their chance at an interview. The duke, as if offended by the notion that he could do anything poorly, mimicked her rounded shoulders and looked down at the floor. It was an improvement, of course, but not a solution. The best thing would have been for her to have come alone.

Her concern was overblown, however, for his lordship agreed with a weary sigh, as if endlessly plagued by meetings with lowly members of the law profession. He told his butler, who had hovered in the hallway to escort them out as efficiently as he had escorted them in, that he would need five minutes. Then he waved them into his study and gestured to a pair of dark-green chairs that matched the rug. He was a tall man, well over six feet, which, Bea thought, most likely explained why he didn't seem bothered by Kesgrave's own height. It would have been very different if he had to look up at the impertinent clerk. "You said you were here on behalf of Charles Wilson? My father's former steward?"

Ah, Bea thought. One suspicion confirmed.

"Thank you again, my lord. I know you are very busy and I promise this won't take long," she said, settling a brown case on her lap. It was filled with old receipts and pages from a book whose binding had torn. She'd felt it was essential to appear to have files if one was to pretend to be a solicitor, as much of their work consisted of the drawing up and executing of contracts. "Yes, it's about Mr. Wilson. I'm sorry to report he has suffered a grave misfortune."

Taunton's brown eyes, appealingly light against his dark complexion—black hair, olive skin roughened by time—flickered with surprise. "Grave misfortune?"

"Yes," she said solemnly, her gazed focused sharply on his. "He passed away on Tuesday."

This information also startled him, but he was better at controlling his surprise, for this time the news barely registered on his face. "I see. It's quite unexpected, I must say, as I had seen him just a few days before and he appeared well. I detected no signs of an ailment, and he did not mention being ill. Indeed, he was full of his plan to buy property near the city and take up farming. Was it an accident?"

Although Bea did not think that the imposing marquess with the rigid posture would regularly associate with a former employee, it did not strike her as unusual that he would occasionally receive Mr. Wilson as a guest. If the books in the deceased's sparsely furnished apartments indicated anything, it was that he had some attachment to his childhood home. He had clearly cherished only a few possessions.

"I'm sorry to say it wasn't an accident but rather a digestive issue," she replied. "It was most unfortunate."

"A digestive issue?" he repeated, rubbing his chin thoughtfully. "As I said, I saw no indication of an ailment during our visit on Sunday, but I cannot say I'm surprised. Wilson spent more than a year in that dreadful country living in what I can only assume were squalid conditions. The surprising thing is that he came back at all. I thought for sure the post would kill him."

If her suspicions about Mowbray were correct, Bea thought, then Taunton's prediction will have turned out to be accurate after all.

"I advised him not to go, but Charles was stubborn

and always did the opposite of what you counseled," Taunton continued. "He had a good job working on our Norfolk estate as steward, a position he assumed after his father died nine years ago. My father had a tremendous amount of respect for Mr. Wilson, which extended to his son, Charles. It was a good life, I believe, but Otley's offer was very generous and he longed to see London. He did not anticipate that his employer would find him so valuable that he would send him to a hostile land such as India." He sighed again and shook his head. "I'm very sorry to hear that he's passed."

Grateful for his unexpected talkativeness, Bea sat quietly in hopes that he would share more of Mr. Wilson's history, for in the space of a few minutes, she'd learned more about Mr. Wilson than during an hour with Mrs. Otley. Taunton, however, had nothing more to say and looked at her impatiently, as if unable to understand why she hadn't already explained the purpose of her call.

Bea was itching to ask about Wilson's visit earlier in the week, but she knew it would be beyond all things inappropriate for a solicitor to try to appease his curiosity. So she hewed closely to the script she'd prepared in advance and informed Taunton that she was the executor of Mr. Wilson's estate and that he had left him several items. As she spoke, she withdrew a sheet of paper on which she had listed the objects. It was a fake document, a ludicrous prop she had created that morning while drinking tea in her room to make her appear more lawyerly. Posing as a steward seemed a lot less fraught than pretending to be a solicitor, and she wanted something else to rely on than just an inexpertly deepened voice and shoulders her aunt described as mannishly broad.

"Among the items are an illustrated copy of the *Faerie Queene*, which your father had gifted to his father for his years of service, and *A Tale of a Tub* by Jonathan Swift. Mr. Wilson felt quite strongly that these cherished books should be returned to the library from which they came.

He also asked that a snuffbox be returned to you, one that you had only recently given to him. It is"—here, she paused as if to confirm the description of the item but she watched for his reaction out of the corner of her eye—"of emerald-green cloisonné inlaid with gold."

As Bea was expecting either one of two things to happen—Taunton would either claim the snuffbox as a gift to an old family retainer or disavow all knowledge of it—she was amazed when he arrived at a third possibility.

"Is *that* where my snuffbox went?" he asked in a tone of sincere exasperation. "I was wondering where it had disappeared to. In fact, I was quite sharp with my butler yesterday morning, for I was convinced he had misplaced it in his carelessness. It was brand-new, and I was particularly fond of it. I saw it in a window on Oxford Street and felt an odd compulsion to have it."

Flabbergasted, Bea stared at Lord Taunton, trying to understand what he was saying. The snuffbox was his, yes, but he hadn't *given* it to Wilson?

Wilson had *taken* the snuffbox?

Kesgrave, who seemed to be struggling with the same surprise but was far more composed, said, "Just to be clear, then, my lord, you're saying you did not present the snuffbox to Mr. Wilson as a gift?"

"Gift a beautifully crafted cloisonné snuffbox to Charles?" he asked, with an incredulous laugh as he stood up, walked to the doorway and called for his butler. When the man promptly appeared, he informed him of the good news. "You can call off the hunt, Perkins. The snuffbox has been found in the possession of Wilson. He took it by mistake when he was here a few days ago. It wasn't your carelessness after all."

The butler's expression remained unresponsive as he received this news, which did not contain an apology for the misguided assumption. "Very good, my lord."

His lordship shook his head as he returned to the room. "I know I should be more circumspect about blaming the staff for the little things that go astray, but nine times out of ten, they *are* responsible," he explained. "Anyway, to answer your question more fully, no, I did not give the snuffbox to Charles. I was fond of the fellow, to be sure, but I would never have given him a present of such shockingly high value. It would have mortified us both. He must have picked it up by accident when he collected his things at the end of the visit. That would explain why he made a point of making sure it was returned to me. He belatedly realized his mistake."

"His mistake," Bea said flatly, as she struggled to reconcile this astonishing piece of information.

Mr. Wilson had picked up the snuffbox by accident.

By accident.

It was not his.

The poison hadn't been meant for him.

He wasn't supposed to die.

Bea shook her head, unable to believe it.

Could it possibly be true?

She looked at Lord Taunton, his face reflecting nothing but relief at the recovery of a misplaced item, and realized that it had to be true. The other option—that he had looked at the two lawyers and deduced the remarkably improbable series of events that had led Beatrice Hyde-Clare and the Duke of Kesgrave to his study—was too incredible to contemplate.

Yes, Kesgrave had slipped up by using his ducal voice while speaking when they'd first arrived, but nothing in the marquess's manner had indicated surprise or confusion. He'd neither paused in his contempt nor looked askance at the impertinent upstart who had questioned him. No one, not even the great Edmund Keen himself, was such an accomplished thespian that observing the high-stepping Duke of Kesgrave in his hallway pretending to be a law clerk with ludicrous facial hair would elicit no reaction at all, not even the merest whiff of recognition.

And then there was the matter of the snuffbox itself,

Bea realized. It was too elaborate. Indeed, it was so patent-ly expensive she'd identified it as the source of the poison almost immediately. If the murderer had been clever enough to poison a man's tobacco, then would he not have been more shrewd in his choice of snuffboxes by selecting one that did not call attention to itself? The craftsmanship on the cloisonné was so expert, it fairly yelled to the observer, "I'm suspicious. Start your investigation here."

That the snuffbox had not been intended for Wilson made far more sense.

Reeling from these revelations, Bea reevaluated other aspects of her investigation and realized how foolish she'd been to think Mowbray's drunken ramblings were the calculated digressions of a diabolical genius. Kesgrave had been right all along, and she felt the faint flush of embarrassment as she recalled the force of her certainty.

As stunned as she was by the discovery of her own prejudices, she was staggered by the immensity of what it all meant—that the man sitting across from her was the victim of a murder attempt and didn't know it. But for the carelessness of another man, he would be dead.

Poor Mr. Wilson.

Contemplating the marquess now, Bea realized she had to tell him the truth. She had little doubt how unlikely it would sound. Nevertheless, she focused her gaze steadily on his and said, "Lord Taunton, in light of this new information, I'm compelled to tell you that the digestive issue that ended Mr. Wilson's life was not brought about by his travels in India or something he recently ate. It was the tobacco in the snuffbox." She paused to see if his mind raced ahead to the logical conclusion, but his demeanor remained unchanged. "It was poisoned."

Nope. Still no light of comprehension.

Bea struggled to clarify without stating it too bluntly. "The poison was in *your* snuffbox, my lord." Another pause. "In the snuff *you* would take."

At first he thought she was teasing, for he started to laugh, but observing her deadly serious expression, he gasped and looked from Bea to the duke in astonishment. "It was meant for me?" he said. "But why would anyone…"

His words trailed off as he grasped the enormity of the event, and he seemed to sink into himself as he tried to assimilate the fact that somebody wanted him dead. He opened his mouth several times to speak and closed it with almost comical swiftness. Watching, Bea felt the weight of the moment and longed to pledge her assistance in discovering the name of this villain. She had enough sense, however, to realize how strange it would be if a solicitor were to offer his investigative skills or volunteer to help him make a list of people who might wish him ill. It was certainly too soon to do anything now, for his lordship hardly had the presence of mind to see beyond the simple fact that his life was in danger.

Bea would have to be patient.

Oh, but it was very hard to sit still while the man who had attempted to kill Lord Taunton was at large and free to try again. There was something almost unbearably exciting about the prospect of investigating a murder that hadn't happened yet.

Immediately, she recalled poor Mr. Wilson, his body wracked with pain, his back bent to an angle so extreme Emily feared he might break himself in half, and felt ashamed of her enthusiasm. Murder itself was a grave enough insult without it being dealt on someone else's behalf. If Mowbray had killed him to preserve his silence about their India deal, he would at least have had the dignity of dying for his own offense.

"This is very troubling," Lord Taunton said softly. "Very troubling indeed. Are you sure? Could there not be a misunderstanding?"

"My examin…um, that is, the surgeon's examination of Mr. Wilson and his situation was conclusive," Bea improvised, uncertain if a surgeon would actually examine anything other than a living, breathing patient. "He was almost certainly poisoned by a substance called nux vomica, which had been applied to the snuff."

Although he'd had a few minutes to absorb the truth, Taunton still could not contain his surprise. "Nux vomica? I've never heard of a poison called nux vomica."

"It's derived from the nux vomica tree in India," Bea explained, wondering who among the marquess's connections would be familiar with the species. With his standing in society and his responsibilities in the House of Lords, he regularly associated with dozens more people than Wilson. Many of them would have connections to the East India Company or connections to those with connections. Suddenly, the pool of suspects was massive, and Bea wondered how she would begin whittling it down. The list of buyers pilfered from the Mercer Brothers was useless, as Taunton had purchased the snuff himself. The challenge was finding the person who'd had access to Lord Penwortham's mixture before Wilson accidentally took the snuffbox.

Bea closed her eyes and pictured the page from Mr. Hamish's ledger, trying to recall precisely when Taunton had purchased the snuff. It was on…the twenty-sixth. Yes, February 26. That was four days before Wilson's visit. Not a particularly large interval, she thought, and the snuffbox was probably not in the marquess's possession the entire time. When it was not on his person, where was it kept? In the pocket of his greatcoat? On the desk in his study? Who had access to both the snuffbox and nux vomica?

No, she thought, not necessarily the box. The snuff might have been poisoned at the source.

Anxiously, she sat forward in her chair and said, "You must be very careful with the remaining snuff. You must check any other boxes you have and make sure the entire canister hasn't been contaminated."

"Yes, yes," Taunton said with an assuring nod. "I've already thought of that. Perkins will throw away the entire batch immediately."

Unable to stop herself, Bea disagreed with that plan, perhaps with more force than was appropriate to the situation. "You must not dispose of it until after you've tested it for poison, for discovering when the snuff was poisoned will help you narrow the time—"

But Taunton was not interested in taking direction from a solicitor and stood up, indicating the visit was at an end. "Thank you, Mr. Wright, for your call."

Bea had no choice but to rise as well. "Of course, my lord. Thank you for agreeing to see us. If I can be of any help to you as you search for the villain who meant you harm, please don't hesitate to ask."

It was on the tip of her tongue to offer him her card, but she hadn't thought to make one for Mr. Wright, solicitor. So much for bolstering her disguise with props!

Her oversight was of no importance, of course, for the Marquess of Taunton was not seeking assistance from a solicitor. "You will send over the items promptly," he said as he opened the door to his study, where the butler was waiting to escort them from the premises. "The snuffbox too."

The dismissal was clear, and Bea, frustrated by his refusal to consider her offer, cast a look at the duke as if to urge him to intercede. She knew it was futile—he couldn't very well tear off his mustache, straighten his hair and say, "Listen, old fellow, do let my associate investigate your potential death"—and yet she could not stop herself from making the plea. She had grown accustomed to utilizing his position to achieve her goals.

Helpless, Bea nodded respectfully and promised to return the items at once, which was an out-and-out lie, as none of them were in her possession and she had no intention of visiting the Melbourne to retrieve the books or wresting the snuffbox from Mrs. Otley's grasping fingers. But perhaps she could ask Kesgrave to send a footman to Wilson's lodging to fetch the books to bring to the marquess.

No, she thought immediately, that would not work, for why would a servant sporting the Duke of Kesgrave's livery have custody of Wilson's books? Causing Taunton to speculate would create an unnecessary link between Kesgrave and the law offices of Mr. Wright.

But if a reasonable explanation could be offered to support the connection, it would provide Kesgrave with an opportunity to insert himself into the crisis as the duke, not a law clerk. Then he could convince Taunton of Mr. Wright's proficiency in scrutinizing matters of this nature.

That would work, wouldn't it? Peers respected the opinion of other peers, and Kesgrave had once mentioned how collegiate the process of working together was in the House of Lords. That would certainly—

"I cannot tell if you are disappointed the wrong man died," the duke said as soon as they were outside, "or if you're disappointed you've been denied a satisfying conclusion."

It was a fair question, and Bea did not take offense. Rather, she marveled at how easily Kesgrave could read her thoughts. "You will think me completely depraved if I say the latter," she observed as he opened the carriage door of the hack he had hired. "So to preserve your good opinion, I'll admit I find both developments to be equally disappointing. I think it's a pity that Mr. Wilson suffered an appalling and painful death for no reason at all. But, yes, it is also incredibly frustrating to be denied the opportunity to investigate this new mystery. Taunton is an entirely different beast than Wilson, which makes it a wholly different investigation, with different motives and suspects. Essentially, I know nothing, a condition I find very uncomfortable."

"And you are trying to figure out how to remedy your ignorance," he said.

That Kesgrave knew her well enough to correctly predict her actions created an uncomfortably bittersweet sensation in Bea's chest, for it affirmed that the connection she felt was far from one-sided, while underscoring its utter uselessness. He owed his lineage too much to let the nebulous emotion he felt for her coalesce into love. It would always remain an unnamed thing he never quite understood.

"Considering the look you gave me earlier, I can only suppose I figure prominently in your plan," he continued blithely, seemingly amused by the prospect of her further machinations. "As myself, of course, not a presumptuous law clerk who doesn't know his place. In full ducal regalia I will present myself to Taunton as ready and eager to assist a fellow peer plagued by an unknown menace. I cannot conceive by what divination I will have learned of his plight, but I'm confident you will supply me with a plausible excuse. With my participation assured, I will then introduce you as"—he broke off as he considered the matter thoughtfully for a moment—"a skilled investigator whose talents are frequently employed by the Home Office and recommend that your input be sought immediately. It's an absurd plan, with several points of impracticality, starting with the fact that Taunton and I have had fewer than a dozen exchanges in the past decade. It would be above all things strange if I were to appear on his doorstep offering to save his life."

Well, yes, Bea thought as he described the method by which they would infiltrate the investigation, *his* plan was absurd. She would never bring the Home Office into her scheme. It was foolish to aim so high when an ordinary magistrate would serve the same purpose while raising fewer eyebrows. Which one in particular she wouldn't be able to say until she'd learned their names and identified the one most likely to indulge unusual policing methods.

"As absurd as it is," he added, the amusement in his tone now tinged with confusion, "I know I will go along with it. How do you do this to me, Miss Hyde-Clare? I recall what you told me while we were on the Strand, about your desire to throw food at my head early in our stay at Lakeview Hall because my air of superiority was too maddening to stand."

"Quenelles of chicken with peas and fruit jelly," she murmured with a smile. "Fish patties with olive paste, eels à la tartare, stuffed tomatoes."

He continued as if she had not spoken. "And I wonder if this was your plan all along—to undermine my dignity not with peas and paste but with plots and plans, to reduce me to this…this creature in a mustache. Do you have any idea how much I enjoyed donning it? My valet thought I was crackbrained when I asked him to procure a false mustache and then insisted he return to the theater to find one that was more effusive," he said with a rueful smile, shaking his head in wonder. "The most fun I've ever had in my whole life was watching you climb over the counter in Mercer Brothers while instructing Mr. Hamish on how to make his sign. You have thoroughly corrupted me," he admitted, "and like any reprobate worth his salt I'm a grateful participant in my own downfall."

It was a remarkable speech.

Oh, indeed, it was remarkable, and Bea could barely breathe for the tumult it stirred in her body, from the pounding in her heart to even a slightly numb feeling in the tips of her fingers. He was so close to putting it all together. Only a minuscule distance—a hairsbreadth—remained between bewilderment and love, and yet it might as well have been a gaping canyon for all the likelihood he had of crossing it. He could say all these astonishing things, he could feel all these astounding emotions, and yet still walk the aisle of St. George's with conscripted dignity.

She felt the truth of that, the dagger-deep despair of that, even as she found herself overwhelmed by the possibility of things that so nearly existed. It was all so close, she would swear she could touch it.

And then suddenly she was.

Mindlessly, recklessly, she made the leap herself, swooping to the other side of the carriage and taking possession of his lips.

Was he surprised?

He had to be surprised.

And yet there was no indication of it at all.

How smoothly he joined the effort, his lips responding

with a disorienting mix of impatience and care, at once eager and gentle. He wrapped his arms around her and pulled her closer to press his body against hers. Softly, he brushed his tongue against her lips, and excited for more, she opened her mouth. Feeling surged through her—incomprehensible passion, undeniable love—and, unmoored by its power, she clutched his shoulders, then moaned in pleasure as his own hands slid beneath her shirt to touch her skin.

He murmured incoherently in response.

Desperate to know the sensation for herself, she dug her hands under his shirt and felt the heat of his back. At the contact, he lurched forward, as if trying to draw her closer, and then pulled her onto his lap.

"Yes, please, Bea, yes," he said, his voice low, husky and breathless.

She heard the pleading in his tone and felt the same insistence, the same driving need. Frantic, she reared up to somehow consume more of him, her lips nibbling on the edge of his mouth, and suddenly found herself chewing, then choking, on a furry, slithery object.

The mustache!

Horrified, she pulled away and threw herself onto the other bench, gagging on the mustache as it scratched the back of her throat. She tried dislodging it by spitting it out, but it was too thick and fulsome and she actually had to reach inside her mouth to remove it.

With a disgusted *yech,* she threw it onto the floor, where it landed only an inch from Kesgrave's shoes and lay like a drowned baby mouse.

It was mortifying in every way possible—the start of the kiss, the end of the kiss, the desperate middle of the kiss where she would have absorbed his body into her own if it were only possible—and although Bea felt lower than a worm on the heel of a gentleman's shoe, she could not help but appreciate the parodic perfection of the moment. It was fitting because her relationship with Kesgrave had been a farce from the very beginning. Their first exchange had been a gross misunderstanding conducted over the cooling corpse of an opium smuggler.

It was always going to end like this.

Certainly, the mustache imbroglio was unexpected and something she never would have predicted in a million years. But the humiliation itself, never mind the method—that had been foretold. There was no other way for a relationship between a smitten spinster and a sought-after duke to conclude.

The embarrassment was crushing, of course, and she wished she could transform into that worm and slink away. But it also typified the essential reality of her existence and was merely the latest manifestation of the truth she'd divined while standing on the doorstep at 19 Portman Square as an orphan: The trajectory of her life was off course. Nothing would ever be right again.

Across from her, the duke inhaled and Bea knew he was going to try to say something mitigating. Despite all his pedantry and superiority, he was a kind man and would attempt to shoulder as much responsibility as possible.

Such evenhanded consideration would only make her mortification worse, and she held up her hand to forestall him. At that very moment, the carriage stopped at the corner of her street and she felt a profound sense of gratitude.

Providence was not kind but neither was it cruel.

Unwilling to wait for the driver, she opened the door and climbed out as Kesgrave called her name.

Calmly, she took a deep breath and smiled with what she hoped was benign good humor. "Goodbye, your grace."

He did not like the finality of her tone—that much was clear from his pained expression—and she imagined he wanted a more decorous ending than two men in disheveled clothes and a soggy fake mustache on the floor. She didn't blame him, for she wanted that too. Alas, it was not in her power to bestow it.

She turned toward her home and began walking.

Kesgrave called after her as he climbed out of the coach, "No, wait, Bea, you must listen."

Bea kept her gait steady and her eyes focused ahead.

She was relying on the indecorousness of the situation to shield her from further contact. The Duke of Kesgrave did not want to be caught in the middle of Mayfair accosting a young man while wearing his steward's clothes. If Jenkins had held the reins then he might have sent his groom to waylay her, but he could not embroil the driver of a public hack in his private affairs. It was an unexpected boon.

The distance to her house was not very great, but with the duke's eyes on her it felt interminable. With every step, she wanted to walk faster and faster, but the thought of the impression that might give him—spinsterish Beatrice Hyde-Clare scurrying away—kept her pace even.

When she finally reached number nineteen, she disappeared down the stairwell leading to the servants' entrance and peered through the window. Confirming that the area was unoccupied, she quietly slipped inside. At once she was greeted by the sound of female voices wafting down the hallway. She had little worry of anyone noticing her absence, as she'd coughed prolifically during breakfast that morning and assured her family it definitely was *not* the early stages of a cold, despite how under the weather she had been feeling. All of them, even Russell, who insisted on going out without a coat in the chilly late-winter weather, visibly winced and scooted their chairs a few inches away from her.

Recalling the scene as she crept past the servants in the kitchen, she marveled at the ease with which she could have conducted a secret love affair with a law clerk named Theodore Davies if such a man existed. That she could find no humor in the irony she laid churlishly at the duke's feet and was pleased to discover she was still capable of annoyance even if amusement eluded her.

Cautiously, she climbed the stairs and emerged in the corridor just as Flora stepped out of the drawing room with her sewing. For several humming seconds, the two women stared at each other. Then Aunt Vera chastised her daughter for halting so suddenly on the threshold, grumbling that her needlepoint had been crushed.

Horrified, Bea felt the color drain from her face.

Calmly, Flora reached out her hand and knocked over a vase sitting on the hallway table. "Oh, no," she said, affecting distress as the porcelain shattered. "I'm so desperately clumsy."

Sparing her cousin a grateful look, Bea dashed to the back staircase, darted up to the next floor as quickly as possible and ran to her room. There, she changed immediately into one of her drab morning gowns and, thoroughly exhausted from anxiety and excitement and desolation, she lay down on her bed.

She knew it wasn't over quite yet. Kesgrave would go home, change out of his steward's clothes and pay a call. When he was refused on account of her cold, he would send a note. When the envelope was returned unopened, he would seek her out at the next social function they both attended. When he failed to get a moment alone with her, he would cease to pursue it. The Duke of Kesgrave was far too well-bred to harass a lady. In another week, two at most, it would truly be over.

Grateful and devastated, relieved and desperate, she began to cry.

A few minutes later, Flora knocked abruptly on her door and opened it without waiting for a reply. "Well, that was a close shave. I swear I thought my mother was about to—"

She broke off when she saw her cousin curled up in a ball sobbing, and asking no questions at all, she rushed over and pulled an unresisting Bea into her arms. "It's going to be all right, darling. Oh, my poor, poor darling, I promise you everything will be all right. You won't miss him forever, I promise," she said softly, naturally concluding that her cousin was still mourning her dead law clerk.

Bea was grateful for the comfort and the gentleness and the warmth of her embrace, and she would never forget the kindness at the exact moment when she desperately needed it. But, no, everything would not be all right.

CHAPTER FOURTEEN

Despite Bea's insistence that she had no desire to attend the Larkwells' ball, Aunt Vera refused to take her preference into account.

"For goodness' sake, Beatrice," she exclaimed crossly as she examined the contents of her niece's wardrobe, "you still have Lady Abercrombie's beautiful blue dress. I told you to return it immediately. Why did you not comply with my directive? Now she will think you intend to keep it. How mortifying for me! It's a shame, really, for the shade of cerulean is so very fine and flatters even your wan complexion, which is somehow more pallid than usual after two weeks of fighting a dreadful cold. Could you possibly…" Abruptly, she shook her head, as if incapable of believing she had been so imprudent as to even consider it. "No, you will wear something else. Like this yellow gown. It doesn't do you any favors, but no scrap of fabric can perform miracles. Now, do get dressed so that we may go to the ball and put to rest all this talk. Annie will be here in a moment."

Taken aback by her aunt's sudden about-face, for the older woman had been quite content to let Bea leisurely nurse a cold, she narrowed her eyes in suspicion. "Talk?"

Aunt Vera, who was now inspecting the vanity for

something bright and sparkly to perk up her niece's appearance, looked at her in confusion. "Excuse me?"

"You mentioned talk," Bea reminded her. "What talk?"

"Nothing," she said, realizing she would have to lend Bea a string of garnets to wind nicely through her hair, as her collection of hairpins was plain and uninspired. "It's just something Kesgrave said in passing."

At her words, Bea visibly started. It was not the mention of Kesgrave that caused the reaction, for his assiduous pursuit of an interview with her had ensured that his name came up frequently in conversation, but the realization that something underhanded was afoot.

"What did he say?" Bea asked.

"How people were beginning to notice your absence, as you had just emerged from the sickroom only to take refuge there again almost instantly," Aunt Vera explained. "It seems some people are concerned that your uncle and I aren't taking proper care of you. Obviously, it's all a hum and I wouldn't listen to a word they say, but there's no reason why you cannot attend tonight's event. As the duke said, it's the easiest way to put the rumors to rest."

"I bet he did," Bea muttered, annoyed that Kesgrave had finally figured out a way to maneuver her into a public space where he would be able to accost her with his remorse. That he still sought a consultation with her two weeks after the incident surprised her. It seemed the more she denied him the opportunity to be gracious, the more determined he was to foist his graciousness on her regardless of her clearly communicated preference. If she had realized refusal would make him more dogged, she would have remained in the carriage and heard him out.

As unbearable as that experience would have been, it would at least have ensured that this episode in her life would be over.

Instead, the duke insisted on visiting regularly, which convinced Flora more than ever that he had somehow developed feelings for Bea—feelings, she believed, her cousin returned. Alas, the guilt over betraying the memory of her first love tormented her, and Flora tried to assure her that Mr. Davies would not mind at all if she found happiness with a duke. Indeed, he would most likely be delighted that she had done so well for herself. After all, he'd had those darling children, had he not, and could not want her pining for him indefinitely.

Her mother, hearing this nonsense, thought the idea of the duke proposing to Bea was the most outrageously amusing *on-dit* ever uttered in a drawing room.

When pressed for an alternative explanation for Kesgrave's repeated calls, Aunt Vera identified herself as the cause, insisting his grace admired her circumspection and restrained attitude toward life.

"We have a very particular friendship," she announced during dinner one night.

Uncle Horace, somehow finding that claim to be credible, began to protest the propriety of the duke's interest and sit in on the visits.

The image of her uncle glaring at the Duke of Kesgrave in possessive jealously over weak tea was the only thing that had made her smile in two weeks.

Annie entered the room and greeted her cheerfully.

As Bea submitted to her maid's ministrations, she affirmed her resolution to elude the duke at all costs. No doubt he thought he had been very clever, but getting her to the ball was not the same as getting her to listen. If necessary, she would recruit Lady Abercrombie, who would be happy to intercede on her behalf, for she remained as determined as ever to help her protégé recover from her infatuation and sent frequent messages updating her on changes to the list of suitors. With the memory of the kiss so fresh in her mind, Bea could not imagine following up on any of the names, but she appreciated the widow's concern and thought often about paying her a visit to talk about the experience. Knowing nothing about love and unable to locate the relevant information in a book, Bea feared she would spend the rest of her life thinking about the kiss, a notion that horrified her. She felt confident a woman of Lady Abercrombie's experience would be able to put her mind at ease on that point.

But the thought of discussing a moment of such staggering intimacy with anyone sent the heat of embarrassment coursing through Bea's body. She couldn't possibly explain the rush of feeling the kiss had unleashed in her, the shock of desire so overwhelming she'd become almost like a wild thing, feral and driven by need.

Who knew what would have happened if not for that fatuous mustache.

As if inspired by the challenge, her mind instantly began to envision several possible outcomes, each one more audacious than the last.

"You are looking better already," Annie said approvingly as the blush bathed her charge's cheeks.

Bea's color deepened as she realized she could feel desire for Kesgrave whilst in the presence of her maid. Appalled by the depravity, she focused on something unpleasant.

The Otleys, she decided, recalling her visit two weeks ago when she had informed both ladies and Mr. Skeffington that Wilson's awful death had been naught but a tragic mistake. Although the Incomparable and her fiancé were relieved to discover the guilty party did not number among the Otleys' household or acquaintance, Mrs. Otley was not as sanguine and insisted Beatrice was wrong in her conclusions. She could not believe that the man she loved had been cruelly taken from her by accident. Surely, his life had more value than just as a warning shot for a man of more noble blood.

"It is part of a dastardly plot to destroy what little happiness I have found in this life," she'd insisted, falling onto the settee as if her legs were no longer able to support her.

It was an unexpectedly passionate response from a woman who had coolly instructed the kitchen staff to remove a tray in the midst of her lover's horrific suffering. But Bea, watching the display, believed the widow was truly dismayed to discover the truth. Unable to bear Mr. Wilson's trivial place in the universe, Mrs. Otley seemed determined to make him vitally important to her own.

Emily did not share Bea's generous interpretation of her mother's needlessly dramatic display, rolling her eyes at the histrionics, but she responded to her outlandish bid for attention by trying to soothe her pain. "There, there," she said softly.

Either sensing the insincerity or too distrustful of her daughter to give her the benefit of the doubt, Mrs. Otley rejected the proffered comfort on the grounds that Emily had never liked Mr. Wilson.

"Well, no," Emily had responded reasonably, "for he was an interloper in your marriage, an opium smuggler and a man of low origin."

At Mrs. Otley's screaming reply, Mr. Skeffington offered to escort Bea to her carriage, and as soon as they were in the hallway, thanked her for resolving the matter so quickly. He showed no reaction at all when the sound of broken glass emanated from the room. Bea flinched and suggested he wed Emily as soon as possible rather than waiting for the full year to be up. Six months was respectful enough.

Bea smiled now as she recalled the note she had received a week earlier announcing their marriage in a quiet ceremony at Lakeview Hall.

Annie wove a string of garnets through Bea's hair and stepped back to examine her handiwork. Her nose scrunched in dissatisfaction, and she adjusted the strand's placement.

"There," she said with approval, "you're perfect."

Bea very much doubted that, but she held her tongue then as she held her tongue later when, on the way to Larkwell House, Flora quietly urged her to hear Kesgrave out. She successfully depressed her cousin's conversation, but the gleam of expectation in the other woman's eye indicated that Bea had been unable to dampen her hopes.

The ballroom was already crowded by the time they arrived, and she silently cursed the custom that required her name to be announced to the entire party. She immediately tensed, as if expecting Kesgrave to emerge from the shadows to accost her.

Naturally, he did not.

Lady Abercrombie, of course, quickly sought her out to chastise her for failing to call on her. "I must say, Miss Hyde-Clare, for someone with your seemingly sturdy disposition, you are awfully prone to ailments. First the bruises that kept you in seclusion for three weeks and now this bothersome cold that kept you inside for two. I find it very vexing. Do recall, we have business to discuss."

Bea rushed to assure the countess that although she had been too ill to pay social calls, she had read every update to the list of suitors and had no quibble with the candidates, all of whom seemed quite suitable. She did not add if they were suitable for her, and the countess did not ask.

Her ladyship nodded in approval, as if she'd expected nothing else, and then said, "However, I am talking about our other business. You are meant to pay a call on me so that we may discuss my referral. It has been almost two weeks, and I trust the other matter is settled."

"Oh, yes, of course, yes," Bea said, flustered because Lady Abercrombie's investigation had completely slipped her mind. In the wake of the disastrous kiss, quite a few things had fallen to the wayside. "I will call on you this week."

Unsatisfied with a vague promise, the widow insisted on scheduling a particular appointment, and while she quietly reviewed the week's engagements, Bea looked up and there he was.

Panicked, she grabbed Lady Abercrombie's hand and squeezed it tightly. "Don't leave me," Bea said.

It took the countess only one second to apprise herself of the situation, and as she gently extricated her hand from her protégé's viselike grip, she said, "I won't, darling." Then she turned to greet the duke as he covered the last few feet that separated him from Bea. "There you are, Kesgrave. I was just about to search you out. What is this I hear about your supporting Johnstone in his proposal to raise the tax on bamboo? You know I'm desperate to own a red panda to go with my drawing room, and red pandas love bamboo so this increase will affect me dreadfully."

Kesgrave, his eyes focused exclusively on Beatrice, seemed almost surprised to see Lady Abercrombie standing there. He darted a look in her general direction, greeted her absently and returned his gaze to Bea, who found herself equally unable to turn away, transfixed by the determination she saw in his stunning blue eyes.

Yes, she reminded herself, determination to apologize for his lapse in judgment and shoulder responsibility for a transgression of which he was but a victim. The prospect of such an exchange was so unbearable, she finally wrested the ability to tilt her head down.

"Very clever, your grace," the countess said with seemingly genuine appreciation. "Pretend I'm not here so you won't have to answer for your heartlessness. I won't be fobbed off by your ploy. I know you are perfectly aware of my aspirations, for when I mentioned the matter to you, you said, 'Tilly, I don't know what a red panda is, but I'm sure it's best for everyone involved if you don't have one.' This happened only a few months ago so you can't claim you don't remember. Regardless, I want you to withdraw your support. Do say you will comply at once."

"Tilly, you are as relentless as ever," Kesgrave said, his tone affable and yet somehow full of impatience. "I will agree to seek out Johnstone tonight and withdraw my support if you will give me a moment to talk with Miss Hyde-Clare. I understand from her family that she has suffered a terrible cold, and I'm eager to inquire after her health."

Bea's heart, which was already racing at an alarming rate, hitched in her chest at these words.

"Yes, of course, you must talk to her and ensure

yourself she is well," Lady Abercrombie said, terrifying Bea with her easy agreement. Had this been her plan all along—vow to help her and then brutally abandon her to Kesgrave's clutches? "I too was worried by the pernicious-ness of her cold. It reminded me of the illness my dear departed Henry caught while he was on the Peninsula. The poor love. How his nose suffered! He could never hold on to a handkerchief in London, let alone in the middle of a campaign. Do let me tell you the tale."

Kesgrave sighed deeply. "I'm sure it's a vastly enter-taining story, but I don't think now is the time."

The countess agreed vehemently with his observation. "You are right, of course you are, for we are in a ballroom and you must dance with"—there was a slight pause as she surveyed her immediate surroundings and settled on a young lady in a pink dress—"Miss Philbin, whose mother expressly sought my assistance in launching her daughter."

The girl in question looked terrified as the famous widow reached out, tugged her arm and drew her into their group.

"I can think of nothing that would more firmly estab-lish her than a set with the Duke of Kesgrave," Lady Abercrombie insisted. "Can you, Miss Hyde-Clare?"

In awe of the countess's manipulations, Bea said, "No, I cannot."

"Very well, then," Kesgrave said mildly.

At his gracious capitulation, Bea's eyes flew to his face and found he was watching her now with an expres-sion of amused forbearance. Although her ladyship had successfully routed him, the extremity of her actions re-vealed her protégé's desperation. She could not know why that entertained him but it did.

"Miss Philbin, it would be my honor," he said, turn-ing to smile charmingly at the young lady, whose terror at dancing with the most eligible parti in all of London was readily apparent on her face. "Miss Hyde-Clare, I look forward to continuing this discussion later."

As Bea watched the couple present themselves to the dance floor, Lady Abercrombie said, "Do you think she could be a Miss Philbin? I rather think she looks like a Miss Philbin, though for all I know, she could be a Miss Cartwright or a Lady Amanda. Truly, I have no idea what her name is or who her mother is. She was merely the first young miss I spotted when I was seeking one. Do you think it matters that we don't know her name?" she asked with a thoughtful note before shaking her head decisively. "It does not. She is far too scared of Kesgrave to correct him, and what I said is true: One dance with him will guarantee her success. Being addressed by the wrong name during the quadrille is really a small price to pay for social acceptance."

Bea surprised herself by laughing with genuine humor. "You are a marvel, Lady Abercrombie, and I do not wonder why my mother loved you."

"Thank you, my dear," the countess said matter-of-factly. "I will not pretend to be unmoved by that sentiment. Now do tell me what happened between you and Kesgrave to create such a tense situation. You were both practically vibrating—you with anxiety and he with impatience."

At her ladyship's observation, Bea turned bright pink, which forestalled the need to answer at all.

"Ah, I see," Lady Abercrombie said with a chuckle. "Take my advice, my dear, and have it out with him once and for all. I understand your dread and frankly share it, but it will be awful and then it will be over. Now, I am happy to protect you when I can, but it's a large ballroom and a long night. You cannot remain glued to my side at every moment. You will have to cultivate other resources."

Bea appreciated both her willingness to help and her perspective, and she stayed as close as she could until the widow was asked to dance by Mr. Cuthbert, whom, Bea discovered a few minutes later from her aunt, was her latest paramour.

"I cannot approve of her manners, for they are far

too free and easy," Aunt Vera said chidingly as she watched the countess twirl around the dance floor, "and given my connection with the duke, I no longer think it's necessary for the Hyde-Clares to court her approval in order to advance our social position. You should consider ending the association."

For a moment, Bea truly couldn't decide which was worse—listening to her aunt's conversation or having a private discussion with Kesgrave—but as soon as she saw the latter approaching, she made up her mind. The apprehension she felt in her stomach at his approach made it as plain as day.

Although it required some effort, she forced herself to stay where she was. Running away too soon would defeat her purpose. First, she needed her aunt to fully engage him in an exchange. Then, when they were both engrossed, she could calmly excuse herself.

Luckily, her aunt took control of the conversation immediately following Kesgrave's greeting, and while he was politely listening to her enthuse about a paperweight Mrs. Scott brought back from Venice, Bea murmured an excuse and walked away. She was so pleased with how well she'd executed her plan, she dared to glance back to admire her achievement.

"You look satisfied," Nuneaton said.

"I am," she admitted, turning to greet the handsome viscount.

"I was hoping you would be here," he said, "as I have not seen you since our strange outing to the Red Corner House. I understand you have been severely under the weather. I trust you are recovered now."

Given her long history of social isolation, it surprised Beatrice how many people had noticed her absence. "I am, yes, and I'm still not prepared to reveal the secrets of Lakeview Hall," she added teasingly.

He shook his head, unconcerned. "I will get the truth out of you eventually, and in the meantime, you have a much more interesting tale to tell. And this one you are obligated to share, as I lent my assistance to the cause."

"Am I?" she asked, amused, wondering if it would be too persnickety to point out that Lady Abercrombie had sought his help, not she.

Before she could answer, the orchestra began to play the opening strains of a waltz and Nuneaton held out his hand. "May I?"

She consented but laughed as she pointed to his ulterior motive. "You just want an opportunity to make your case."

"Untrue!" he insisted as they took their position on the dance floor. "Your obligation precludes my having to make any effort at all."

Although she wasn't sure she agreed with the validity of his argument, she saw no reason to demure and told him the particulars of the investigation, altering the names of the participants by reducing them to their first letter, even Andrew Skeffington, who was in fact Nuneaton's distant cousin. It was the first time she had considered the inquiry since sharing her findings with the Otleys and Mr. Skeffington, and even then she had provided only the broadest strokes. The events in the carriage immediately after her interrogation of Taunton had eclipsed the murder, and the fact that she would never have the satisfaction of identifying the culprit because the real victim refused to consult with her reaffirmed the uselessness in pondering it. In any event, Taunton was surviving quite well without her assistance, for she had seen him moments ago on the dance floor with the ersatz Miss Philbin.

"So it was all just an error?" Nuneaton asked at the end of her narration, appalled by the seemingly unpredictable machinations of an indifferent universe. "W died because someone was trying to kill T?"

"Yes," she said, glancing at him as they spun. "If W had not taken the snuffbox, then he would be alive today and T would be dead."

"Caught in the crossfire as if on a battlefield," he said softly. "What a thing. Who could have ever anticipated such a peculiar turn of events?"

At his words, Bea stumbled, losing her step in the waltz as his words called to something deep inside her.

Who could have anticipated such a peculiar turn of events?

The handkerchief, she recalled suddenly, with the initials on it. JBW. In the dressing room of his apartment at the Melbourne. The locket from George on the shelf.

I must ask him about my ring, my talisman ring.

That was Mowbray. Mowbray had muttered those words in his drunken stupor.

"Miss Hyde-Clare," Nuneaton said firmly, concern evident in his voice. "Are you all right? 'Twas only a slight trip, and we are steady now."

Bea looked at him, almost surprised to find herself still in his arms on the dance floor. "Yes, yes, of course," she said but her tone was abstracted as she considered the staggering possibility that Taunton was the murderer after all.

During their conversation, he had practically confessed.

About Wilson's position in India, he's said, "I thought for sure the post would kill him.... I advised him not to go, but Charles was stubborn and always did the opposite of what you counsel."

Could it have been that simple to murder a man? Find an irresistible object you know he would steal because he had a habit of taking things that were not his, fill it with poison and let the man damn himself.

At once, Bea's throat went dry and her heart began pounding.

It would, she thought, explain why he'd been surprised to hear the name of the poison. He had not used nux vomica but something similar that produced the same reaction. She had no idea what it could be. Something readily available in London, she decided.

Why had Taunton wanted him dead?

He'd spoken of him fondly enough, and Wilson was merely the estate's former steward. Could it have gone back to their childhoods? Could it have been jealousy? Had young Charles usurped the old lord's affection or did his father treat him more kindly than Taunton's did him? Or was it a more recent resentment? How had Mr. Wilson earned such violent retribution?

Consumed by her thoughts, Bea hardly noticed that the music had stopped and she realized Nuneaton had said her name a few times before she heard it.

"Are you sure you're all right?" he asked, genuinely worried now. "Perhaps you are suffering a relapse of your illness."

Bea looked at him and was touched to see anxiety in his deep brown eyes. "No, I'm sorry. I just—" Spotting Taunton out of the corner of her eye, she watched as he strode across the dance floor toward the gallery opposite. Agitated, she walked off hurriedly to follow, calling belatedly back to Nuneaton that she was fine.

She caught up to Taunton just as he reached the entrance to the balcony, and she followed him out onto the empty terrace, too agitated to notice either the unusually cold air or the significant breach in custom she was committing by addressing a superior to whom she had not been introduced.

"You knew he would take it," she said accusingly as she crossed the terrace to where he stood along the far railing.

Smoothly, he removed a cheroot from his pocket as he said, "My dear lady, I can tell from your tone that you think I've committed some offense. I assure you, my conscience is clear."

Bea took another step closer and said, "The snuffbox. You knew he would take it because he took everything. Was the Swift book given to him or did he steal that as well?"

Now he narrowed his eyes as he examined her, and finding no resemblance to any person he knew, he insisted again that she was mistaken. "I do not know to whom or to what you refer, but I find you impertinent and not at all interesting. Do remove yourself from my presence immediately." He turned away to light the cheroot from one of the torches stationed at regular intervals along the balustrade.

"I am referring to the murder of Charles Wilson, my lord," she announced forcefully as he carelessly took his first puff. "I'm referring to the snuffbox you left out so that your father's light-fingered former steward would steal it. I'm referring to the poison in which you bathed the snuff so that he would inhale it and die a gruesome death. That's what I'm referring to and you do know it very well. If it wasn't nux vomica, what was it? That is what I cannot figure out. What poison was administered?"

Hearing the words *nux vomica* loosened something in his memory, and he shook his head as he realized who she was. "Good God, Mr. Wright, can that be you?" he asked, amusement mixing with surprise. "How considerably more feminine you look in that gown than your lawyering suit. It's charming to see you in your altered state. I must concede, I'm impressed with how clever you are to have figured it out. I didn't think anyone would." His voice rang with what appeared to be genuine appreciation. "You are clearly a cut above the common female. What did you say your name was?"

"I did not say," she informed him, "as I have no interest in introducing myself to a murderer."

The charge did not unsettle him in the least, and he smiled before inhaling sharply on his cheroot. "You are very rude, but for some reason I find it appealing. As your reward, I will answer your question: The poison I used was obtained from a public house near the docks. One of my footmen procured it. It's called strychnine, and the tavern keeper adds it to the beer he waters down to make sure it's sufficiently bitter to fool the customers. I understand it's quite a common practice. I trust it goes without saying that they use it in far smaller quantities or they would be losing patrons at an alarming rate."

Strychnos nux-vomica, she thought, recalling the name of the tree in India. It must derive from the same source.

"Why?" she asked. "What had he done to you?"

"My dear, what *hadn't* he done?" he said, amused by his own question. "He was a mincemeater of the highest order, always looking for a way to squeeze or sharp you. From the moment he was put in leading strings, he was bleeding the estate. Always an extra slice of pie or another comfit. The older he grew, the worse it became. First books for school, then tuition itself. My father found his constant grasping diverting, but it bothered me to no end. It was as if he felt entitled to what was mine. Mine, not his. I almost didn't mind the stealing because it was in some respects more honest than the incessant wheedling for more and he at least displayed a talent for it. He was a real rum diver, our Charles. But then he took a miniature of my father only a few months after he died and that was not diverting. My mother was distraught when she couldn't find it and assumed it was her own carelessness, which somehow made it all the more devastating for her. She fell into a decline from which she has yet to entirely recover."

"So you decided to kill him," she said, aghast that the accumulation of small peccadillos could drive a man to such extremes.

"No, I decided to send him to India, where the *elements* would kill him. I'm not a ruffian, my dear. I saw Otley was looking for a steward and knew it was likely that any candidate would eventually find himself looking after his business interests in India, so I arranged the position. When that did not work as I expected, I was forced to come up with another plan. But my goal was never to kill him. It was always to see if he would kill himself. If he made a poor decision that ultimately led to an excruciating death…" He trailed off with an apathetic shrug. "The snuffbox was mine, not his, and he knew it. Nobody can blame me for his death. I did nothing."

His confidence was infuriating, more so because Bea

feared he might be correct. He had arranged for Wilson's death in a slippery way that was at once illegally dubious and morally reprehensible, and it was only the gleeful malice in his tone that made his intentions clear. If he affected sincere distress at Wilson's death, he might very well come across as blameless. Truly, she didn't know.

But she was more than willing to find out.

"You think so?" she asked tauntingly. "Let's return to the ballroom right now to share your story and discover together how innocent the *ton* finds you. I own I'm quite curious to see what your peers think."

Taunton laughed and took another puff of the cheroot, not at all concerned by the threat. "Please, my dear, feel free. You think anyone will believe you? For one thing, you are a woman, so immediately your truthfulness is suspect. For another, I have no idea who you are, which means your standing in society is insignificant. Lastly, you are plain. Nobody notices plain-faced women unless they are attached to a sizable dowry and we know you are not, as we've already established your insignificance. You may return to the ballroom and say whatever you like, just as I am afforded the same privilege. What might I say, you ask?" he said mockingly, enjoying the game now. "I will tell them about our very satisfying tryst on the balcony, as I'm sure at least one person saw you follow me out. I'm delighted to inform you, my dear, that you are an extremely skilled woman, quite daring in your tastes, but, alas, so very bitter at being rejected. Obviously, I cannot be expected to wed an insignificant woman with no dowry. Nobody would doubt me, for you are too old for me to consider you as a marital prospect."

It was a good threat, indeed a very good one, for even as she remained inured to its persuasion, she felt the mortification of being known as a woman who was quite daring in her tastes. It did not matter that the specifics of such a designation eluded her.

Nevertheless, Bea suffered no actual apprehension at

his words because she had a significant advantage of which the villain knew nothing. The Duke of Kesgrave would believe every single word she said and would make sure the truth was shared with the magistrate. He would not be swayed by a self-satisfied lord bragging about his conquests and would certainly never believe anything so low of Bea. He had far too much admiration for her intelligence to doubt her conclusions and too much respect for order to allow a murderer to go unpunished. Even if the magistrate decided there wasn't enough evidence to bring charges against Taunton, everyone in London would know he had cold-bloodedly arranged for the death of a family retainer.

The House of Taunton would be disgraced, and the sixth marquess would endure the consequences whatever they were.

Looking into her eyes, his lordship perceived something that unsettled him, perhaps her complete lack of fear, for Bea noticed the first crack in his implacable confidence as confusion, then worry, crawled across his face.

Good, she though, he's not invulnerable after all.

Satisfied, she spun on her heels to return to the ballroom and had taken no more than a step when Taunton reached out a hand and grabbed her arm. He wrenched her to his side, slammed her back against the stone balustrade and said with chilling scorn, "You silly, insignificant little nobody. Did you really think I would allow you to spread gossip about me? *This* is what's going to happen. First, I will snap your neck. Second, I will throw you over the balcony. Third, I will return to the ballroom as if nothing happened. Don't worry, my dear, it will be fast and painless. Are you ready? On the count of three, then. One…"

Bea had barely processed the threat, his cold indifference to human life, before she began to struggle against it. Terror piercing through her, eyes darting wildly, she writhed under his weight as she fought to free herself from his grasp.

The torch!

It was so close.

If she could just squirm an inch or two to her left to reach it....

Twisting, she gasped for air. The bash against the railing, hard and brutal, had knocked the wind out of her, and his body pressed against her chest with so much force she couldn't regain it.

"Two..."

Squealing with anger and hate, writhing in desperation, every bone in her body reeling in terror, she thrust her head forward and rammed it into his chest.

Bam!

The blow, landing in the middle of his rib cage, stunned him for a moment. Briefly, fleetingly, his grip loosened, and she slithered a fraction of an inch closer to the torch. She stretched out her arm—she...was...so...close—and screamed with frustration when her fingers couldn't touch it.

Taunton, so much larger than she, lurched forward, immobilizing her with his bulk, and took her head into his two large hands.

"And thr—"

"Goddamn it, Bea!" A furious voice rent the cold night air. "Is it not enough that you torture me with Nuneaton? Must you flirt with every man?"

The sound, the question, the anger, the company—something caused Taunton's grip to slacken, and Bea, her back scraping the stones as the force of her struggle propelled her to the side, finally reached the torch. Frantically, she wrapped her hand around the cradle, pulled it free, and whacked him over the head with it as hard as she could. Staggered, he stepped back as Bea dropped the torch to the ground, then screamed in terror as burning tendrils of hair seared his scalp. Horrified, Bea threw all her weight against him and knocked him to the ground, a maneuver made considerably easier by the fact that he was already collapsing in a faint. Her movements frenzied, she pounced on his head and smothered the flames with her dress before the blaze could do little more than singe him.

"Is this what you mean by 'quite daring in my tastes,'" she shrieked at him as she sat on his chest, pounding his head with her fists and skirts. "Is this what you mean?"

And then Kesgrave was there, kneeling beside her, halting her assault by pulling her into his arms and saying, "No, my love, no. You are safe. He is vanquished." He kissed her cheek and her forehead and her lips and her eyes.

But Bea couldn't stop, her arms still flailing wildly even as she let the hem of her gown fall. Kesgrave grasped her shoulders to calm her thrashing and looked into her eyes. "I love you, you daft woman. I love you madly. And if you had allowed me to speak any time in the past two weeks, you would have known it already and not be sitting here on a villain after extinguishing flames in his hair."

The pedantry!

By all that was holy, he was pedantic even now, the esteemed Duke of Kesgrave, with his fastidiousness and his precision and his battleships listed in order of appearance, unable to declare his love without also ensuring that the facts were appropriately aligned.

The clarity of it sliced cleanly through her terror, and she felt an overwhelming surge of calm wash over her, as paradoxical as it was peaceful. She inhaled sharply, relieved to finally catch her breath, and leaned into the warm strength of his embrace. How wonderful he felt, how solid and safe, and she stayed firmly there, her arms around him, perched on an insensible murderer, far longer than was decent.

As much as there was to explain, she couldn't bring herself to say a single word. Not now. Not yet. Soon enough they would get into all the gruesome details—Lady Victoria, she thought in amusement, as much as Lord Taunton—but for now she was content to let her pounding heart slowly quiet.

Finally, she lifted her head and said, "I must beg to disagree, your grace, as there is no cause and effect that ties the two events together and I defy you to come up with one."

Oh, he liked that.

Kesgrave liked that very much indeed, and despite the fact that she was sitting on top of the Marquess of Taunton, whose groan of pain seemed to indicate a growing awareness of the situation, he leaned forward to press his lips against hers. It was a gentle kiss, soulful and sweet, and Bea's eyes fluttered shut as her heart settled into place.

"I love you," she breathed softly.

"I love you," Kesgrave said, resting his forehead against hers for several lovely, serene moments.

How long they would have stayed like that had Taunton, fully awake now from his faint, not begun to struggle, neither one could say.

"Judging by the assault I just witnessed—and do note that we will be discussing at a later date your ill-considered decision to confront a murderer all alone—I can only assume Taunton did in fact kill Wilson?" Kesgrave observed mildly.

Although Bea wanted to protest his characterization of the confrontation as "all alone," as they were at a ball attended by hundreds of the *ton*'s finest, she paused to acknowledge the partial validity of his complaint. Additionally, the marquess was flapping his arms wildly as he tried to dislodge her from his chest, and it didn't seem like the proper moment for a protracted debate.

"You are a fool, Kesgrave, if you believe a single word this hussy says," Taunton snarled through gritted teeth as his efforts yielded no results. He squirmed, shifting his weight from one side of his body to the other in an attempt to throw Bea off balance. "I am quite cut up by my friend Charles's death, so cut up I felt compelled to step away from the gaiety of the ball, for how can I enjoy myself when the poor fellow had been killed in my stead? It's a terrible burden to bear, quite, quite terrible. And this woman here, this brute of a female, sensed my weakness and tried to use it against me. She thought I would be easy prey for her wiles, and when I proved impervious to her seduction, she turned violent. You saw it yourself, Kesgrave. This harridan launched a brutal attack on my person and then set me on fire."

The marquess could have no idea how ridiculous he looked making these charges against Bea, his cheeks red from his exertions, his forehead flecked with ash, half his head of hair singed away. Amused, she shook her head at him and tsk-tsked disapprovingly. "Insulting a man's fiancé—I'm not really sure that's your best strategic maneuver in this particular situation. Would you like to consider another approach?"

Taunton gasped.

Kesgrave's lips twitched as he looked at her. "You're not going to let me propose?"

Bea smoothed the front of her dress primly, a wasted effort as it merely spread the soot more evenly across the silk, and held out her hand to request his assistance in standing. "It took you more than two weeks just to declare yourself. I cannot trust you to act with sufficient resolve."

"She's not what you think, Kesgrave," Taunton cried as they both rose to their feet. "She's a charlatan. She dressed as a man and pretended to be a lawyer to swindle me. She will swindle you too."

Paying the marquess no heed at all, Kesgrave helped Bea straighten her gown, which, though ruined beyond repair, was still presentable. "I'm not sure I can be held responsible for that. I did visit every day and send a dozen letters that were returned unopened."

Bea was likewise happy to ignore Taunton, who was now shouting that she had stolen several invaluable objects from him, including a priceless snuffbox. "I seem to recall you were adept at climbing trees at Lakeview Hall. Was a brick wall more than you could manage?"

"Oh, I see now. So I was meant to atone for my sins

like Hercules performing the twelve labors," he replied as they crossed the balcony to the building.

She listed the few labors she could remember from her lessons as a child—steal the Mares of Diomedes, capture the Erymanthian boar, slay the nine-headed Learnaean Hydra—and observed that scaling the wall of a London town house was a minor challenge in comparison.

"Slay the nine-headed Learnaean Hydra, capture the Erymanthian boar, Steal the Mares of Diomedes," he corrected with pointed emphasis. "If you're going to list some labors but not others, the least you can do is put them in the correct order of appearance in the story."

Smitten beyond reason, she said softly, "HMS *Goliath*, HMS *Audacious*, HMS *Majestic*."

The recitation of the ships in the Battle of the Nile in their correct order was more provocation than his grace could withstand, and even though Taunton had finally managed to rise unevenly to his feet, Kesgrave paused in the doorway to kiss her languidly.

"And to think I once foolishly believed I could desire your mind with every ounce of my being," he said softly as he released her lips, "and not crave your body with every breath. We must get married at once, my love, for I am not accustomed to the sting of self-denial."

Although his confession had an unsettling effect on her body, for she suddenly felt at once delightfully loose-limbed and agonizingly taut, she smiled and offered to provide him with a few helpful tips on abstemiousness, a subject on which she considered herself an expert. Before Kesgrave could respond, she heard the hum of a growl and stepped back in surprise. Eyes blazing with anger, Taunton charged at them, determined, it seemed, to cause as much damage as possible before his inevitable disgrace. Bea barely had time to let out a gasp before Kesgrave raised his fist and plowed it into the side of the marquess's face. The other man dropped to the ground like a sack of apples.

Bea watched Taunton for signs of movement, and

assuring herself he was quite unconscious, turned to the duke. "May we leave him there?"

Kesgrave nodded, stepped into the gallery and closed the doors. "I think so. He'll be out for a while, and in the meantime, I'll send one of the servants to get a Runner."

"An excellent plan," Bea said, discovering, now that the danger had passed, she was desperately parched. Fighting for one's life was thirsty business. "While you do that, I will avail myself of the refreshments. Do come find me when the Runner arrives so I may make my report."

Kesgrave agreed, then tilted his head to the side and asked if she didn't think it was perhaps a little unwise to return to the ballroom in a filthy dress and tousled hair.

Although Bea knew his comment was entirely reasonable, something about it struck her as unbearably funny, and she dissolved into a fit of giggles. As she struggled to regain her breath, as the gales of humor continued to undermine the effort, she silently conceded the likeliness that her excessive mirth was the product of her relief at not lying on the garden paving stones with a broken neck.

Calmer now, although still deeply amused, she said, "Your remark demonstrates how little you understand life among the lower stratum of society, your grace. I am plain, six and twenty and insignificant, so no, I do not think it's unwise for me to return to the ball in my slightly disheveled state. What I *do* think is unwise is not to fetch a class of ratafia, for it feels as though I swallowed an entire desert of sand. Now please excuse me."

But Kesgrave was not quite ready to let her go, for he tugged her hand and drew her close. "Oh, but you are very significant now," he said foolishly, lowering his head for another kiss.

As much as Bea appreciated the sentiment, she could not let it go without making a mildly satirical comment, and when her lips were free, she said, "Because you find yourself utterly incapable of drawing your next breath without me?"

Now the duke laughed with sincere amusement. "No, my love, because you are marrying me, and I'm a leader of society whom everyone holds in high esteem."

Of course that was his answer. His arrogance knew no bounds. "You are giving yourself far too much credit, your grace, but I will leave you to your misconceptions because I'm far too thirsty to argue the matter."

"That is for the best," he said, his blue eyes twinkling with such delight it actually took her breath away, "for you would surely lose."

"A challenge," she said with relish, pleased to discover that love had not made her facile. His beautiful face might addle her lungs, but it left her brain unimpaired. "As you know, there's nothing I enjoy more than skewering your towering self-regard, and it will be quite lowering when you realize not even your credit is enough to carry me over the finish line. Now, if you'll excuse me, I'll be at the refreshment table imagining Lord Taunton being led through the ballroom in chains. You will make sure to instruct the servant to tell the Runner to bring chains, won't you?"

And with that said, she stepped free of his embrace, spun around on her heels and walked through the galley toward the ballroom. She had taken no more than two dozen steps, however, before she found herself suddenly engulfed by a swarm of sweet-smelling hostesses inviting the future Duchess of Kesgrave to tea.

ABOUT THE AUTHOR

Lynn Messina is the author of more than a dozen novels, including the best-selling *Fashionistas,* which has been translated into 16 languages. Her essays have appeared in *Self, American Baby* and the Modern Love column in the *New York Times,* and she's a regular contributor to the *Times* Motherlode blog. She lives in New York City with her sons.

47696764R00137

Made in the USA
Middletown, DE
09 June 2019